WALK-THRU PEOPLE

A BILATERAL SITUATION

AN AMAZING COULD-IT-HAPPEN
FROM

A.D. HOWARD

Copyright © A.D.Howard - 2015

All rights reserved. No part of this publication may be reproduced, stored in a retrieval system, or transmitted, in any form or by any means, electronic, mechanical, photocopying, recording or otherwise, without the prior permission of the copyright owners and the publisher.

A.D.Howard asserts his right to be identified as the author of this work in accordance with the Copyright, Designs and Patents Act 1988.

This edition published in Great Britain in 2015 for
BOOKAHOLICS PUBLISHING
by
Farthings Publishing
8 Christine House
1 Avenue Victoria
SCARBOROUGH
YO11 2QB
UK

Cover design by Emile Bale, Bernard Bale and Darren Hendley

http://www.Farthings-Publishing.com
E-mail: queries@farthings.org.uk

ISBN: 978-1-326-19461-1
February 2015 (c)

ABOUT THE AUTHOR

Born in a small North Hertfordshire market town in the late 1940s when rationing was still in use, the author had shown some writing talent at an early age but was far more interested in music and entertainment.

He freely admits that he was not the most successful of students but still managed to forge quite a career for himself in the electronics side of the entertainments business and especially the music industry, working with many major international stars.

A change of lifestyle when ill-health took over meant that he could at last fulfil the long-held desire to write and especially to create a novel that had been on his mind for many years.

Walk Thru' People is that novel, a great tale and a great way to realise an ambition.

CONTENTS

Chapter 1	Discovery	9
Chapter 2	Changed	26
Chapter 3	Assignment	39
Chapter 4	Hospital	53
Chapter 5	Exploration	77
Chapter 6	Commencement	96
Chapter 7	Acceptance	116
Chapter 8	Investigation	137
Chapter 9	Convergence	158
Chapter 10	Computation	181
Chapter 11	Possibilities	203
Chapter 12	Resolution	228
Chapter 13	Conclusion	256
Chapter 14	Epilogue	269

CHAPTER 1

DISCOVERY

The bright light of the morning sun, shining in his face, finally woke Gary up. He had fallen asleep on his sofa, fully dressed, after returning from a night's drinking. Had he drawn the curtains on his return home, he might well have had a few more hours sleep. But as it was, he was too drunk to think of things like that. It had been difficult enough getting home anyway and then he had the problem of getting the key in the lock. But that was all last night, he was awake now and had to decide what he was going to do.

Sitting on the edge of the sofa he tried to flatten his unruly hair with his hands. As he ran his hands down the back of his head, he paused and then winced. There was a lump on the back of his head. He had either banged it, or had been hit with something and now that he was aware of it, it started to throb.

Somehow, he managed to manoeuvre himself into the kitchen area, only to find that the cupboard was empty. If he wanted breakfast, it would mean a trip to the local shop. The intensity of the throbbing in his head wasn't helped by the bang of the door as it closed behind him and with his eyes scrunched up against the sunlight; he set off for the shop. The lift was still out of action, no surprise there, so he prepared himself to descend the eleven storeys.

He was not really paying attention to how far he had

gone, when he turned to descend another floor. In the stairwell, at the turn of the stairs, stood two men who were engaged in conversation and were blocking the way. As he got closer to them, he thought it strange that he could not hear their voices and that they made no attempt to get out of his way. Gary started to feel a little uneasy, something didn't seem right. This feeling was proved justified, for when he attempted to tap one of the men on the shoulder, he was horrified to find that his hand went straight through him, as if he wasn't there. 'This must be a dream' he thought, 'this can't be happening'. While the weirdness of the situation was sinking in, he was slowly backing away from them and ended up cowering in the far corner of the stairwell. At that moment, Gary heard a noise on the stairs below and looked through the handrail to see his neighbour Mrs Johnson, returning from the shop that he was heading for. He stood up so that he could clearly see what would happen when she approached the two men. Her shopping trolly was bumping up the concrete stairs behind her, when she looked up and saw Gary. "Morning Gary love" she said cheerily "everything alright? You look a little out of sorts this morning. Been out drinking again?". She continued on up the stairs, one at a time due to her bad hips, not seeming to notice the men standing there, who in turn were not paying any attention

Step by step the elderly lady got ever closer to the duo and then Gary thought that his head was going to explode, as he saw her walk straight through them. "You best get some rest dear" she said, "you don't look at all well". Somehow, Gary managed to get past the men and descend to the next stairwell, where he stopped and turned to look back at the two men. It was at this point that the hairs on the back of his neck stood up and he shivered when they both looked directly at him and one of them appeared to mouth, "Do you think he could see us?". Gary couldn't get out of there quickly enough, although he knew that he would have to return by the same route. He was still hoping that this was some strange sort of interactive dream, possibly caused by the bang on his head, but he quickly began to realise that it wasn't. Maybe it was the DT's, after all, he had been drinking rather heavily in recent months. He just couldn't fathom it out. Not only had he been able to see the two men, they had seemed very surprised that he could see them.

At the shop his mind wasn't really on what he was doing, which was not surprising after what he had been through. His confused state was noticed by Ahmed, as he served him. "You alright Gary?" he asked, "you don't seem your self today". "If I tried to explain, you just wouldn't believe me" he replied. After paying for his shopping, Gary set out on his return journey. As he was deep in thought, he never noticed that the closer he got to the tower block, the more his pace decreased, but he eventually got there. He was worried about what might happen, knowing that his mind just couldn't cope with another shock like the one he had already been through. Peering through the doors he couldn't see anyone, the coast was clear. Fortunately, the lift was working now and a sigh escaped from him as the motors whirred into life as he pressed the button for the eleventh floor. When it reached its destination, the lift shuddered to a stop and the doors opened. Gary did not step straight out, he wanted to make sure that no-one was about. He was looking along the walk-way towards his flat, when he nearly jumped out of his skin, as he heard a voice from behind him shout "Hold the lift, love". Gary slowly turned to look, not knowing what to expect. But he need not have worried, it was just two women going shopping. As they stepped into the lift, he heard one of them say, "He's a bit jumpy, isn't he?". "On drugs I would think" the other replied. 'If only you knew the truth' Gary thought, 'your minds wouldn't be able to cope with it'. In fact, Gary was having a difficult time dealing with his recent experiences and he shuddered as he relived it all. An intense feeling of relief washed over him as he entered his flat and locked the door behind him. He felt safe now, but he realised that at some point in the future he would have to leave his flat again.

Gary kept running through the day's events in his mind, getting more and more worked up as he did so. He tried to empty his mind of such thoughts, he'd had enough for one day. To help him forget, he decided to drink the first of the many cans of lager that he would consume that night. He hoped that everything would straighten itself out; but in the back of his mind he knew that's not the way things happen. By ten that evening, he had drunk himself into unconsciousness, the final partially consumed can emptying itself onto the floor, until it finally fell from his hand. Eventually, Gary rolled off of the sofa onto the floor and to keep himself warm, he wrapped himself in the rug. He lay there in his drunken stupor, while his brain took him on an extraordinary journey, until he woke with a start the next morning.

You would think that with all his experience of drunkenness he would take the first few moments slowly, but he didn't. He had experienced hangovers before, but this one was the grandaddy of them all. He couldn't open his eyes as the light was too bright, even though he'd closed the curtains this time. If he tried to stand up his head spun like a top and his hearing was so acute he was sure he could hear his finger nails growing. Eventually, all the symptoms started to ease, as he re-hydrated his body and became more used to moving about. But the thought of food was still too much for him, so breakfast was out for one day, even though there was food in the cupboard, for once. He was now just about able to look around his flat. Seeing the large number of empty cans scattered all over the place, he tried to remember if anyone had been drinking with him, but he soon realised that it was all down to him. A quick look in the fridge, where he kept his lager, proved that he had downed a spectacular amount of drink the previous evening. This prompted his usual "I'm never gonna drink again" statement, which was forgotten almost as quickly as it was spoken. He thought that a walk out in the fresh air might help, but he was apprehensive about leaving the flat, following the previous day's events. The need to replenish his stash of lager was the thing that finally helped him to make his decision. "After all, I can't stay in here forever," he said. So he prepared himself to venture outside. Wallet, roll—ups, lighter and keys, he was ready.

Taking a deep breath, he opened his front door and looked out. The coast was clear and he hoped that the rest of his shopping trip would turn out to be uneventful. As he left Ahmed's shop he realised that his appetite had returned, after all it was almost midday and he hadn't eaten for about twelve hours, as far as he could remember. A short walk brought him to his local cafe where, to his surprise, he ordered and enjoyed a large fry-up. It must have been his regular consumption of large amounts of alcohol that enabled him to shake off its effects more quickly than the normal drinker, or maybe he was just lucky this time. Whatever it was, he really enjoyed his food and it was followed by a large mug of strong black coffee and a roll-up. It was a revitalised Gary that set off on the journey home. He hadn't felt this good for a long time, he was unsure why that was, but all his recent troubles seemed to be unimportant now. The air smelt fresher, the sunlight brighter and for once, life felt good. Even though he had all these positive feelings, he was still relieved to get back home without any strange events taking place. He settled down on the sofa, planning to watch the afternoon's racing on TV. Of course he had the obligatory can of lager to keep him company, but he was contented and felt at ease with the world.

    The next couple of weeks went by uneventfully, as far as people-who-weren't there were concerned, but Gary now had a new girlfriend, Suzy. They had seen each other while in the company of others, but a relationship had never developed before. They had both just drifted into it and spending time together seemed the right thing to do. They decided, that for now, they wouldn't live together, as the council was always checking up on those who claimed to be living alone but that didn't stop her visiting.

    One evening, when the drink had loosened his tongue, Gary related the account of the two men on the stairs. To start with Suzy swore that Gary had made the whole thing up, but his insistence that it had really happened, along with his description of how he felt at the time finally convinced her.

    "You're not going off your head, are you?", she said

and then asked, "Have you had any other similar experiences? Do you still see things?",Gary began to get upset. "You think I'm going loony, well I'm not. It all happened just as I told you and let me tell you, I was scared stiff". An argument seemed to develop from there, with insults and accusations being fired from both sides. This continued until Suzy jumped up, threw her can across the room and shouted "I've had enough of this, you're a bloody nutter. I'm leaving". She grabbed her coat, which was draped over the back of a chair and stormed out of the door, slamming it behind her.

"Well, that didn't last long" Gary said to himself, as he walked over to the fridge to get another can, not bothering about the can Suzy had thrown across the room which was draining itself over the kitchen floor. He did eventually clear the spill up - after he had slipped on the wet floor and landed on his backside, banging his head on a cupboard door in the process.

'Sod this' he thought 'I'm going down the pub'. That's where he spent the remainder of his evening, barely thinking about Suzy at all, although she did occasionally crop up as his mind flew from drinking to strange experiences and to her.

A couple of days later, Gary was travelling down in the lift. It stopped on the seventh floor and the doors opened to allow two women to enter. Gary thought it strange that they weren't talking to each other, not even a few cursory words, as women usually have something to talk about. Anyway, these two were silent and even though the first woman acknowledged his presence the other one ignored him. Eventually the lift reached the ground floor and the doors slid open noisily rasping on their runners. Then it happened.

The woman that had entered the lift and ignored

him, started to walk out of the door, When-the other woman did the same. They both occupied the same space at the same time, overlapping slightly as they moved through the door. 'It's happening again' thought Gary, 'I must be going loopy'. He just stood there, rooted to the spot, his mind reeling. The lift door opened again, to admit a young woman and her children, one of whom was in a pushchair. "What floor do you want?" she asked. "I just want to get out of here" Gary mumbled as he pressed the 'Door Open' button and then forced his way through the doors before they had completely opened.

All this left the young woman with a puzzled expression on her face. Her little boy watched Gary and then said "Is that man alright?"

"I'm not sure" his mother replied as the lift doors closed.

Gary must have seemed very strange as he cautiously walked down the road, peering around corners and making large detours around anyone that came within his proximity. As he continued on down the road, this extreme behaviour slowly began to ease, although he was still very jumpy. His mind was in a state of confusion following the experience in the lift. He was trying to work out the meaning of it all as he rounded the corner of a block of shops and walked straight through a man walking in the opposite direction. He did not react immediately, as his mind was unable to cope with this new experience. He slowly turned around, expecting to see the man's retreating image. But he wasn't walking away, he had stopped and turned to look at Gary. When he saw Gary turn and look straight at him, a look of surprise spread over his face. "Can you see me? If you can please, please tell someone".

Of course Gary heard none of this, but he could lip read well enough to understand what was being said and memories of his encounter with the men on the stairs flooded back into his mind. He turned and ran. He ran harder than he had ever done before, as fast as his smoker's lungs would let him. Not knowing where he was heading didn't matter, he just had to get away from there as quickly as he could. Of course, he could have been heading into a more difficult situation, but his brain didn't consider that possibility, as the instinct to flee from danger had kicked in.

Eventually, he had to stop, he couldn't run anymore. He stopped in an underpass, sinking to the ground on his haunches, as he struggled to breathe. He wouldn't normally hang about in a place like that, as the chances of being mugged were quite high, but he had to get his breath back and the underpass provided temporary shelter. Strangely, he lit one of his roll-ups, which is not the best thing to do if you're trying to increase your oxygen levels, although the nicotine kick seemed to do him good. After he had finished his smoke, he felt ready to face the world again.

As he emerged into the open, he realised that it had started to drizzle. The fine mist-like drizzle that seems to penetrate everything. By the time that he reached the pub, he was quite damp, but he now felt that he was in a place of safety. He removed his wet coat, hanging it on the coat-stand by the door. As he settled himself on a bar stool he emitted a loud sigh, loud enough to attract the attention of the other drinkers, who quickly returned to their previous conversations. Gary looked up as the barmaid approached. "Lager as usual?" she said. "Not today" Gary replied, "I've had an unsettling morning. So make it a double Vodka"..

"It must have been quite a shock," the barmaid said as she turned toward the optics, Garry's glass in her hand.

The Vodka went down in one gulp. It left a warm, stinging glow inside his gullet, the sudden influx of alcohol giving his system a boost. While he was still enjoying the glow from the Vodka, he bought a lager along with some crisps, salt and vinegar were his favorites,and then sat down at a table. While Gary was on his third drink, two of his friends came into the pub, ordered drinks and came over to Gary's table. They then related their experiences that morning. The job centre had called them both in to discuss their continued jobless state. "They'll be after you soon Gary" Dave said, with a smile on his face, "I don't know how you've managed to stay out of their clutches this long".

"Just very skilled" Gary replied, "They don't seem to have positions for the professionally jobless". "So that's it!" Nigel chipped in, "You're professionally jobless".

"Correct" said Gary "I've been in training all my life to become unemployable."

I won't say that they haven't tried, as each new manager has a go, but I've beaten them every time, so far." Nigel said, "That applies to all of us. Let's enjoy the fruit of our labours and have another drink.".

In that happy atmosphere, Gary almost forgot about the morning's events, that had concluded with him in the pub. In reality, he didn't want to remember, but he had no choice, the images were in his brain. Blotting these memories out with alcohol seemed the only option, but he now realised that it was only a matter of time before the situation cropped up again.

"Gary....Gary," Dave said, trying to attract his attention. "Where were you then? It's not like you to be so deeply engrossed in thought. Anyway, it's your round".

"Sorry" Gary replied, "I'll go and get the drinks now" and walked over to the bar, the three pint pots in his hand.

"Do you know what's up with him Nigel?" Dave asked.

"I was going to ask you the same thing. It's not like Gary to let something bother him like that, especially when there's a drink involved. Let's see if we can drag it out of him when he comes back".

When they were all reseated, fresh drinks in front of them, Dave made the first move. "Gary, do you mind if we ask you something?".

"I was expecting this Dave. Go on, ask away"
"Well," Nigel said, "It's obvious that something is playing on your mind and we were wondering if there's anything we can do to help? After all, we've all been mates for for a long time".

"I'm not going into great detail" Gary said, "but you're both right. There is something going on in my life that's worrying me, in fact it's frightening me. It happened for the first time on the morning following a really heavy night's drinking and I thought that was the cause. But today it happened again, twice.

"I don't think I'm going mad, well I hope I'm not, although although something is definitely going on in my life that I don't understand. Anyway, that's all I'm going to say. If I go into any more detail, you'll really think I've lost it".

The three of them agreed to leave it there, although both Dave and Nigel strongly advised Gary to visit his doctor and see if he could provide some relief. Gary said that he would think about it, even though it had been a long time since he'd seen his doctor. The reason was the lecture about his drinking he received, the last time he had been. The doctor had described to him, in graphic detail, the effect that his drinking was having on his body, so he hadn't been back since then. The three of them agreed to leave it there, although Dave and Nigel were very worried about Gary's state of mind.

The days drifted by, without any unusual happenings. Gary's mental state began to return to what he called normal. There was one change though. He had started to cut down his alcohol consumption, equating the lack of incidents with the decrease in his drinking. He even began to feel a little better in himself. 'Perhaps the doctor was right after all,' he mused. Anyway, he definitely had more money in his pocket, now that he wasn't spending every penny on drink. Suzy had also returned to his life, their upset having been forgotten long ago. She was impressed by the reduction in Gary's drinking and the physical changes that this had brought about. Although he thought that giving up his smokes, was a step too far, at present, he had nevertheless found himself toying with the idea of giving them up..maybe in the future. Suzy had plucked up enough courage to try and cook a meal for the two of them. Gary was sent off to the shop, with a list of some necessary items, while Suzy prepared some vegetables.

'Vegetables', Gary thought, 'Who would have thought it possible.'Up to this time he had lived on a diet of microwave meals and take-aways. He found the thought of a properly cooked meal some-what appealing as he couldn't remember the last time he had had one.

Gary realised that he was singing to himself, not out

loud, just going over some favourite songs in his head. He didn't normally do anything like that, as his head was always fuggy and never seemed able to remember anything. So he put this down to another positive aspect of cutting down on the drink. He had lost the apprehension that he felt in the days following the previous incident, but it was always in the back of his mind.

As he started walking past the row of shops, heading for Ahmed's, he began to feel uneasy. He stopped and looked around, just to see how many people were about. Apart from him, the place appeared deserted, although there could have been some people in the shops. So he shrugged his shoulders and entered Ahmed's shop.

He always loved the mix of aromas, the smell of exotic spices, ground coffee and the special meats that hung from the ceiling filling the air with a sensual haze. It always astounded Gary that no matter what you asked for, Ahmed would find it tucked away somewhere. He wasn't disappointed this time either. Suzy had asked for some items that he'd never heard of before but Ahmed soon had them on the counter.

Gary looked longingly at the neatly arranged display of lager cans. What a temptation for him. He could so easily undo all the progress of the past few weeks but he was very pleased with himself for not giving in. Even Ahmed had noticed the change in Gary's lager purchases, but instead of encouraging him to buy some, he actually congratulated him on his resistance.

"I've seen too many times the effect drink can have on people" he said, "and I know I sell the stuff, but I'm a businessman providing a service. If they don't buy it here, they will just go elsewhere, my business will suffer and make it more difficult for me to keep the shop open. But if someone has the strength of character to turn their back on it, I congratulate them. As a Muslim, I don't touch it myself, but sadly some of my countrymen have fallen into the trap".

"Thank-you" Gary said in reply, "I didn't think you'd notice."

"Being a small shop keeper is a fascinating job, especially if you are interested in people like I am. Watching how people and their habits change over time".

What's the damage?" Gary asked, as he gave Ahmed a twenty pound note and then took the change.

"See you later" he said over his shoulder, as he stepped out into the street. Not knowing that it would be a long time before he saw Ahmed again.

In the future Gary was never able to clearly recall what happened next, even though it was only too obvious at the time. As he left the shop, he saw two women walking towards him. Instinctively, demonstrating that he still had some manners, he stepped off the pavement, to avoid a collision. As he walked past them he noticed, out of the corner of his eye, that they had stopped and were turning to watch him walk by.

'Why on earth are they doing that?' He asked himself, as he turned to look back at them. He rationalised that their reaction was due to the fact that he shouldn't have been able to see them. He didn't realise that his thinking was being shaped by his previous experiences. His worse fears were confirmed, when a group of small boys ran straight through them. That was the final straw and Gary's mind snapped. He dropped his bags of shopping, spilling their contents across the footpath and he fled.

He finally came to a halt behind the row of shops, where he tucked himself between two industrial waste bins. He was laying on the floor, curled up like a ball and was muttering to himself.

A few moments later, the rear doors of 'Pick-O-The-Bunch' florists swung open, allowing the shop assistant to emerge, her arms full of rubbish for the bin. Hearing the sound of someone moaning, she peered around the corner of the bin, only to see Gary laying there. She screamed, dropped the rubbish on the floor and ran back into the shop. She re-emerged along with the shop's owner, to show her the cause of her fright. They decided to call the police, after all, "He could have escaped from somewhere".

The police duly arrived and immediately assumed that Gary was drunk, even though he didn't smell of alcohol. They bundled him into the police car and drove away, heading for the police station.

When they arrived, they half carried, half dragged Gary to the custody desk. They managed to identify him from the details in his wallet. The sergeant decided to place him in a cell as he wasn't able to stand and then called for the FME.

A few hours passed before the doctor was able to see Gary and he quickly established that excess alcohol was not Gary's problem. As far as the doctor could determine, following a few more tests, Gary had suffered a complete mental breakdown. They all tried to make out what it was that Gary was muttering, but after many attempts, the best that they could come up with was something about 'See-through-people'.

This was dismissed as total rubbish, not knowing how close to the truth they had come. The doctor felt that the best place for Gary was in the Psychiatric Hospital, as they had the facilities to help someone in his condition. As a further precaution, he thought it advisable for Gary to be 'Sectioned', for both his own and the public safety. He made a couple of phone calls, filled in the paperwork and fifteen minutes later the ambulance arrived.

It didn't take the desk sergeant very long to complete his paperwork, as Gary was to be released without charge, not having committed any offense. The doctor said his farewells to everyone and left to continue with his duties:Before he drove away, he removed a white card from his wallet and dialed the number printed on the card, on his mobile phone. His call was answered by a young woman. "Help line" she said. "Hello. This is Doctor Rodgers. I've just attended a patient at Station Road police station, that I think you might be interested in. He seems to fit the criteria I was given".

"Thank you for responding" she said, "It's really important that you answer the following questions as accurately as you can". The call lasted for about another ten minutes, after which she thanked the doctor for his co-operation and reminded him to call again if anything else cropped up.: He put the phone back in his jacket pocket and tucked the card away in his wallet. 'I wonder who I was talking to and what her department's function is,' he thought. 'Why was she so interested in my patient? I suppose I'll never find out what's going on, but something's happening'.

Back in Gary's flat, Suzy was not a happy girl. It had been a long time since her vegetables had passed the 'well done' stage, most of them having turned to mush. During this period, Gary was called some very unpleasant names. It had been ages since he was supposed to nip down to the shop and then come straight back.

"God knows what he's got mixed up in this time" she said aloud, "I've had enough, I'm going home. Sod him".

She turned the cooker off, grabbed her coat and bag, turned off the lights and once again slammed the door behind her. She was not to know that at that very moment, Gary was strapped down to a stretcher in the back of an ambulance, heavily sedated and on his way to the Psychiatric Hospital.

***

CHAPTER TWO

CHANGED

It's a bit of a cliche, but Theo worked all week just for the weekend, when he would go out clubbing with his mates. His job at a supermarket didn't exactly stretch his mind, but like many of his contemporaries he had left school with minimum qualifications and with minimum expectations. He had eventually found this job at the supermarket and although he couldn't see himself in the same job in ten years' time, it did for now, as it put money in his pocket. Money that he felt he put to good use at the week-end, although he usually started the new week broke and spent the week looking forward to his next pay day. He was fortunate to have a mother who only asked for a basic rent from him, so the remainder of his wages was his to use as he wanted. As he prepared himself for another Friday night on the town, he never realised how much his situation would change that evening and the effect that this would have on those who cared for him.

There was nothing to indicate that this Friday was to differ from any other. He drank, chatted to girls and even danced with some of them. Nothing ever seemed to develop from these meetings, but it was nice to have the female company and enjoy the type of music he liked, rather than the 'muzak' he had to endure at work every day. Because of drug problems in the past, the club that Theo and his mates preferred had to close early.

Although they still chose to frequent it as substances to heighten the evening's experience could be obtained with a word to the right person.

The restrictions to the club's opening hours had done little to stop the flow of illegal substances. Even if they had closed the club altogether, those who sold such things would soon find a new way of contacting their potential customers. But the police and local council had to try and do what they could, within their prescribed limitations. The club had to close at one a.m., although they all wished it could stay open longer. Still, a few hours were better than nothing.

Theo and his mates started chatting to a group of girls they had met up with as they left the club and their animated talking and laughter added to the general noise and bustle. Even the strongest bladder has its limit and Theo's had reached bursting point, no doubt due to the large amount of drink he had consumed during the evening. What was he going to do? He couldn't return to the club, as it was all locked up. now. So he scanned the area for a suitable location, where he couldn't be spotted by any passing police patrol car. An alley across the street seemed to fit the bill, especially as there were some rubbish bins to hide behind. "I'll be back in a minute" Theo said to the group.

"Don't flood us out" his friend Bob said as he laughed at Theo's panicky discomfort.

As Theo walked across the road, the need to pee became ever more urgent. He reveled in the feeling of relief and hoped that it would never end, but of course it did. He had just zipped up his trousers, when he heard a voice behind him. "Don't turn around, just give me your wallet and mobile". Theo hesitated. Was someone playing a joke on him? He wasn't sure, his brain confused by the combination of alcohol and drugs. The owner of the voice was becoming very impatient. "Come on, quickly!" it said. Then out of the blue, a sudden push from behind smashed his forehead into the brick wall. This was the final straw, as far as his body was concerned. After the initial blinding flash as his head hit the wall, everything went black and he fell to the ground, unconscious.

Eventually, consciousness returned, although he had no idea how long he had laid there. His watch was gone and it was obvious that his pockets had been rifled. Everything of any value had been taken by his unknown assailant. He realised that his head really hurt and reaching up to his forehead he felt brick grains embedded in his skin. As he lifted his hand away he noticed the blood. 'He must have really pushed me hard' Theo thought and then he noticed that his head had started to pound."I'd better get home and get this wound, cleaned up' he said to himself.

When he had left home that evening, the last thing he expected was that his night out would end up like this. Although he knew that this kind of robbery regularly occurred, he had never expected to become a victim himself.

As he started to walk out of the alleyway, he felt the warm trickle of blood as it ran down the side of his head. 'I need to get this bleeding stopped before it ruins my best shirt' he thought to himself. A slight concussion now adding itself to the rest of his problems.

As he started to walk back to the road, he staggered all over the place. Adding the bang on his head to the effects of the evening's festivities it was a wonder that he could stand, let alone walk. As he reached the road, he was pleased to see that there was still a large crowd outside the club. Looking around, trying to locate his friends, he noticed that a group of girls walked straight past him, but didn't even look in his direction. 'What's the matter with them, am I invisible, or something?' he thought. Theo would have at least expected a look in his direction, if only briefly, as he must have looked quite disheveled, plus he had blood running down his face. Then he saw his friends, still standing roughly where he had left them. He walked over to them, expecting some smart comment from one of them, but there wasn't any reaction. It was as if he wasn't there.

"I wish Theo would hurry up" Andy said, "he must have pee'd enough to fill a reservoir by now".

"What's the matter with you all?" Theo said in response, "I'm right here, stop messing about. You're frightening me. I've been mugged and I need help".

There was no response and to his horror Theo realised that they weren't having him on. There were no sniggers, no sideways glances and no recognition in their eyes.

Since Bob was closest, he reached out to grab hold of his shoulder. His hand went straight through him. Shocked and terrified, he pulled his hand back and looked at it. He could feel it alright, so he tried again. The result was the same. Maybe he was having an hallucination caused by the bang on his head. This theory was quickly disproved, as his friends along with the girls they had picked up, turned to leave.

"I'll go and see where Theo's got to." Bob said and headed towards the alleyway. It wasn't long before he returned. "Well, where is he?" Terry asked. Bob had a very puzzled look on his face. "There's no trace of him, anywhere" he said.

"Knowing Theo, he's picked up some tart and forgotten all about us" Terry replied, with a big grin on his face.

Theo was now screaming at the top of his voice, "I'm here, please respond. I'm right here in front of you". For the first time in many years, tears rolled down his cheeks and dripped off his chin. But his friends turned to go home, without reacting to him in any way. Theo tried to side-step out of their way, but was not quick enough and Andy walked straight through him, as if he wasn't there and to-them, he wasn't. Theo then realised that he had to come to terms with the fact that they really couldn't see him and as far as they were concerned, he didn't exist anymore.

What was he going to do? Was he on his own? Were there others in the same situation? Realising that he felt cold, he pulled his coat tightly around him. The thought of having to survive the night on his own, without food or shelter really frightened him.

There were still quite a few people around and he wondered if any of the pairs of eyes that were looking around, belonged to someone in a similar condition. He noticed that a man in his thirties, seemed to be watching him very closely. He ambled across the road towards Theo and spoke some words of greeting.

"Are you surprised that I can see you?" he said. Theo hadn't noticed, then it suddenly hit him. His friends had totally ignored him, obviously because they couldn't see him, but this person had specifically picked him out.

"How did you know?" Theo asked.

"It's quite simple really and by the way, I'm Phil. I suppose this is all very new and strange to you".

"Well, go on. Tell me how you knew that I had been altered, in the way I have?" Theo questioned.

"Actually, it took a while for me to work it out, when it's really quite simple. Let me show you, come down the road a little way. Look at me and tell me what's missing".

Theo looked Phil up and down and even walked around him, all to no avail. "You've got me. I can't see anything".

"Let's try it a different way" Phil suggested, "What's missing? What should you be able to see, but you can't?" Then, Theo realised. Phil was standing next to a street lamp, but he didn't cast a shadow.

"You haven't got a shadow" Theo exclaimed, "is it really that simple?

"Yes" Phil replied, "You would think that if we didn't cast a shadow we wouldn't be able to see, but we can".

Theo now felt relieved, there was hope after all. Others had obviously travelled on this voyage of exploration before him and most importantly, had been able to find solutions to help them cope with their new situation.

"Let's get away from here" Phil suggested, "That wind is getting a bit cold now, so let's go and get something to eat and drink". Theo hadn't even thought about it, but then realised that he did feel hungry. After all, his body had used up a great deal of energy during the past few hours. Normally he would be home by now, enjoying a bacon sandwich and a mug of coffee, while he was interrogated about his activities. He suddenly thought about his mother, she would be getting concerned by now.

"Phil," he said, "Is there any thing I can do to put my mum's mind at rest?";

"Sadly, there isn't. It's not for lack of trying to communicate, but without any success so far".

Theo, normally the carefree young man, started to worry about his mum along with his sister, even though they fought most of the time.

"Let's go and meet up with the rest of our little group" Phil said as he started to walk off and beckoned Theo to follow. His comment gave Theo a boost. They were not the only two in this unusual situation.

Theo was not sure where he was, as he only came into this part of town at the weekends to go to the club. So he followed Phil, as he felt at ease with him. After what felt like hours, they entered an old abandoned building. Theo was relieved to see a number of people gathered around a fire. 'A chance to get warm at last' he thought, although the walk had taken the chill off. He also noticed that he didn't feel so frightened anymore.

"Come on in" Phil said gesturing to him to join them. "We're not going to harm you. You're a member of an exclusive little club now".

Theo was ushered into the small gathering and lapped up the warmth from the fire. "Here, have something to eat". He turned to see who had spoken and saw a middle aged woman offering him a sandwich. "Cheese and pickle" she said "most people like a nice piece of cheese. I hope you do".

Theo hadn't thought about eating, but he suddenly felt very hungry. He took the sandwich from her hand and quickly gulped it down. He was surprised that he could hold the sandwich, unsure how it was possible, but he didn't let his concerns mar the enjoyment.

"Thank you so much" he said, "I hope that I can return the favour to you one day, I'm sorry, I don't know your name".

"I'm Jennifer," the woman replied and then went on to introduce the rest of the group, that comprised three women and now, with the addition of Theo, four men: Theo looked them all over, trying to determine if there were any commonalities between them. But if there were, they eluded him.

"We've all been through this time of re-adjustment, but you will get through it I assure you," an older man said. "But to start with I think it would be a good idea to get that wound on your head cleaned up. Then if you're up to it, we'd like to know how this happened to you and we can tell you what we have discovered about the new way of life you have now entered. There are certain limitations and restrictions you need to be aware of."

A little while later, after his head wound had been seen to, Theo related the evening's experiences to them. When he reached .the part about discovering his new state and how it made him feel, they all nodded in agreement. "....and that's what happened right up to the time that Phil rescued me" Theo said.

The others went on to relate their own experiences and a pattern started to emerge. All of them at the time the change occurred, suffered some form of head trauma, coupled with an unusual mixture of chemicals in their system. Regardless of the variations, the outcome was the same. They appeared to slip out of phase with the rest of humanity, existing within their own environment.

By two a.m., Theo's mother was getting really worried. His sister Jasmine, had been home for some time and had stayed up to keep her mother company. To start with, she thought that he had decided to spend the night with one of his friends, but that assumption was dashed by a phone call from Bob, asking if Theo had got home yet. When he was told that he hadn't, he related how he had just seemed to disappear and that no-one seemed to know where he had got to. Bob said that he would phone around all Theo's friends, to see if he had decided to stay the night with any of them.

A half hour later, Bob phoned back. As the phone rang, his mum raced across the room to answer it. "Theo, is that you, are you alright, where are you?".

"I'm sorry Mrs Brown, this is Bob again. I can't find any trace of him at all. I don't know what else to do".

"Thank you for all your efforts Bob" she said, "I think I'll phone the police, to see if he's been picked up somewhere and if they don't know where he is, I'll try the hospital. If I find anything out, I'll let you know".

She put the phone down and started crying. Jasmine sat down next to her mum and put her arm around her. "Don't worry mum, he'll be OK you know he will, this is Theo we're talking about".

"Thank's love" she said, "hand me the phone book, so that I can find the number of the hospital".

Four phone calls later, there still wasn't any news of Theo. The police hadn't picked him up and the hospital had no knowledge of him. They didn't have any unidentified casualty patients either. "If he comes breezing in here in the morning, with that stupid grin of his on his face, I'll kill him" his mother said.

Jasmine brought a duvet down stairs and mother and daughter huddled up together on the settee, waiting for the phone to ring and bring them news of the errant Theo. Time slowly drifted by, without any information about Theo arriving. The two of them finally fell asleep and there they stayed until morning.

Theo had been, thinking about what his mother must have been going through and the thought that he was making her very unhappy really bothered him, although he realised that there was absolutely nothing he could do about it. He had to learn how to live with his condition, so that if there ever was a way to return, he would be able to explain to his mother in person.

"So then" he said, addressing the group, "What is it that I can and can't do? Who's going to explain it all to me". T

he group agreed that as Jennifer was their most senior member, not by age but by experience, it would be best if she took on the task. So the group settled down and Jennifer took centre stage. "You won't be surprised to learn that we are not the only ones in this situation. To our knowledge, there are about twelve more like us in this area, but in the whole country, I wouldn't like to say. We all seem to have had similar experiences and have the same limitations. As you have found out, we cannot be seen by people in general and are unable to touch them. This appears to apply to all animate life, so if you used to enjoy contact with animals, I'm afraid that it's no longer possible. But this is not like a sci-fi story where you are able to walk through walls, they may feel softer to you, but I have yet to meet one of us that can achieve that feat. Somethings you won't be able to touch at all, you'll find out what they are by experience. Now, as far as food is concerned. Most foods we can touch and consume, so eating is not a problem, although access to food is something you'll have to learn. Phil, perhaps you'll help Theo to learn the more practical aspects of obtaining food".

Phil said that he would be happy to do so. Jennifer continued, "It's strange that any food and drink we consume seems to effected by our altered state and disappears from the outside world. Sadly, because of our condition, the only way we can obtain food is by stealing it. That goes against my morals, but what else can we do? We don't have any other way to obtain our needs, apart from stealing from shops. If anyone can come up with a better method, I'll be pleased to hear it. Well Theo, that's the induction into your new world. Any questions?".

"I'm sure I'll think of something later" Theo said, "but for now, thank you for explaining it all to me and thank you everyone for helping me through this difficult time".

While Jennifer had been speaking, Theo had been surreptitiously watching a young woman, about his own age as far as he could determine, and he had noted that she was called Emily. He was pleased when he caught her taking a good look at him, when she thought he wasn't looking. But of course, he noticed.

'Well,' he thought, 'there's one thing about me that hasn't changed'. He was getting very sleepy by this time and as he had lost his watch earlier, had no idea what the time was.

"You'll feel quite sleepy for the first few days," Phil said to him, "This change seems to take a great deal of energy out of the system. You'll have to ensure that you eat well over the next few days. I'll help you out with that."

Turning to the group, he suggested that they all get settled down for the night. Theo didn't need much encouragement and was soon asleep, as were the rest of the group. Theo's last thoughts, as he faded away, were the questions he had forgotten earlier and would forget again by morning.

The morning was bright and clear and the group slowly stirred, rousing themselves from their slumbers. As was their practice, the food was pooled and shared out equally. This was an aspect of Theo's new society that he found quite novel, but it made sense. After all, food was not that plentiful and all they had was from the previous day, so it made sense to use it up. Theo managed to manouevre things so that he ended up sitting next to Emily, which, he was pleased to see, didn't bother her at all. It didn't take long for the two of them to become engrossed in conversation and sharing their portions of food and drink. On the other side of the group Jennifer turned to Phil and said "It's nice to see that Emily has someone of her own age to spend some time with. She actually has a smile on her face. That's the first time she's looked happy since she became one of us".

"I think it will do the both of them good, a semblance of their old way of life which should help them deal with their new situation," Phil replied.

The two youngsters had no idea that they were the subject of scrutiny by the rest of the group, they were too wrapped up in each other to notice. Finally the food was consumed and it was time to prepare for the day's activities. It would have been so easy, for any one of them, to become overwhelmed by the situation and sink into a depressive state. But as there-was a group that looked out for one another, it helped to prevent that happening. Although to start with, when Jennifer was on her own she had felt like giving up on a number of occasions and had it happened, who would ever have known. But that possibility was avoided by Phil's arrival and the two of them kept each other going during the difficult early days. The group paired off, Theo with Phil as arranged the previous evening and they all started to drift off to their various activities. Theo's day was made for him, when Emily ran back to him and kissed him on the cheek. "See you tonight" she said, before running off to catch up with Jennifer.

"1 think you've made a conquest there," Phil said chuckling to himself. But Theo didn't hear him, he was too busy watching Emily, as she walked away.

***

CHAPTER THREE

ASSIGNMENT

Superintendent Jack Hargreaves leaned back in his chair, if he had been allowed he would have lit up his pipe now. But the no smoking legislation had put paid to that. How things had changed since he joined the force a life-time ago, but now, just two more years and he could retire with a full pension. He didn't approve of some of the more recent innovations within the police force, feeling that 'good old-fashioned' police work that obtained results, had been pushed to one side to make room for new-fangled ideas, which were constantly being revised, because they didn't work. He also didn't approve of university graduates being brought into the higher ranks, as they tended to make judgments based on academic theories, rather than experience. What else could they do? They hadn't spent time on the beat learning the practical aspects of policing.

That's the way he felt and most people in the station knew Jack's feelings about modern police practices and was, in a sense, humoured for his 'out of touch' views, although he was renowned for getting results with his old school ways.

The majority of the younger detectives liked working with Jack, as they knew that he would be straight with them. No station politics, he just wanted to get the job done and get a result. It seemed as if there was a waiting list to join Jack's team, as promotions occurred and spaces became available. But it had to be admitted, that officers who had been trained and honed by Jack became some of the best senior officers in the force.

Jack was deep in thought, when his phone rang. He was taken aback and looked at his watch. 'Who's still here at this time of night?' he thought as he answered the insistent ringing.

"Superintendent Hargreaves" he replied.

"Jack, it's Arthur. Would you come up to my office for a few minutes, before you go home".

"OK" Jack said, "I'm on my way. Five minutes later and you would have missed me".

"I'm glad that I didn't" was the response.

Ignoring the lift, Jack started to climb the stairs towards the top floor. He liked to use the stairs as he felt it kept him in trim and prevented his hips from seizing up. So far it had worked. He was fortunate to be in good physical shape for a man of his age, even though he liked to smoke his pipe, when he was allowed.

He arrived at the top floor without puffing, a feat many younger officers could take note of. His knock on the door was quickly followed by a "Come in". As he entered the room, he looked around to see if anyone apart from his boss was there and was surprised to see the Assistant Chief Constable.

Jack's superior, Detective Chief Superintendent Arthur Richmond, waved Jack into the room. "Come in Jack and sit down. The ACC has something special to ask you, something that should provide you with a real challenge for what may well be your last case. That's if you choose to accept it" he said and added, "By the way, would you like a cup of coffee? I think you'll need one after this".

The ACC pulled his chair a little closer to the others, as if to prevent anyone overhearing what he was about to say. "Jack, I've specifically asked for you on this case, as I feel that it needs the touch of old style police techniques, utilizing the instincts that you've built up over the years. I know that this goes against all the public statements that we make about modern policing, but this case needs someone who sees things in a different way and I think, along with the agreement of other senior officers, that you're the right man for the job."

"Thank you" Jack replied, "I must say that I'm rather intrigued by what you've said, it does sound like quite a challenge".

"Right then" the ACC said, "From now on all that I say stays between the three of us. If you accept the case, you will obviously have to choose some officers to work along with you. Officers that can be trusted to keep quiet and not talk about the case with others, regardless of the pressure that may be put on them. Alright so far?"

"Yes, I understand what you're driving at and I can think of a few officers who would fit the bill. I presume you want people who are good at puzzles and crosswords and are able to make lateral jumps in their thinking?".

"You've got the idea", the ACC replied. "Now we'll move on to the reason for all the secrecy. This is a report from the Home Office" he said, holding up a folder, "A copy has been sent to each Chief Constable, along with instructions that its contents be divulged to as few people as possible".

Jack's interest was really roused now and he paid

41

close attention as the ACC continued to speak. "The situation is this. A strange phenomena has been noted all over the country. People have been disappearing. Now, before you respond, I know that people have always gone missing, it's happened since the dawn of time. But this is different, something strange is going on, something out of the ordinary. Usually people go missing for a reason, not always an obvious one, but if you dig deep enough there's usually one there. Most are usually traceable and turn up either living or dead, but there are a few exceptions that are never located. Nowadays, there are an increasing number that just disappear without reason, often at the strangest times. Some have disappeared during a night out, others while engaging in a variety of everyday activities and a few have even disappeared from closed rooms. One moment they are there, the next they are gone. No explanation and no discernable reason. I'm sure that you can both see why this has been kept quiet, if it got out, it would cause a panic. Well Jack, do you feel like taking this on?. I would have asked you, even if you weren't getting close to your retirement. I feel that it would be best for you to think about this overnight and give us your decision in the morning".

"I agree,"Jack said, "There's a lot at stake here and I need to be sure that I can handle it. What about clearances? I may have to ask questions in places that don't like having to give answers"

"You will get all the clearances you require" the ACC said "and I must tell you that all the members of your team will need to be screened and cleared. I'm sure that you can understand why. Come and see Arthur in the morning morning and let him know your decision."

"That should give me enough time Sir" Jack replied,

"So long as I don't disappear overnight".

Jack found it difficult to concentrate as he drove home that night. The veil of secrecy was obviously working, as he hadn't heard of the problem before. Yet he had been chosen as the officer that the 'powers that be' felt could unravel this mystery. He was comforted by the fact that other officers were facing the same task and no doubt were similarly daunted by the prospect, as they conducted investigations in their part of the country.

"You're late tonight" Jack's wife, Joyce, said as he came in through the front door. "Yes I am, sorry about that. I hope dinner isn't ruined".

"No need to worry, don't you think that I'm used to allowing time for such things, after all these years" she replied.

As he lowered himself into his favorite chair, he was finally able to light his pipe. "Do you want a drink, love?" he called through to the kitchen, trying to make himself heard over the rattle of plates and the clatter of cutlery.

"No thanks, I'm fine for now, maybe after dinner" Joyce said. They sat together for their evening meal, facing each other across the kitchen table, as they had done for so many years "You're very quiet tonight, anything bothering you, anything that you can tell me about?" Joyce enquired, "You usually bring me up to date with the day's activities, while we have dinner."

"Just before I left tonight, I was summoned upstairs and when I got there the ACC was waiting for me" Jack said.

"You haven't been naughty, have you?" Joyce said while laughing.

"Tonight, I was offered what will most likely be my

final case but it's all very hush hush. So I can't even unburden myself to you about it and I'm really going to miss that opportunity. I have to let them know in the morning whether I'll take it, or not. I'm not too sure at the moment, but it certainly would be a great challenge. So if I seem lost in my thoughts this evening don't worry".

They sat together in the sitting room for the remainder of the evening, watching TV. If you asked Jack what he had watched, he wouldn't have been able to tell you, as he was lost in his thoughts.

Sleep did not come quickly to Jack that night. His head was full of thoughts prompted by the meeting earlier that evening. There were so many possibilities to consider. Where to start? Who would make up his team? What could be behind it all? So many variables. After these thoughts had been going round and round inside his head for ages, he looked at the bedside clock. It was after two am. He realised, from the direction of his thoughts, that subconsciously, he had convinced himself that he should take the case. Looking across the bed at Joyce, who was sleeping soundly, he wondered, 'How would I feel, if she just disappeared without a trace?'. Yet this had already happened to a number of families and so far, no explanation had been uncovered. With all these thoughts bouncing around his mind, he fell into a fitful sleep.

It's quite common after a troubled night's sleep to wake early and that is exactly what happened to Jack as he woke an hour early. He decided to get up rather than just lay there and possibly wake Joyce.

Preparations for the day got under way and then he went downstairs, for some breakfast. It seemed unusual to be having breakfast alone. Although it did happen from time to time, especially if he was part of an early morning raid. Jack thought that it would be nice if he prepared Joyce's breakfast for once, after all, she looked after him every other day. He made a fresh pot of tea and then assembled a breakfast tray.

As he was ascending the stairs, the alarm clock went off. Joyce had just switched it off as he entered the room. "What's all this?" she said. "Well, I was up early, so I thought it would be nice if I looked after you, for once," Jack replied.

A smile spread across Joyce's face, "That's really kind of you Jack, I'll really enjoy this. I can't remember the last time I had breakfast in bed."

Jack sat down on the edge of the bed and they chatted, while Joyce ate her breakfast. When she had finished, Jack picked up the tray and said, "I'm off to work now, there's no point sitting around here, planning what I'll do when I get there. It would be best to go in and get started. Why don't you have a lie-in for once"

"Do you know, I think I will" Joyce said, " and by the way, are you going to take that new case?".

"Yes, I think I will. It's the kind of challenge my old brain could do with. It should blow some of the cobwebs out" Jack said as he left the room, waving goodbye over his shoulder.

Jack was first into CID that morning. He appreciated that it was too early to see the DCS, so he started to clear up all his outstanding paper work. He wanted to start the new case with a clear desk and without people pestering him for paperwork that he should have completed. A couple of junior officers came in and noticed Jack in his office. "The old man's in early today, isn't he?"

"Yes, he's not normally in this early. Do you think he's starting a new case?"

"It's possible. You know how he likes to clear his desk when he's starting something new. I think we should keep our eyes and ears open. I don't know about you, but I would really like to be part of one of Jack's teams".

They moved to their respective desks and started the day's work. Over the next half hour the majority of the officers arrived, apart from those who were already out on police business.

Jack looked at his watch and without realising it, he confirmed the time with the office clock. He picked up the phone and dialed the DCS's office.

"DCS Richmond's office" the female voice answered. "This is Superintendent Hargreaves, I'd like to see the DCS as soon as possible". "He's been expecting your call" she said, "and is ready to see you now".

Jack put the phone down and sat in silent reflection for a few minutes. 'This decision could change my life forever' he thought 'and possibly place my officers and myself in some unusual situations. After all, there are people and departments out there that will go to extraordinary lengths to protect their secrets'. "It will do them good to emerge into the daylight for once". He realised that the last statement was spoken out loud, but fortunately there wasn't anyone close enough to hear. Or so he thought. He didn't realise that his comment had been overheard by a DC who happened to pass Jack's door, which was slightly open, at the moment he spoke aloud.

"You'll never guess what I heard the old man say just now"

"Go on, tell me" her colleague replied.

"Well" she said, "he was just sitting there, obviously working something out in his head, when he suddenly blurted out something about people having to come out into the light for once".

"That confirms it," her fellow DC answered, "There's been a buzz going round the office this morning that he's starting a new case and what you overheard seems to back that up. Something is definitely going on. Let's keep our wits about us and try to fathom it out. A few moments later, Jack stood up, smoothed his jacket down and walked out of his office. His mind was too wrapped up in his thoughts to notice all the pairs of eyes watching him and of course, he never heard the chatter that started as the doors closed behind him.

Jack entered the outer office, where he was greeted by the owner of the voice that he heard on the phone. Now he recognised her. Seeing her face and hearing her voice triggered his memory. "Go on in", she said "he's expecting you". Jack thanked her, knocked on the DCS's door and walked in.

"Morning Jack. How did you sleep last night? I don't mind telling you, that thinking about this problem kept my mind whirring for a long time".

"I was the same. I was totally engrossed. Even after I got to bed I couldn't stop thinking about it, with all the implications going round and round in my head"

"Well then Jack. I have to ask if you've reached a decision, as the ACC needs

to know. Will you take on this case, or not?".

"To start with I was unsure, if I'm honest. Especially as this could involve dealing with civil servants and the like and they tend to rub me up the wrong way. So that made me apprehensive at first. But then I realised that I had to put my personal feelings to one side. After all, my job as a copper is to protect the public, regardless of how I might feel about the people I have to deal with. So I effectively talked myself into accepting the challenge"

A look of relief passed over the DCS' face at first and then it lit up and he said, "I'm so glad that you've decided to take it on, Jack. As. the ACC pointed out last night, we needed a special kind of detective for this case and you really are the best detective we have. I'll phone the ACC and let him know."

Jack got up, ready to leave, "No, don't go Jack. I've a few more things to discuss with you, after I've made this call. Why don't you help yourself to some coffee while you wait".

Jack walked over to the coffee percolator and poured himself a cup, while the DCS phoned the ACC to inform him of Jack's acceptance of the case. They then spoke about some unrelated matters until the call was completed.

"Right Jack, come on over and sit down. The next thing you'll need to do is to start picking the team that you want to work with you, Any thoughts at the moment?".

Jack didn't respond immediately. Finally he said, "For my number one, I thought about DI Dave Grantham".

"That's a good choice" the DCS replied, "I had a thought that he would be one of your choices. Any others?".

"Not at the moment. I need to take my time and think carefully about this. Once an officer becomes part of this team, there's no going back, it's for good. You cannot retract the information they'll become privy to, so it's important to get it right first time".

"I agree," the DCS said, "Don't think that I'm trying to force your hand, but I'll need to know who else you want by the end of the day. I have to let my superiors know and ensure that the chosen officers are released from their current duties. Also, there's the little matter of security checks. They will have to be performed on the officers you choose and by the way, you're already cleared"

"Thanks very much" a surprised Jack replied, "I didn't realise that it was being done. You must have had great confidence in me making the decision you wanted."

"Well Jack, we've been working together for many years now and I think we know and understand each other pretty well. Don't you agree?"

Jack had to agree. They had been together during their training at Hendon and their paths had crossed on a number of occasions over the years. "The rest of your team by the end of the day, please Jack" the DCS said as Jack walked out of the room.

Back in his office once again, Jack requested copies of the service records of the officers on his short list and concluded the phone call by saying, "Any problems, ring the DCS and he'll clear it with you". Within half an hour, the files were on his desk. These were all officers he had worked with before and had a great deal of respect for as-he.knew that he could rely on them. By lunch time he had pretty well made up his mind over his list but decided to mull over his choices while he ate. Anyone that tried to engage Jack in conversation that lunch time didn't fare too well, as his mind was totally occupied with the important decision that he had to make. As he drank the last of his coffee, he was happy with his choices and left the canteen for a wander around the car park. By doing this he could enjoy his pipe before re-entering the building and seeing the DCS, to inform him about his choices.

Within the hour, he had returned to the DCS's office, having taken the service records of the relevant officers with him. "Right then Jack, who have you chosen? I'll make a note of the names, so that I can get the security checks under way and let me assure you that they won't know that it's happening, just in case one of them doesn't get accepted".

"I thought about that possibility" Jack replied, "so I've a couple of extra names that I can fall back on if required".

"Good thinking. Right. Give me the names and we'll fast track these checks and then you can interview each one of them, without giving too much away and see if they're interested. If they are, I'll arranged for them to be released from their current duties".

"Right then, here goes. As I told you earlier, I would like DI David Grantham for the senior officer position, along with DS Sarah Mitchell and finally DS Clive Barron.

"Is that it?" the DCS asked, "Just those three officers?"

"Yes. A small closely knit team should work well" Jack replied, "Less chance of security lapses that way and I do appreciate that DS Barron is quite a young officer to be a DS, but he has an exceptional mind, that I feel will be of great benefit to the team".

"I can't foresee any problems there," said the DCS, "You're not involving half the station, or anything like that, are you. I don't think you'll have any problems getting your choices accepted, so long as the wretched security checks are alright and with these officers I don't think you'll have any problems".

On his way back down the stairs, Jack was thinking

about his next move. What would he ask his chosen officers when he interviewed them? How much information could he release in answer to their questions and how could he impress on them the importance of security during the investigation? He decided to see DI Grantham first and get him on board, if he was willing. Then he could move on to the two junior officers. By the time that he was back at his desk, he had arranged it all in his head. Now to see if it would all pan out the way he hoped that it would. He spent the afternoon working out strategy for the investigation, trying to plan it out as he would have done with any other case.

It didn't take Jack long to realise that the usual rules and techniques didn't really fit the situation. If it had have been a murder that he was investigating there would have been a body, which would have provided information, along with the victim's friends and relations. All these items would have provided a place to start from, but none of that applied in this case. He couldn't examine the victims, so he was unable to determine what had caused their problem and there wasn't a weapon that had caused their disappearance. He could interview the families and friends of those missing and could uncover some instances where someone had left of their own accord. But the disappearances he was going to investigate were the ones that had no logical explanation, so where on earth was he going to start? The sooner the team could be united the better, four minds working together, approaching the situation in different ways could soon determine the first step to take.

All those working in the CID office that afternoon, did not fail to notice that Jack spent the whole time in his office, alone. He was obviously working on something important. Since the first observations that morning, the rumour mill had been in operation, providing some ideas about the case that Jack was thought to be working on. although none of these speculations came anywhere close to what he was actually doing. Jack had been astounded when he was first told about the situation and the other experienced officers in the CID office would have been as well. It was because of the security so far, that had managed to keep the lid on it all, but it did leave Jack wondering. What else could be going on, that had also been kept quiet?

He spent the remainder of the afternoon planning and speculating, until it was time to go home. As he was just about to switch off the office lights, he realised what he had done. His writing pad, covered in all his doodles, questions, names and speculations had been left on the desk for all to see. This was the simple kind of security lapse that had to be avoided, although he was pleased that it happened, as it demonstrated how easily-the things could take place. "I must be more careful in the future" Jack said, as he turned to leave, wondering what the next day would bring.

***

CHAPTER FOUR

HOSPITAL

The ambulance's right hand indicator flashed as it turned off the main road, into the tree lined avenue that was the entrance to the Fairview Psychiatric Hospital. The avenue was one aspect of the welltended grounds that surrounded the hospital and were a pleasure to walk in, also providing a healing environment for the patients. As the ambulance drew closer to the main entrance patients, along with their nurses, could be seen either walking in the gardens, or spending time sitting on one of the many benches, enjoying the view and the relaxing atmosphere.

    Gary was oblivious to all of this. The injection that the doctor had administered had sedated him to the point of semi-consciousness so that he didn't harm himself and made him easier for the medics to deal with. The ambulance pulled up beside the front door, announcing it's arrival by the squeal of it's brakes and the banging of doors. As the rear doors of the ambulance were opened, the bright light flooded in and made Gary squint his eyes. This was one of the few voluntary movements that he could make, as his arms and legs were strapped to the stretcher. The two ambulance men then removed the stretcher from the ambulance and Gary was bounced about as he was wheeled up the ramp into the reception area of the hospital. Had he been more aware of his situation, he would have realised how difficult it was to steady yourself when your arms and legs are restrained, but he was too far gone for that. He heard voices talking, but they were unintelligible, sounding distant, just out of reach. What was actually happening was the change-over from the ambulance stretcher to the hospital gurney, so that the ambulance could get on its way.

"Make sure that he doesn't start thrashing about when he feels the restraints loosened," a voice said. This was timely advice, as at that moment Gary realised that he was able to move his arms and legs and tried to make good his escape. All to no avail. The combination of the drugs in his system and two burly orderlies quickly ended Gary's bid for freedom. The orderlies had dealt with too many patients in the past, to be overcome by Gary's feeble efforts and quickly subdued him, restraining his arms and legs to the gurney. The ambulancemen and the orderlies stood chatting for a few minutes and then parted. As the ambulance drove away they radioed into base, to tell them they were finished at the hospital and were now free to take another call. Gary was wheeled to his room, while the receptionist waited for the police to arrive and provide them with Gary's details, as at that time they didn't have any idea who he was. Gary didn't know what was happening, as he watched the ceiling lights pass above him with a hypnotic rhythm. Eventually he had to close his eyes, as the constant flashing of the lights was making him feel ill. Finally the motion ceased, as he was moved into his room. They placed him on the bed, restraining him once again.

"We'll get him changed later, once the doctor has seen him. Any idea why he's here?"

The other orderly replied. "I heard that he flipped

out at some shops and then hid out between the rubbish bins. Apparently he put up a good fight when the police arrived, but they soon sorted him out".

"Poor sod" the other one said, "If only he knew what was ahead of him".

As they left the room, the double action lock clicked into place as the door was shut. He was alone. Silence reigned as he laid there on the bed, while the full effect of the drugs took over as the external stimuli had stopped and he fell asleep.

About an hour later, the police arrived. "Where on earth have you been?" the receptionist asked, "we've been waiting for information on the man that you had in the cells". "We were right behind the ambulance when it left the station, but we were called to a domestic as there wasn't anyone else available".

"Well, I'll let you off, this time", she said, "So what can you tell me about your prisoner, as we can't do anything with him until we get his personal information from you".

One officer smiled and said "I'd hate to know what you lot are going to do with the poor bloke."

"Come on now," she responded, "We're not that bad. We have moved on from the dark ages. Anything we do will be for his own good. Our doctors really care about the welfare of the patients, although I wouldn't fancy tacking some of the medications they dish out. Anyway, that's by the by. Who is our mystery guest?". The other officer reached into his tunic pocket and removed a folded wad of A4 sized papers. "Here are the committal papers from the FME to place him in your secure care and, wait for it, his name is Gary Sandowski."

"Slow down. How do you spell that name? I haven't come across that one before".

The next few moments were spent putting Gary's details onto the hospital computer system, which sent a memo to the doctor who would be overseeing Gary's treatment, during his stay in the hospital. Now that he was officially a patient, Gary's outdoor clothes were removed. This was needed as they had picked up the odour from the bins he had sheltered between at the shops and to be honest, they weren't that clean to start with. He was put into clean hospital pyjamas and placed back on the bed. He struggled a bit, when the restraints were re-applied but he was told that they were for his own good. This was an expression that he would hear many times in the days to come. But Gary was oblivious to all of this happening, as he wallowed in a drug-induced sleep and there he remained until the following morning, when he awoke with an intense head-ache.

As his eyes opened Gary's first thought was 'Where the hell am I?' and then he started to panic when he realised that he couldn't move his arms and legs. "What's going on" he shouted, "Let me out of here you bastards. You can't keep me in here," although at the time he didn't appreciate that they had the legal power to do just that.

He engaged in another brief bout of fighting against the restraints, but as he began to tire himself out, he realised that he wouldn't be able to break free. The only way was to have them removed by those who had attached them in the first place. Of course at that moment in time, he hadn't any idea who was behind his detainment and there was one other thing that had escaped his notice. Tucked away in the corner of the room, high up, close to the ceiling, was a camera with an integrated microphone, placed there so that the patients could be monitored from a central point.

All of the patient areas were fitted out like this. Even in the open wards, where the patients were free to move about and, under supervision, go out for walks in the gardens. But Gary was in the secure part of the complex, as he had displayed uncontrolled and violent behavior, when he was first brought in. So the doctors would not know what they were dealing with until they had been able to speak to him and that could only happen once he had calmed down. Gary accepted that he was defeated and lay back on his bed, exhausted.

A strange new emotion enveloped him, something that felt alien to him and he struggled to identify it. Then it came to him. It was an overwhelming feeling of hopelessness. With this thought running through his mind, the drugs overpowered him once again and he fell asleep.

He woke with a start, as he heard the door being unlocked. The passing hours had loosened the grip of the drugs and he was more aware of his surroundings. The door swung back against the wall and three people entered. Two men and a woman, who introduced herself. "Good afternoon Gary. I'm Dr Hedley and I will be looking after you during your stay with us".

"How long have I been in this place?" Gary asked.

"You've been here four days now and we kept you sedated to allow you to calm down following your traumatic experience, which I'd like to discuss with you tomorrow. But for now, I'd like to see how you cope if the restraints are removed. Don't go getting any ideas about escape, as you wouldn't be able to get out of here. Even if you managed to get past the orderlies and out into the corridor, that's as far as you'd get as the doors are all locked and have a keypad entry system. So you would quickly be recaptured, be brought back in here and restrained once again. You'll soon learn that behaving yourself is the best policy and that it's for your own good. "

There was that statement again and that wouldn't be the last time that he heard it. "Right Gary," she said "I'm going to get the orderlies to remove your leg restraints first, so please don't start thrashing your legs about".

He noticed that as she said this, the two burly orderlies moved right into the room, to follow her instructions as up to this point they had stood behind the doctor, almost in the doorway. After the leg restraints were removed, he waited until the doctor stood back, in-case she got the wrong idea when he started to move his legs about. He had never appreciated having the freedom to move about as you wanted before and looked forward to the restraints that held his wrists to be first loosened and then removed.

"How's that?" the doctor asked, "Do you feel ready to have the other ones removed?".

"Yes. I'm ready" Gary replied, "I can't wait to get them off" and watched closely as the orderlies moved in to follow her instructions. As the restraints were removed, Gary felt large hands grasp his wrists, to prevent any punches being thrown. "If I ask them to release you now, no funny business, OK".

Gary understood. For the moment they had the upper hand and he knew that fighting back would be futile, so he agreed to her terms. The orderlies removed their hands and Gary looked at them closely. He had seen muscular bodies before, but their hands were impressive, like dinner plates and he now understood how they had held him down so easily. He was free, able to move as he wanted. He had always taken such freedom for granted, but he now valued it more than ever before.

"Well, how do you feel?".

He didn't answer, as he was engrossed in his thoughts.

"Gary. How do you feel?" she asked again.

"Alright" he replied, "I'm a bit woozy, but I suppose that's from all the stuff you've injected into me."

"That's only to be expected," the doctor said, "We had to sedate you when you were brought in, as you were in such a state. It won't be completely removed because you need to unwind, but I'll give you a lower dose overnight, along with something to stop you seeing things".

Gary was going to blurt out that he wasn't seeing things, but thought better of it. At least he was free to move about now, so he decided to keep his mouth shut. He knew that there would be other opportunities for him to discuss what he had experienced. He suddenly realised that the doctor was speaking " ..... so that's what we'll do and then you'll be brought to my office so that we can talk about what's been troubling you. I suppose you're feeling quite hungry as you haven't had much to eat over the last few days".

"What do you mean 'had much' you've been starving me!" Gary replied angrily. "Well that isn't entirely true" the Doctor said "You did have a drip-feed in your arm, which supplied you with nutrients and liquids. Look at your left arm, you'll see the mark where the needle was inserted".

Gary raised his left arm, pulled the jacket sleeve out of the way and sure enough, there was the tell tale red mark where the needle had entered his vein.

"So we have been looking after you despite what you may think" the Doctor continued by saying "I'll get some food sent up to you and then you should start to feel a little happier."

Gary liked that idea. He hadn't appreciated how attractive the thought of some food could be. Gary looked up at the doctor and smiled, "I don't suppose there's any chance of a nice cold can of lager with my food, is there?"

"Sorry Gary" she said with a laugh. "No alcohol, especially with the medication you've had".

She turned on her heel and was followed out of the room by her entourage. Sure enough, while Gary was exploring his room and having a look out of the barred window, a nurse with an orderly in tow, arrived with his meal.

"I'll come back and collect your tray in a little while and give you your medication at the same time. Is that alright?"

"Yeah" Gary replied and he noticed her smile as she turned to leave the room, making Gary feel at ease with her, unlike the doctor, even though she had been pleasant enough. He had always been wary of doctors and the power they wielded. He couldn't help feeling that she hadn't been totally honest with him, as far as her intentions had been concerned. He'd heard about places like this before and some of the treatments they meted out, leaving people without personalities, or to use the vernacular like 'vegetables'.

'If there's any suggestion that they intend to do something like that to me, I'm out of here, no matter what it takes' he thought to himself. Then he tucked into his meal, which by hospital standards, was surprisingly good. When he had finished he felt bloated as he washed it down with the beaker of juice. He examined the cutlery and quickly established that there was little chance of doing any damage with any of them.

Gary smiled as he thought, 'They're smart buggers, they don't miss a trick'. So that means of escape had been refused him, for the moment. Maybe things might be different if he was able to ingratiate himself with the doctor and be allowed to join the general population. But this was all speculation, he hadn't even been outside his room yet. So when the opportunity arose, he had to take note of everything he heard and saw. Filing it away for a time when the information would be useful.

He was mulling these points over, when he heard the lock in the door and the nurse, along with her keeper, walked into the room. "How was that Gary? I hope you don't mind me using your first name".

"That's alright by me" he said adding "Abby", having read her name on her ID badge.

"Well" she said, "Your brain is operating normally and your sight's obviously alright as the printing on these badges is quite small. Right then, are you going to let me give you your injection, or am I going to have to get my friend to help me?". "You go ahead" Gary replied, as he had already realised that at present, nothing was to be gained by fighting them. So she administered his injection, picked up his tray and the two of them left the room. His mind was exploring his various options, schemes and plans to get out of the hospital, so he could return to his normal life. The combination of his full stomach and the medication lulled him into sleep, his mind still exploring the possibilities in his dreams.

Sometime after the sun had risen on a new day, Gary slowly emerged from his sleep, finally ending up sitting on the edge of his bed. He just happened to look down at his hands and noticed that he was shaking. He lifted his hands closer to his eyes, only to notice that the shake extended into his arms as well. Incorrectly assuming that this was a side effect of the medication he had been given, he decided to mention it to the nurse, the next time he saw her. That was not very much later, as she, along with her body guard, arrived with his breakfast.

"Good morning" she said, "My name is Jill". "What's happened to Abby?" Gary asked. "Abby is on the night shift this week and I'm on days. We tend to chop and change quite regularly. Why are you asking about Abby?".

"It's just that she was kind to me when I was going through a difficult time and she stuck in my mind," he said answering her question.

"She'll be back on this wing tonight, so there's a good chance you'll see her again. After all, we want our patients to feel at ease with the staff as that will aid their recovery".

"By the way" Gary said, "I've noticed that my hands are shaking. Is that from all the stuff you've been pumping into me?".

"Well, there are side effects with all drugs, but your shaking isn't down to us. You've caused that".

"Me? How have I caused it? I've been stuck in this bed, in this room for days". "That's the reason why this shake has developed. Just think. What used to be a major part of your life, that you haven't been able to do since you've been in here?"

Gary hesitated before he answered and then said "Well, I haven't been able to get a drink since I've been in here. Is that it? Have I been drinking so much in the past, that when I stop I get the DT's?"

"That's it, you've hit the nail on the head. It's your enforced withdrawal from alcohol that's caused the shaking. I'll get you a couple of paracetamol to take the edge off things, but I'm afraid you'll have to go through the remainder of your withdrawal on your own. I don't think it will be too bad as you've already been through the worst. I'll bring the paracetamol along with your medication, when. I come back to collect your tray."

That's how Gary's day started and once again, as the medication took hold he started to feel sleepy so he lay down on his bed. A new thought started to drift through his mind. 'How do they always pick the right times to come to my room. How did they know when to bring my breakfast this morning?' As he drifted away he realised that he must be under surveillance, how else could they know when he was awake and would need his food.

"Gary, Gary". He woke with a start, as the nurse shook him by the shoulder. "Gary, it's time to get up and go to see Dr Hedley".

He stretched, looking around while his eyes came into focus and he could see the nurse smiling at him. He swung himself round onto the edge of the bed and then cautiously stood up. "Come on, put this dressing gown on and slip your feet into your slippers, then we can take you for a ride". He hadn't noticed the wheelchair before.

"I don't need that thing," he protested.

"Sorry, it's hospital policy,", she replied, "And as it's a while since you've walked any distance your legs will be a little wobbly. Especially as it's quite a way and it'll do you good to see some other parts of the hospital".

Gary knew that there wasn't any point in arguing, as he looked at the man mountain hovering by the door.

So he gave in and sat himself down in the wheelchair. "I've never been in one of these things before" he stated, "So please drive carefully".

Off they went, the orderly pushing the chair, the nurse walking alongside pointing out relevant features as they passed them. Gary had seen the hospital from the road, when the bus had passed by, but he never realised what an extensive building it was. If he was ever going to get himself out, he appreciated how much information he had to remember. They carried on walking down corridors, even travelling in a lift at one point, until they finally arrived at an ornate wooden door that bore a brass plaque, engraved with the name 'Dr Marion Hedley'.

The nurse knocked on the door. "Come in" said a voice, that Gary recognised from the day before and he was wheeled in.

"Good morning Gary," she said, smiling at him. That was something that always made him wary. When doctors tried to be nice to you, it was time to keep your wits about you. "OK nurse, you can leave now and you as well Frank, I don't think Gary and I will have any trouble".

Gary noted that that was the first time he had heard an orderly called by his name. It was good to keep that name in mind, as he never knew when that piece of information might come in handy in the future. The nurse held him by the elbow, helping him up out of the wheelchair and then into a leather seat, carefully positioned in front of the doctor's desk. Then she, along with the orderly, exited the room. This left Gary under the gaze of Dr Hedley, who seemed to be looking him up and down, as if she was sizing him up. She sat down behind her desk and opened a beige card folder that

Gary just managed to glimpse and see that it was embellished with his name.

Doctor and patient sat facing each other, neither knowing how the interview would develop. The doctor started the ball rolling, by asking a question. "Right Gary. I'm going to ask you to tell me what you can remember about the situation that landed you in here?".

He struggled to locate the relevant memories, but they eluded him, there seemed to be a large black hole where those memories should have been. So he decided to ask the doctor for some information, that would kick-start the thinking process. "Where did you find me?", he asked.

"Can't you remember?" She replied and when Gary indicated that he couldn't, she decided to help him out. "The police found you behind the shops on Redmile Walk, does that help?".

Gary's mind started racing. The shops, yes, now it was coming back to. him, but why was he at the shops in the first place? He just couldn't figure it out. The doctor closely examined Gary's expression and realised that although he wasn't saying much, he was trying to remember. She jumped out of her seat, when Gary suddenly shouted, "Suzy! God she's gonna be mad".

"Who's Suzy?" the doctor enquired, "Are you beginning to remember?"

"Yes, parts of it anyway. Suzy's my girlfriend and she sent me to the shops to get some bits and pieces, as she was going to cook my dinner".

"It's really good that you can remember that much. So why were you found behind the shops, hiding between two of the refuse bins. Was somebody chasing you?". "I'm sorry," Gary replied, "There's a gap between going to the shops and ending up here. I just don't know what happened. Where do you say they found me?". "Cowering down between two of the shop's refuse bins, the industrial kind they keep behind their premises. Anyway, I don't want to push you too far today and end up with you in a bad way again. Let's complete our record of your personal details, so we have an accurate record of your history".

That's how they spent the remainder of their time together that morning, the doctor hoping that by going over familiar things, it might help Gary's mind to start filling in some of the gaps he currently had. Eventually, she rang for the nurse to come and collect Gary, to return him to his room, once again.

While they were waiting for her to arrive, Gary asked "How much longer am I going to be cooped up in that room as there's nothing to do, or anyone to talk to". "Maybe a couple of more days, until we're sure that there won't be anymore incidents. But I can get some books and magazines sent into you and we'll give you a table and chair as well so that should help you pass the time".

"Thanks" said Gary, "It's a long time since I've read a book".

The nurse and orderly arrived and prepared to return Gary to his room. "I'll see you again tomorrow Gary. Would that be alright?".

"That's OK," Gary replied, thinking to himself 'As if I had a choice'.

Gary was soon back in his room. "The orderly will be in with your table and chair and

"I'll get your reading materials," the nurse said, as she was leaving.

'I wonder if they are trained to smile like that" Gary

thought 'it certainly makes it easier to accept what they do and say'.

True to their word, within the hour, he 'was fitted out with a plastic table and chair, along with a selection of books and magazines.

As he slept that night, he experienced some unusual dreams. He saw people walking in a street where they walked through other people, rather than bumping into them: The location seemed familiar, but it was altered in some way that made him unsure. These dreams were caused by his mind trying to unravel the memories it held including the recent experiences that he'd been through. So he awoke in a somewhat confused state, although he felt that his memory was a little more complete now..The more he thought about the recent events, the more they began to clarify in his mind.

By the time that his breakfast arrived Gary had pretty well remembered what had happened to him. As some parts of it seemed too fantastic to be true, he thought that his memory was still playing tricks on him. He mentioned to the nurse, that he felt his memory was beginning to improve.'

She responded. by saying, "It's surprising what a few day's rest, along with some peace and quiet, can do for you. Dr Hedley will be pleased to hear that your recall of events is improving, you'll have to tell her everything that has comeback to you".

Gary wondered if that would be such a good idea. If he told her that he was seeing people that he could walk through, she might think that he was a complete nutter and put him back on the knock-out drops. So he thought about this while eating his food, coming to the conclusion that leaving some things out, might well be in his best interests.

He felt more confident as he was being wheeled to Dr Hedley's office that morning, after all, he thought, 'Information is power. I've got it and she hasn't. So long as I keep my wits about me, I'll be OK'.

"Good morning Gary. The nurse tells me that your memory is improving. That's good. Get yourself settled and we can have a talk about what you can remember" He settled himself into the chair, deducing that the chair was nice and comfortable to help the patients feel relaxed, so that they would let it all out. This deduction was totally correct. They wouldn't pay out good money for a plush patient's chair, without good reason.

"Would you like a coffee?" she asked.

'This is new,' thought Gary, 'I wonder why she is being so pleasant today?'. "Yes please" he blurted out, without thinking, "black with two sugars".

So they both settled into the session, each with their own agenda firmly fitted in their mind and planning on getting the upper hand. Dr Hedley started the proceedings by asking Gary to relate his trip to the shops, along with any incidental information, no matter how insignificant it seemed to him. Basically that's what Gary did, although he decided to miss out the two women who had

been 'walked through' by the young woman and her children.

"So, why do you think you reacted so acutely to this experience, had something happened to you before?" the doctor enquired. This was the point where Gary had planned to deny any previous incidents. But his mind was determined to unload all it's unpleasant memories. So it all flooded out, starting with the two men on the stairs, the woman in the lift and the incident of walking through the man, once again, at the shops.

Dr Hedley didn't say a word. She leaned back in her chair, going over all that Gary had said. Meanwhile Gary's mind was working overtime as well. 'Why on earth did I blurt all that out' he thought, 'She really is going to think that I'm mad now and lock me up for good'.

The doctor finally broke the silence that had seemed to last forever, but was really only a couple of minutes.

"Is that all of it Gary, are there any other experiences that you feel I need to know about?".

Gary let rip. "Isn't it enough for you that these people are everywhere and that I can see them even though I'm not supposed to. So what you gonna do now, lock me up and throw away the key?".

She tried to be reassuring. "Gary, don't worry. There's no chance of that. This may surprise you, but I was hoping to meet someone like you".

He looked up. "What do you mean?".

"I'll explain" she said. "I've one other patient that has had similar experiences to yourself and I have been waiting for someone like you to come along. Then I might be able to help both of you by using the information you provide coupled with the information I already have".

"Well" Gary said, "are you going to tell me who it is?".

"I'm sorry" she replied, "but because of patient confidentiality I'm not allowed to. Although I can relate your experiences to the other patient and in time, I will relate theirs to you. That's all I can do".

"Well that's better than nothing, I suppose," Gary said, "But it is helpful to know that I'm not alone and there may well be others out there that we don't know of, who had been through this".

"Right then" said Dr Hedley, "You've been through a lot today and I don't want to stress your mind, as it's still in a delicate state. We'll meet again tomorrow and we'll discuss moving you into the general population".

"That would be great" Gary replied, "It would be really nice to have some people to talk to".

"If you feel that you are ready, I'll get that arranged and as I said, I'll see you again tomorrow".

As soon as Gary, the nurse and the orderly, had left the room, Dr Medley reached down for her handbag and lifted out her purse. She unclasped the fastener and reaching inside, removed a small white card. Turning to the phone, she dialled the number that was printed across the center. In fact that's all there was on the card. No identification that would indicate whose number it was, or anything else. She waited until the call was answered and then said "Good morning. This is Dr Hedley from the Fairview Psychiatric Hospital, concerning a patient that you're interested in. That's right, Gary Sandowski and what you thought about him has proved to be correct. It appears that he can see these people, so I'll need you to tell me how you want him to be handled....Alright then, I'll keep you up to date with his progress, along with the other patient we discussed. I'll speak to you again," she said to conclude the conversation and then replaced the phone on its holder.

Within a few days Gary had been moved into a room in a less secure part of the hospital and was looking forward to his time in the common room. He was looking forward to meeting the other patients and to be able to have a conversation with them. The day arrived and Gary was led from his room to the common room, which was in the opposite direction than he was used to going when he saw Dr Hedley. He also found the experience more pleasant, as he was only accompanied by a nurse, aithough the orderlies were still around and could be called on for help, if things got out of hand. The nurse pushed open one of a pair of doors and beckoned Gary through. As he stepped across the threshold, his brain was confronted with an avalanche of sensory information including light, colour, noise and he was also delighted when his lungs filled with air that carried the smell of tobacco.

"Am I allowed to smoke in here?" he asked, if only to confirm his observations. "Yes you can" the nurse replied, "We are exempted from the 'No smoking in a public place' legislation that applies to almost everywhere else. So make the most of it".

Then she left, allowing the door to swing closed behind her. Gary looked around the room, sizing up its inhabitants and trying to pick out someone that he liked the look of, Someone he felt that he would be able to make contact with. It didn't take very long for him to realise that contact would not be possible with all of them. Some were obviously lost in some strange reality that they couldn't escape from and also cut them off from any contact with the outside world. He chose an old armchair to sit in, so that he could survey this new environment more closely and to make his first 'roll-up' for some time.

He felt a wave of enjoyment wash over himself as he drew the smoke deep into his lungs and then expelled it from his mouth in a series of rings. A middle aged man, who had been slowly edging closer, said: "That's a neat trick. Never smoked myself. Hi, I'm Benny".

"Gary" he muttered in reply, unsure whether it was

safe to get to close to this man.

"It's alright" Benny said, sensing his caution. "We're all safe in here, otherwise they wouldn't let us out of our cages in case we fought with one another" "I'm glad about that," Gary replied "I was a little unsure as to how much contact it was safe to have. After all, you're all strangers to me".

"Look around you," Benny said "how many orderlies can you see?".

Gary hadn't noticed before, but they were all on their own, no-one standing around watching them all in case of trouble.

"You may not see them" Benny continued "but they're watching all the time. Look up in the corners of the room, can you see the cameras?. That's how they keep track of us, along with the cameras in the corridors and in each room".

Gary hadn't noticed, but as he looked around, there they were.

"When you go back to your room, have a good look around. You'll see the cameras tucked away in the corners of the room. Always keeping an eye on you. So if you get, any ideas about having some fun with one of the female patients, you'd better find some place out of their gaze," he said, with a big grin on his face. "I suppose you know where they are, don't you?" Gary, asked, hoping that he'd reveal the location to him.

"How would I know something like that" Benny replied, while laughing "After all, you may well be a plant, put in here to gather information for the doctors. They're a crafty lot and they've tried that before. So I'm not saying anything. That's if I had anything to say in the first place".

Gary watched Benny as he ambled away. He hadn't

realised how big he was. 'I bet he could do some damage,' Gary thought to himself. But the seeds of caution had been sown. Were the doctors really that devious? Well, that fitted in with his feelings towards them and at the moment, they had total control of his life. So he decided to be very careful about what he said and who he said it to. He no longer felt that he could trust any of the people in here with him. After all, it was a psychiatric hospital, not a health spa, so they all could have their own agendas and plans. The last thing he wanted was to be drugged and restrained again, so erring on the side of caution seemed to be the best course of action. At least until he got to know his fellow patients a little better and knew who he could trust.

As the days passed by, Gary became more integrated into the group that occupied the common room. Some were more introverted than others and took a little longer to accept him, but they eventually came round, if only in a limited way. Gary grew to enjoy sitting in the common room, as he could look out of the windows down onto the main entrance and watch the people come and go.

One sunny afternoon he was watching the activity, as usual, when he saw something that disturbed him. A young woman was walking across the staff parking area and was looking up at the building. At first, Gary couldn't work out what it was that bothered him, but he knew something was amiss. Then it struck him. He felt a cold sweat envelop him. The girl had no shadow. He looked away and then looked back again to confirm what he had seen. But he was too late, as she had moved out of his line of sight. 'Did she have a shadow, or is my mind

playing tricks on me?' he thought, without really

convincing himself.

    The experience put him on edge and made him a little jumpy. About half an hour later, one of the orderlies came into the common room to collect a patient that Gary had not been able to make any contact with: He huddled himself into a ball and always remained facing into the same corner of the room. It took quite some time for the orderly to entice him out of his corner, so he could be taken to see his doctor. Gary had never seen him standing up before and was quite impressed by his height and physical size. 'I wonder what could make a person like that huddle away in the corner of a room' Gary thought to himself, 'it must have been something pretty traumatic" and then thought back over the sequence of events that had caused him to end up in hospital, not forgetting the state he was in when he arrived.

    Although this provided him with a distraction for a few moments, his previous line of thought was re-established when he saw something that shook him to the core. As the door was closing behind the orderly and his patient, he saw the young woman he had seen in the car park, nip in through the gap. He sat there, his eyes transfixed on her, watching her every movement. Everything was alright to start with, although he did notice that he seemed to be the only one looking at her. She examined the common room and its inhabitants, wandering about the room. Then she noticed Gary watching her and gave him a little wave. He instinctively waved back and instantly regretted his action, as it confirmed that he could see her. If she was normal and he had ignored her it wouldn't have been so bad, after all he was a psychiatric patient and could act as he pleased.

The young woman responded to his wave with a large smile and started to walk toward him. 'OK' thought Gary 'everything's normal so far'. But then it all changed. She was about twenty feet away from him when Benny came ambling across the room in his direction, getting ever closer to the young woman. Gary looked down and saw that he was gripping the arms of the chair so tightly, that his knuckles had turned snow white. Looking back up, he saw the two of them getting closer and closer, until they briefly occupied the same space and then parted. Gary jumped out of the chair so quickly that he knocked it over and then he backed into the corner, pulling the chair in front of him, like a shield. Although he didn't realise it, he had started shouting. "Get her away from me. Don't let her near me". The orderlies saw and heard the commotion and rushed into action. They ran across the room towards Gary, one of them calling for a nurse on his radio. People started to appear from all directions and the young woman just melted away in the resulting confusion.

The orderlies managed, eventually, to extricate Gary from behind the chair, although he was clinging on for dear life. They finally managed to pin him down on the floor, enabling a nurse to give him an injection in the buttock, which quickly subdued him and rendered him unconscious. He was then taken back to his original room and the restraints were put back in place once again.

By now, Dr Hedley had arrived and they discussed among themselves about the trigger for this episode. Try, as they might, they were unable to fathom out what had happened. So it was decided that it was best to ask Gary, when he was able to tell them and they left him to sleep off the effects of the drugs.

***

CHAPTER FIVE

EXPLORATION

It took Theo some time to get used to walking along a crowed street, without having to move out of peoples way. He instinctively stepped to one side, or off of the pavement. But he still had to take care when crossing the road, as he could still be hurt or even killed, even though he was invisible. As Phil was Theo's guide for the day, he took him round all the various outlets where they were able to gather food and water, mentioning that late night shopping had proved to be a boon for them and sometimes, when the weather was cold, they were able to spend the night in these shops.

They were walking along Bridge Street, when Theo suddenly stopped in his tracks. "What's the matter?" Phil asked, but Theo was speechless.

Walking straight towards him was his group of friends. Bob, Andy and Terry all dressed in their finery. They were on their usual weekend quest, pulling girls, if they could. Theo just stood there, mouth open, as they walked past him.

"Do you know them?" Phil enquired.

"They're my mates. They were with me when this change happened. Although they have no idea what's happened to me". Theo was a little upset that they just seemed to be carrying on as normal, but, as Phil pointed out, what else could they do. This brought home to Theo just how remote his old life had become. He was like a spectator on the side-line, having to watch his old life drift by, without being able to take part in it. For the first time since the change had occurred, he started to feel really sad. Phil noticed the change of expression on Theo's face. "Don't worry" he said, "We all went through a sad phase when the full realisation of our situation hit us for the first time. But it will pass, as you adapt to your new circumstances. You wouldn't want your mates to be sitting around, as if they were in mourning, would you?".

"No, I suppose not. After all, what can they do about it" Theo replied and started to feel a little more at ease with his mates' presumed indifference to his disappearance. How could he know what they really felt.

"You're in a unique position to find out exactly how they feel. Make use of your current situation, go on, follow them and listen to what they're saying. I'll see you back here in an hour's time".

"But I haven't got a watch, mine was stolen," Theo said.

"Let's go and get you a watch and then you catch up with your mates," was Phil's reply.

It didn't take Theo very long to locate his mates, who were still in Bridge Street, sitting at an open air cafe while they enjoyed their individual choices of coffee. He was surprised and relieved to hear that he was the subject of their conversation. "Well, I don't know what's going on. No-one's heard from him".

"His mum's going frantic, she's phoned the police, the hospitals and each of us a number of times".

"I still think he's shacked up with some bird".

"You would. But even if that was the case, he'd phone one of us, if only to brag about the situation. Anyway, he wouldn't let his mum get into such a state, without letting her know that he was alright, even if he didn't say where he was".

That last comment really hit home. Theo had always made it a practice to phone his mum if he was going to stay away for the night, of if he was going to be much later than planned. He was often mocked for doing it, but he felt happier if she wasn't worrying about where he was. So he realised what a state she must be in at the moment. It was getting on for twenty four hours since he had last seen or spoken to either his mum, or sister and he felt guilty for causing the current situation. But as Phil had pointed out, what could he do? Then it came to him. What about sending a text message.

So he waited until Phil returned and made the suggestion. "That's a good idea, but I'm afraid that it won't work" Phil said, dashing his hopes. "I think it's something to do with the electronics inside the phone, although I'm no expert. We've all tried that before, but mobile phones don't seem to work for. us".

"I'm not going to give up trying to work out a way to make contact" Theo said, "I'm only young and could have plenty of years to experiment in. But I would like to go home and see my mum, even if I can't talk to her. Would you come with me? I don't know if I could do it on my own".

"I would be honoured to accompany you," was Phil's reply. So they started to walk across Cathedral Square, on their way to the bus station. At least in their condition it didn't matter how full the bus was, as they could always manage to fit in.

Once the bus reached Bretton Way, they had to wait until it pulled up at a stop, so that they could disembark, even though it had gone past the stop they wanted. It really didn't matter, as Theo knew all the passage-ways between the houses, so they were soon in his street. Theo was surprised by the flood of emotions that greeted him, when he saw his house. Would it ever be his home again, he wondered. He had complained about it so many times in the past, but it now seemed like the most wonderful house in the world.

"Do you mind if we wait for a while?" He asked.

"Not at all" Phil replied, "Are you waiting for something in particular?"

"My mum has a part time Saturday job at one of the shops in the centre, just up the road and she should be coming home soon".

"I can't think of a better reason for waiting. I think that it will do you good to see her" said Phil, smiling. To while away the time, Theo regaled Phil with stories of his school days and the many tricks that he and his mates used to get up to. Phil chipped in when he could, with similar accounts from his childhood, until Theo suddenly exclaimed "There she is!"

There in the distance was Theo's mum, struggling up the road, loaded down with bags of shopping. Phil noticed a tear in Theo's eye, as he heard him say, "That's too heavy for her to be carrying. I used to meet her at the shop when she'd finished work and help her carry the bags home".

"You obviously are a good son" Phil said, trying to comfort him, "and I'm sure that one day you'll be able to help her once again. Once we've got all this sorted out. I'm sure that someone, somewhere, is looking into our situation as we speak. So don't give up hope. Are you going to follow your mother into the house?".

Theo hesitated before he answered. "No I don't think I will. It would be a bit too much for me to cope with at the moment. Maybe I'll come back again another day".

"Shall we go then?" Phil asked.

"Yes. I think that would be best. I'm feeling really emotional right now and I'm not used to feeling like this, it's very disconcerting. Let's go".

So the two invisible figures turned to leave, heading back the way they came but with Theo leaving an occasional teardrop on the footpath.

Back in the town centre, Saturday afternoon was in full swing. There were people everywhere, each trying their best to reach their destination. Of course, none of this mattered to Theo. The town centre could have been deserted, for all the difference it made to him. He could go wherever he pleased, without any delay or interference. Phil said that he was going to gather some food stuffs, but felt that as there were a lot of people about, it would be best if Theo did not accompany him, until he'd had a little more experience. Theo saw the sense in this, after all he wasn't an accomplished shop-lifter, as this was another aspect of his new life that he had to learn.

"I'll see you back here in about half an hour. Is that OK?" Phil asked him and Theo agreed.

On his own, free to move about unhindered, Theo's mind started to think of all the places that he could go now. Places where he was denied access before. He also began to realise, that as he was free to move about as he pleased, the prospect didn't seem quite so exciting anymore. 'I suppose it wouldn't hurt if I just peeked into a ladies changing room, just this once' he thought to himself. He was surprised how little persuading was needed to convince himself that it would be OK, just this once. He walked towards a ladies clothing shop to fulfill his need to look at something forbidden, feeling quite excited as he entered the shop. It didn't take him long to realise that the forbidden, when easily obtained, isn't as wonderful as his thoughts had convinced him it would be.

As he left the shop, the worse thing possible happened. He walked slap, bang into Jennifer and Emily. He didn't know if it was still possible for him to turn red, but he felt that he could.

"Oh Theo, you didn't did you?" Emily said, looking both sad and disappointed, at the same time.

"Don't be hard on him" Jennifer responded, "What young man wouldn't exploit his condition if he could. I'm sure that it's a one-off, isn't it Theo?".

Inwardly Theo was thanking Jennifer for helping him out of a tricky situation. "I was waiting for Phil, while he obtained some food and the next thing I know I was in there. It's the only time that I've done something like this and I'm really sorry if I've upset you Emily, it's the last thing I would want to do".

"I'll put it down to a young man's curiosity. The desire to see something that's always been forbidden," Emily said.

"Thank you for being so understanding" Theo replied, feeling happy that Emily seemed to care. 'She must have some feelings for me, otherwise she would have called me a pervert and left it at that' he thought to himself.

Phil walked over to join them at this point and looked towards the shop. "I suppose you gave in to your hormones, Theo?" he said.

"Yes he did" Emily retorted, "But I've forgiven him".

"I'm pleased to hear that" Phil replied, "We can do without disunity in our little group. But Theo's reaction to his situation is a quite normal one. I don't know of many men who wouldn't have done the same, or something similar".

"You're all sex mad" Jennifer said, while laughing. "But we women do tend to play on that, don't we. So let's close the subject now and forget all about it. All agree".

When the group gathered that evening, they each related the day's events. Theo told them about his trip home and what an emotional experience it had been for him, but said that he planned to return there in the future. Emily just couldn't hold herself back from relating Theo's experience in town, which left him

feeling very self conscious and embarrassed.

"Come on," Jennifer said, "We agreed to forget about that, didn't we. But I must admit that the look on Theo's face when he walked into us, was priceless".

"All right" said Theo, starting to feel a little angry that Emily had raised the subject again. "I've been a bad boy, but I've said that I won't do it again and I mean it". "We'll see," he heard Emily mutter, under her breath.

"I heard something interesting today" Frank said.

This surprised them all, as Frank didn't normally have much to say, tending to keep to himself, in the background.

"I was sitting in one of those open air cafes that they have nowadays and I overheard two women talking. I ascertained from their conversation that they were nurses at the psychiatric hospital. This in itself is nothing particularly special, but what they were discussing was. They were talking about, no, joking about a patient who claimed that he saw ghosts who tried to speak to him. That struck a chord with me, what do you all think?".

Phil joined in the conversation at this point. "I had an experience a while ago, that seems to fit in with what you overheard Frank. I was in an area of town that I'm not familiar with, just exploring near a group of shops and as I turned a corner a man walked through me. Nothing unusual in that, but I'm sure that he could see me, because he stopped and turned to look at me. I even tried to get a message across to him, but I don't think that it was successful. Whether that was the same man the women were talking about, or not, I don't know. But it does give credence to the rumour that there are people out there that are able to see us".

"Well then, what do you think about all of that?" Jennifer asked the group and a lively discussion ensued, carrying on for the remainder of the evening. Many different theories were proposed that evening, some sensible and some quite outlandish. But the prospect that there were some people that were able to see them, seemed to instill a sense of hope in the group. A hope that held out the possibility that one day they would be able to return to normal, resuming their lives and rejoining their families.

The following morning was not as pleasant as the previous day had been. The wind speed had increased overnight and it was raining almost continuously. This was another new experience for Theo, as he had no idea how the rain would affect him in his altered state. So he did the sensible thing, he asked the group to relate their experiences.

This was a new departure for Theo. Normally, the 'know-it-all' attitude of youth would have prevented him from asking older people for help. But he now found it an easy thing to do. This was a positive development that his changed state seemed to have brought about, it had helped him to mature as a person. Any-way, asking for help seemed the most logical thing to do, learning from those that have experience of the situation.

Theo was surprised when Frank, the quiet one of the group, offered to explain. "Put your hand out in the rain and see what happens" he suggested. "Alright" Theo said and walked over so he could place his fore-arm out into the rain. He was shocked when he felt the rain striking his flesh, but even more so by the rainfall being interrupted by his arm, just the way it had always been.

"What's this mean?" he enquired.

"It means that if you go out in the rain, your outline will be visible, because you will leave a space where the rain should be," Frank explained.

"As we can see each other, we think nothing of it," Emily interjected, "But to the normal people we will seem like phantoms moving about in the rain. I'm sure that you can appreciate the problems that that could cause"

"I can imagine the panic if that happened," Theo continued. "I suppose that it could be used as a method for them to track us down, if they wanted, looking at a worse case scenario. So what do you do on days like this? Do you hide away, or what?".

"At times, that is the only course open to us" said Jennifer, the most experienced member of the group, "Or we can venture out, if we're very careful."

Theo decided that he would not venture far from them all that day, as he had already begun to feel safe and secure in their presence.

As they settled in for the duration of the rain, Theo raised a new topic for conversation. "Do you think that we are the only ones in this state around here?". A lively debate followed, covering many different points of view, but eventually coming to agreement that there were bound to be others like them, somewhere. After all, not all people wish to be part of a group, being content to remain alone. Although dealing with the invisible condition on your own could be a somewhat daunting prospect. But the human spirit is very resilient and even people on their own would quickly adjust to their new circumstance. There was a general consensus, that they should keep on the look-out for more like themselves, as they could well be out there. If they were successful and those discovered wished to remain separate, fair enough, they would be left alone, but the invitation to join the group would remain open. It was decided that a record should be kept of how many like themselves were in the area. Who knows when such a list might become invaluable. If a cure for their situation was ever discovered, it would be necessary to locate all those in their condition, to correct the situation. At this point, Frank made an interesting comment.

"What if they don't want to be changed back to the way they originally were, prefering the anonymity of invisibility?".

No one had thought of that. It had been assumed that everyone would want to change back. But would they? It was a distinct possibility that some would not want to revert to the way they had been in the past, feeling that their lives were more to their liking in this new state and found it easier to cope with life this way. Others might have different reasons, but it was certainly something to think about. Theo couldn't wait to get back to normal and be able to tell all his mates about his experiences. He didn't ask the other members of the group how they felt, as he thought it might be a little intrusive to ask a question like that, especially as he'd only been one of them for a short time. But as far as he was concerned, he was sure that girls would want to spend time with him, because of the fame all of this would bring. Then he looked across the group at Emily, who noticed him looking at her and smiled. Strangely, he didn't feel the same way about her as he had done with all of his previous female friends. He felt a different bond with her and hoped that she had similar feelings for him, as there was something really special about her. He had felt it the very first time that he saw her. Maybe she would turn out to be the special girl in his life, after all, the chances of them meeting up in the world of the 'normals' was remote, but who knows. Perhaps fate would have brought them together, whatever the circumstances. He sighed.

"Is that how she affects you?" A voice behind him said. He turned round and saw Frank standing there.

"I suppose she does. I was just thinking about her and the chances that we would have ever met, if it wasn't for our current situation" Theo responded. "

Well, you've met her now, so make the most of it" was Frank's reply. Somehow, Emily realised that she was the subject of their conversation and looked over at them both, but chose not to say anything, feeling that the answer to an enquiry could make her feel embarrassed.

In the early afternoon the rain started to ease off and the sun attempted to shine through the clouds. Conditions were now more amenable to going out, as the chance of being spotted had disappeared along with the rain. So the group members drifted off to fulfill their specific tasks, helping to supply the group's needs. Theo had paired up with Frank, for the first time and was a little unsure how to treat this large, quiet man. He soon managed to answer that question, once he had managed to break through the outer shell and found that a very pleasant person lived inside. They were soon chatting as if they were old friends. Frank noticed the easing of the tension that had initially been there between them and began to open up a little. As they were walking through the park, the sun was starting its downward journey towards the horizon and was casting a warm light over the displays of flowers, growing in the various beds. Theo had never thought of himself as some-one who admired such things, but now for the first time he really appreciated the natural beauty that was spread out before him. He'd only been here before with his mates and then it was the girls, not the flowers, that drew his attention. He now realised how much people can miss when they have a blinkered outlook on things. This was the second time that he had acted out of character and was beginning to prefer this new version of himself, compared with the way he had been in the past. In such an idyllic setting he felt at ease and decided to ask Frank about two people who were part of their group, but never seemed to be involved with the rest of them.

"You mean Linda and Michael, don't you?" Frank asked. "Yes" Theo replied, "They're always together, with Michael appearing to look after her. Is that the case? What's their history with the group? I hope you don't mind me asking as I'm intrigued. The rest of the group just leaves them to go their own sweet way and never involves them in anything. I'd just like to know".

"Let's sit down here" Frank said, "and I'll do my best to answer all your questions". So the two of them sat together in the early evening sun, on an out of the way bench, where there was less chance of disruption.

"Michael became part of our little family before I did, arriving not long after Phil. But Linda was found wandering about the town centre, unable to understand why people wouldn't answer her when she spoke to them. You see, she's in the early stages of dementia and cannot comprehend things very well. So she was totally confused, as you can understand".

"She must have been terrified," Theo stated, "As she does seem to be getting on a bit".

"You're right there" Frank said, picking up the conversation once again, "I would think that she's in her late sixties, maybe early seventies, but it's difficult to determine. She has no idea where she came from, or how she came to be in the town centre. She had been with us for at least three weeks before she said her name was Linda".

"So what's all this with Michael and her then?" Theo asked, "Why does he look after her? They're not related, surely".

"Well, you've only to look at them, to realise that it's quite unlikely for them to be related," Frank stated, "After all, Linda is a typical English woman, although a little frail now and Michael is a sturdy, well built Caribbean man, roughly in his thirties. But Michael used to work in a nursing home and took on the task of caring for Linda without being asked. He said that it was what he had been trained to do and that he was the best qualified member of the group, as he had cared for similar patients in the past. Since then, the two of them have become inseparable and Linda won't let anyone else look after her. After all, what woman in her early seventies wouldn't like to have a nice young man to look after her?". So that was it. Frank had explained all that Theo wanted to know about them and satisfied his desire to learn about his fellow group members.

It had become a warm balmy evening by the time that all the group members had re-assembled and as was their custom, they shared out the food and drink that had been 'obtained' during the day. The usual evening discussion of the day's events and activities followed, while they enjoyed the wide variety of food before them.

Theo had difficulty stopping himself staring at Linda and Michael and saw that it was obvious to anyone, that they really cared for each other, but in a purely platonic way. Michael was carefully helping Linda to eat and was wiping her mouth when she needed it. Theo thought to himself, that it must take a special kind of person to care like that. Of course, if he had ever been in hospital, he would already understand and appreciate the many caring people that work in healthcare, just as Michael had done before his change of state.

As was normal for the group, the evening was spent in discussion and the sound of the voices brought Theo out of his thoughts. During the evening, many different theories and plans were raised, discussed and often discounted as impracticable. Theo suddenly came to the realisation, that if he had been asked to spend an evening in discussion with a group of friends, say six months ago, he wouldn't have considered it. But once again, a positive result from his change of situation had come to light. He was becoming a more rounded and complete person, something that wouldn't have happened in the old scheme of things.

As the evening progressed, a plan slowly developed in his mind and by bedtime he had plucked up enough courage to put it into action. Walking over to Emily he said "I would deem it a privilege if you would spend the day with me tomorrow". No-sooner had the words escaped from his lips, he thought 'Deem it a privilege..., I never speak to girls like that', but he realised that it must be his emotions taking over, as he had more respect for Emily than he had ever had for a girl before.

"I would love to" she replied.

He was speechless for a few seconds and then started to speak. "That's great. I want to show you where I live and meet my family, within the limits of our condition, that is". "That sounds as if it should be very interesting," Emily said and added that she was really looking forward to their time together.

Theo's head was spinning, as he tried to get to sleep that night. He had never felt so exited by the prospect of a date before, 'What's happening to me?' he wondered. Whatever it was, he decided that he liked the experience and with these pleasant thoughts on his mind, he finally fell asleep.

As they walked through the town centre together, they looked just like any other happy couple, except that they were not visible to the crowds that surrounded them. 'If only my friends and family could see me now' he thought. They were both pleasantly surprised at how easily conversation came to them, after all, they were total strangers until a few days ago.

"Which bus do we need" Emily asked, as she was not too familiar with Theo's part of the city since she lived way over in the opposite direction. "If we get the Citi Bus No 3, that will take us to the area that I live in," Theo answered, "They run every few minutes, so we won't have long to wait". Queuing was not a problem for

Emily and Theo, as they were able to move through the people without hindrance. The journey was the same as he had made with Phil, just a few days earlier, so it wasn't long before they were standing outside Theo's home.

"What's your family like then?" Emily enquired, "Are they as bad as I used to think mine were, before all this happened?".

They sat on a wall nearby, while Theo explained the make-up of his family. He described how his father had left while his mother was pregnant with his sister. "What was your dad like? What was his name? Can you remember?" Emily asked.

"I can't remember much about him, just a few vague memories. His name was and I suppose still is, Arthur although he was always called Art by everyone. I know my mum still keeps photos of him in her bedside cabinet. When I was much younger I found them and when she saw me, she quickly gathered them up and put them away. But I'm sure that they're still in the same place".

"Do you think she still has feelings for him?"

"Strangely enough I think she does, even after all these years. If he arrived on the doorstep one day, I'm sure that she would accept him back, even now". Theo noticed that he felt a little saddened by the thought of his dad. He had always found it difficult at school, when the other boys were bragging about their dads, that he couldn't join in and was the butt of some cruel jokes by some of them. 'Come on' he thought, 'Snap out of it. You're out with a girl you really like, so be happy'.

"Let's change the subject, shall we. Tell me about your family" Theo said. So Emily gave Theo a potted family history and details of the various family members.

Theo asked her, "That comment you made earlier, the one about how bad your family were. Do you still think that?".

"Not now. I realise how well off I was and long to be back with them. Do you now have similar feelings about your family?".

"I used to think my family were the worst in the world" Theo replied, "But now I feel the same as you. I long to be back with them again and to be able to go for a drink with my mates.

Theo was in the middle of describing his group of friends to Emily, when he suddenly stopped and pointed."That's my sister Jaz, coming down the road". He was surprised to feel a twinge inside him, as this was the first time that he had seen her since the change had occurred.

"She's a lovely young woman" Emily said, "She's younger than you, isn't she?". "That's right. You're a good listener. Yes, that's Jaz, or Jasmine, my sister. I often longed for her to shut up and now I just wish that I could speak to her. Come on, let's follow her into the house".

So they got up off the wall and followed Jasmine into the house. Theo showed Emily around and noticed that the only change that he could see, was that a picture of himself now took pride of place on the mantlepiece.

Emily noticed the picture and said, "They're obviously missing you", but decided not to say anything further in case it upset Theo. Theo heard a key in the front door, which opened to let his mum in. Theo loved hearing their voices again, although in the past, he used to hide away in his room to get away from what he called 'female banter'. Now he found great pleasure in hearing his mum and sister talking. After a while, he said to Emily that they should make a move, to get back to the group before it got too late. So they waited for a chance to leave to present itself and a little while later an opportunity arose, when Theo's mum went outside to the bins. They slipped out while the door was open and started their journey back to the group of like people, which for the present, they called home.

It didn't take them too long to get back and they bounded, hand in hand, into the group's meeting place, bursting with the details of their adventures. They quickly realised that something was not right. Theo looked around and noticed that Linda and Michael were missing. "Where are Linda and Michael?" Theo asked, "It's not like them to be away at this time of day".

Jennifer said that she had been the last one to speak to them earlier that afternoon and that Michael had said that they would go for their usual afternoon walk. But I haven't seen them since. They all realised that something must have happened, as it was unlike Michael to keep Linda away, for such a long period of time.

About fifteen minutes later, a tearful Michael appeared.

"It's Linda," he said, "She's dead". T

They all fell silent. Frank was the first to speak, "Come and. sit down and tell us what happened". It took Michael a few moments to pull himself together, a hot drink helping to steady his nerves and then he started to speak.

"I know you're all aware of Linda's condition and because of it, I'm always very careful when I take her out for a walk, especially if there's traffic about. Somehow, she slipped out of my grasp and walked straight out into the road. Almost immediately, she was struck by a van, The driver, realising that he had hit something applied his brakes, but it was too late. The poor man didn't stand a chance, after all, he couldn't see Linda anyway. But then something amazing happened. It was obvious from the comments of the people who had witnesses the accident that they could see Linda. She was visible to them. Then the ambulance arrived and they confirmed that she was dead. To them it was an every day road accident, an elderly lady walking out into the traffic without looking. I was totally confused and shocked. Shocked by Linda's death, but also by the fact that they could see her. The condition that effects us all was rectified, but at what a cost".

It was obvious that he could say no more, as he was in a state of emotional collapse. Theo thought that it was so sad to see a strapping healthy man like Michael sobbing like a little child. It conveyed to them all how strong his feelings had been for Linda, a lady who could barely remember his name, but that he felt compelled to care and provide for. Her death though, had raised an interesting fact, that they could all change back, if only a less drastic way of implementing that change could be brought about. They decided that they should keep a close eye on those that would be looking into all of this and see if they could, in their own special way, help to find a cure that would leave them alive, to be discovered.

***

CHAPTER SIX

COMMENCEMENT

Peter instinctively raised his arm across his face, as the car hurtled towards the crash barrier. Just before contact was made, a lorry hit the back of the car, spinning it round so it ended up facing the wrong way, jammed between the crash barrier and the lorry's cab. Peter checked himself over and fortunately he seemed to be alright. Looking across the car, at the passenger seat, he saw that his girlfriend, Christine, was motionless, her eyes closed. Panicking, he felt her neck for a pulse and uttered a sigh of relief he located it. She was alive, although he had no idea as to how injured she might be. It was as he looked away from Christine, that he saw something unexpected in the rear-view mirror.

There was a young woman in the back seat and she didn't look too well, her body being twisted in a most unnatural way. Who was she? They didn't have anyone with them when they left and they hadn't picked up anyone along the way. His thoughts were disrupted by the appearance of two policemen, closely followed by the paramedics and a few moments later they were joined by the ambulance and fire brigade.

They were taken to hospital and fortunately were not too badly hurt, just cuts and bruises. But the unknown young woman in the back had sadly died, having been killed by the impact of the lorry. Both Peter and Christine stated repeatedly that they didn't know the young woman and had never seen her before, not knowing that she was in the car with them. Their explanation was finally accepted and the police told them that she had probably sneaked into the car while they were stopped at the services. This provided them with something to enter on the accident report and were willing to leave it there. However, that was not the true explanation.

Following the post postmortem, investigations were carried out to establish who she was and were surprised by their findings. Her name was Sally Wright, aged 27 and she had disappeared following a night out in Portsmouth, some eight months earlier. Since that night there hadn't been a single trace of her, but now, knowing she had been located would bring some relief to her parents, who had been desperately looking her all those months. However, the fact that she had died was a cruel blow for them. They had found her and lost her in the same instant.

The unusual circumstances surrounding the young woman's appearance in the car, guided the paperwork involved in the investigation to become the contents of one of two files that were waiting for Jack, when he arrived that morning. The second file contained an account with a similar theme. A local shopkeeper, a Mr Habib Ali the owner of a general store, had opened up his shop one morning, only to find the body of an elderly man. He was discovered at the rear of the premises and had obviously been helping himself to some of the food.

Mr Ali insisted that the man wasn't in the store when he had locked up the previous night, as he was always very careful to check that someone hadn't tucked themselves in some corner because of his stock of tobacco and alcohol. Anyway, he had called the police and they arranged for the body to be taken away. It was obvious that the man hadn't been living on the streets, as his clothes were neat and tidy and he appeared to be in good physical shape. The post postmortem revealed that he had died from a heart attack and as he was locked inside a shop when it happened, there wasn't anyone to help him.

An investigation to locate his family was soon under way and because of his age, they soon located his details which were on file from his days of National Service. He was identified as George Bailey, aged 78 and had lived in Winchcombe, north east of Cheltenham. Once again, the same pattern emerged. He had been involved in a car accident and had received a head injury. Then one evening he just disappeared and try as they might, his family couldn't find him. The official explanation was that he had become disoriented and wandered off, possibly having some form of accident, which would account for him not showing up. His family could not accept this theory and continued their search, hoping that someone might have seen him in the six months that had passed. It was if he had vanished from the face of the earth. Which was what had happened more or less, but only a few knew of the possibility of that happening.

'So,' thought Jack, 'It's started. The information is beginning to come in. I think I should go upstairs and let them know who I have chosen for my team'.

He phoned DCS Richmond's secretary, who told him to come up in fifteen minutes time. 'Well, I'm certainly getting the red carpet treatment these days,' Jack thought, as he got himself a coffee and read through the two reports again. By then it was time for his exercise up the stairs, to keep his appointment.

"He'll be with you in a moment," the secretary said, "He's on the phone at the moment".

A few minutes later the door opened and he was ushered into the office.

"Right Jack. What have you to tell me. By the way, what did you think of those two reports?".

"I thought they were quite exceptional accounts, seeing what we know." Jack answered, "And I don't think they will be the only ones we receive".

"I think you're right there," the DCS replied. "Now, as this seems to be kicking off, have you chosen the officers you would like to work with you?"

"I've just chosen a team of three. I thought that the more involved the greater the chance of information leaking out".

"Very wise thinking Jack".

"So I would like, if possible, DI David Grantham, DS Sarah Mitchell and DS Clive Barron. That's it. Each of these officers have proved themselves in the past and I feel that I can rely on them for this case".

"Well, that's a nice little team Jack and I echo your sentiments as to the quality of those officers. I'll get on to Division to get them re-assigned, for this special project. I think we'll call it the invisible investigation. That covers its purpose and remit, also serving as a distraction for any nosey-parkers. What say you?"

"I'll go along with that," Jack replied, smiling, "It's like a war-time operation isn't it". "Well, it's just as important to keep it under wraps, as it was for operations during the war. It's not exactly that lives are at stake, but indirectly I suppose they could be, if you think of the panic if this got out. So just keep in mind the war-time poster campaign, 'Careless talk' etc".

"Message received and understood," Jack replied, in keeping with the war-time parlance.

"I'll let you know when you can gather your officers and get the investigation under way. Under the circumstances, I don't think Division will hang about," the DCS stated.

As he returned to his office, Jack started to think about the officers he wanted to involve in all of this.'How would they react?' he thought to himself, 'Would they want to be part of the team, or would it be too much for them to take on?'.

He didn't think that they would reject his offer. After all, he knew them all personally, having worked with them in the past. Weighing it all up, he felt that he had chosen the most suitable officers that he could, especially as he was able to cherry-pick the officers he wanted. Normally, you would inherit a team that consisted of good and not-so-good officers, so he realised that he should think himself lucky that he could pick who he wanted, to become members of his team.

True to their word, Division responded a couple of days later. Jack received a phone call, mid afternoon, to inform him that his choices had been accepted and he could start to interview the officers the following day. Following his enquiry, he was told that their superiors had been informed and that this would be taking place.

Jack phoned each of the officers in turn and arranged to see them at fifteen minute intervals, starting at 9:30 the next morning. He also impressed on them that they were not in trouble, but that he would be discussing a confidential matter with them and that they were not to talk about it to anyone.

By now the grape-vine was in full swing, with all

manner of wild predictions about what Jack was working on. It was obvious that he was working on something new, but for once, no-one could find out what it was. So the wild speculation continued, although none of the theories even came close to the reality of the situation that he was investigating.

DI Grantham was first to be interviewed. "I have asked for you to be my second in command on a new case that I'm taking on," Jack said, while watching the expression on his face. "This is a highly secret case, not a word about it is to be discussed with anyone who isn't part of the team. Do you understand?".

"Yes Sir" he succinctly replied.

Jack then continued with his explanation. "The hours will be variable and possibly long, with overnight stays a possibility. The team will be small, comprising of myself and three other officers, with you hopefully one of the three. But I must emphasize again that the whole investigation will be under a shroud of secrecy. Other officers are bound to quiz you about it, but details about it cannot be leaked, under any circumstances, no matter who asks. This may well leave you feeling isolated at times and if that happens, come and discuss it with me. So, after all of that, I need to ask you. Are you interested?".

"It sounds just like the kind of case I've been dying to get my teeth into. It would be a privilege to join you, sir", he replied.

A smile spread across Jack's face, as he said. "Welcome aboard," reaching his hand out across the desk to shake DI Grantham's hand strongly.

Jack then said, "When I've seen the other prospective team members and hopefully received their acceptance as well, we'll all meet together as a team for the first time. At that time, I will be able to acquaint you all with the details of our investigation. Until that happens, I'll say thank-you for now".

Every pair of eyes in the office had been watching all this taking place and the speculation gathered momentum.

As DI Grantham left Jack's office and walked through the main office area, he passed DS Mitchell, walking in the opposite direction. Their eyes briefly met, as they passed each other. Just before he left the office, DI Grantham turned and paused for long enough to see her enter Jack's office. 'I wonder who the fourth officer will be' he thought and and started to speculate what the case was about. Jack followed the same pattern with DS Mitchell and then DS Barron, as he had done with DI Grantham and was pleased that all three of them agreed to join the team. As DS Barron left his office, he congratulated himself on the choices he had made.

After interviewing the three of them, he felt that he had chosen a strong and versatile team. After all, that's the kind of team needed when dealing with such an unusual case. He wondered how they would all take it, when the full details of the case were revealed and they became aware of the task they had signed up for.

After he had spoken to each of his prospective team members and received their positive responses, he phoned DCS Richmond to inform him of the outcome and that the team was now in place.

"Right then, Jack. The next step is to let them know the nature of the investigation. I suggest that as this is all a little out of the ordinary, that we all meet together in my office this afternoon. How's that sound to you?".

"I think it will be a good idea to do it that way. It

should impress upon them the serious nature of the investigation" Jack replied.

"How about we all meet after lunch, say 2pm?".

"That's alright with me. I'll phone each of them and let them know that the veil of secrecy has descended over them all, as of now".

So Jack contacted each of his chosen officers in turn and inform them about the afternoon's meeting. Telling them to spend the remainder of the morning finishing off any—thing that they were working on. He then phoned their commanding officers, to inform them that they would be losing the officers for the foreseeable future. A couple of them weren't very happy, but they had been directly contacted by division, so there was little they could do but complain to Jack about the situation. Jack was not surprised by their reaction, after all, he had taken some of their best officers and had he been in their situation he would have complained as well. Jack felt that when all was finally revealed, they would understand why it was all necessary.

A few minutes before 2pm, Jack arrived at DCS Richmond's outer office and was pleased to see that his team were already there, together for the first time.

"He's expecting us all at 2pm," Jack told the secretary.

"He told me to show you all in, the moment you were all assembled," she replied. "Come on then" Jack said, turning to his team, "Shall we all go in. Are you ready?".

In they trouped and Jack realised, that for his team members this was the first time that they had ever been in the DCS's office and could sense their nervousness. As they were arranging themselves on the chairs that had been set out for them, DCS Richmond briefly spoke on the intercom, to his secretary.

"The ACC is due in fifteen minutes, so please show him straight in. After he has arrived, no phone calls or interruptions, OK?".

"Yes sir" she replied.

He released the button on the intercom and then looked up at Jack and his team, who were sat in a semi-circle in front of him.

"Right then, down to business" he said. "To emphasize the seriousness of the case that you all will be investigating, the ACC will be joining us in a little while. But until he arrives, I have some necessary paperwork that has to be dealt with". He handed a copy of a document to each of them and then sat back down. "You will see from the heading, that you will be working under supervision from the Home Office. This document is an extension of the official secrets act. You will understand why when the full details of the case are revealed to you".

"When will we be told the details?" DS Mitchell blurted out, "We've all signed up for a task, without knowing what it is. We've worked out that it's something pretty special and this document confirms that assumption".

"I can appreciate your impatience," DCS Richmond said in reply to her inquiry, "DS Hargreaves knows the details and that helped him in his choice of team members. I need each of you to sign your copy of the document and if anyone does not want to, please leave now before you hear something you shouldn't". They all looked around at one another, to see if any of them were going to leave. When it became obvious they they all were staying, pens were removed from pockets and the signing commenced.

"By the time you've filled in the forms and checked them over, the ACC should be here and he will then pass on to you all the information you'll need. He'll also answer any questions that you may have and Jack, there's more for you to find out about as well, so I was told this morning".

The documents were duly signed, by all four of them and handed back across the desk. "I'd get yourselves a drink, if I were you, as this could well take the rest of the afternoon. You'll also find note-books over there, so you can take any notes you deem necessary. But, for now, the note-books won't be allowed out of this room, until we can arrange a secure facility for you. The same procedure will also apply to the number of files that will be transferred to the team. Please remember, that these will be for your eyes only. We must all be very careful about all we say and do. No pads or files to be left on desks, where prying eyes could gain access to information. It will soon become second nature to you, but for now, keep a watchful eye on each other, as a mistake can easily made, but very difficult to undo".

As he was explaining all of this, the door opened and they all stood up respectfully as the ACC entered the room. He was carrying a briefcase with him and after placing it on the desk, removed a number of files from it. Each of the files had a diagonal red line across the cover and the words 'EYES ONLY' stamped in crimson ink.

"Are we all ready?" the ACC asked, looking around the room, "Right then, here we go".

Jack had placed himself at one end of the semi-circle of chairs, so that he could watch the expressions on the faces of his team. These were all experienced officers and had seen many extreme things while fulfilling their duties, but nothing had prepared them for the information that the ACC released to them. Jack thought back to the evening when he had been told about all of this and remembered how he felt at the time. It all seemed unbelievable, but the evidence was there to back it up. As he watched them, it was obvious to see that they were shocked by the whole situation and were looking at one another for confirmation that they had heard correctly. But as they watched the expressions on their colleagues' faces, they realised that they had indeed fully heard and understood this strange case.

When he had finished, the ACC turned to them and said, "Well, what do you think about all of that?".

DI Grantham was the first one to speak. "Are you sure that this is real, that it isn't some kind of elaborate hoax?".

"Oh, it's real enough. Do you honestly think that all we senior officers would be party to a hoax of this nature, a hoax that extends right up to the Home Office?" was the ACC's response.

"But it's so fantastic, people just disappearing without a trace" said DS Barron, "I can understand why there's been so much secrecy about all of this".

"So you can understand why it has to be kept under wraps. We six are the only ones who know the details, in this division, and it has to be kept that way"

DCS Richmond added, "The people in this station will soon pick up that something's going on and will do their best to nose out what they can. Therefore great care needs to be taken with paperwork and of course, we all know what the press can be like. If they just get a whiff of this all hell will break loose. It would be front page on all the nationals the following morning. So one word, one comment or one piece of paper in the wrong hands, will cause irreparable damage to our investigation".

At this point, Jack decided to add a comment on his own. "This need for secrecy demonstrates how we must watch each other, until security becomes second nature to us all and that also applies when we leave the station. A wrong comment when we mix with the public, will be overheard by someone and who knows where it will end up".

"I wish you all success in your investigation," the ACC said, "and that this matter can be resolved as quickly as possible. You'll have all the resources that you need, but I emphasize again the need for security. Just think of the recent scandals regarding missing 'Lap Tops' and memory sticks. We can't afford to join those statistics, so please be careful".

The ACC got up from his chair, walked across the room and as he was standing in the doorway, he turned and said, "I wish you all a speedy result" and then he was gone. It was all over, they knew the full facts now, so there was no turning back.

They were just preparing to leave, when Jack turned to DCS Richmond and said, "You mentioned earlier about something you learned this morning?".

"Oh yes" he replied, "All of you, come back in and close the door behind you. I was told of a case at the Psychiatric Hospital, of a man who was admitted after he claimed that he could see ghosts. The doctors would normally put this down to a mental illness, but as they are also involved in this investigation and knowing what we do, tends to cast a somewhat different light on it. don't you think?".

"I certainly do" Jack answered, "He may well be

worthy of a visit".

"I think it would be an excellent idea," the DCS replied, "We might be able to persuade him to work along with us if his condition can be stabilized". The two old friends shook hands and then Jack, along with his team, left the office.

As they stood together in the outer office, Jack turned to his fledgling team, "I think that it would be OK if you all took the rest of the day off, after all, you've got plenty to think about and remember, not a word about this to anyone outside the team. If you want to discuss it among yourselves, make sure that no-one can overhear you. Right then. My office, first thing in the morning, alright?". They all thanked him, left the office and headed for the lifts.

The office that Jack had presided over for so long, was buzzing with rumours and counter rumours. Even though all the officers concerned had important work to do, most of their attention was directed towards the group that had gathered in Jack's office. But no matter how wild their speculations were, they never came close to the truth and would have been shocked if they had known.

"Good morning" Jack said to his team, "This will be the last time that we will meet together in this office as there are too many prying eyes in the vicinity".

As he said this, they all looked through the glass and a dozen heads suddenly dropped to look at their desks.

"You see what I mean," Jack said. "So a new office is being arranged for us, on the next floor up and we will be moving there in a little while. I'm going to speak to those in the office outside, so use the time to introduce yourselves to each other". All eyes were on Jack, as he entered the main office.

"Could you all gather round for a moment," he called. They didn't take much persuading, as they were dying to know what Jack was up to.

"As you may have gathered" he said, "I am working on something new and will be joined in this venture by the officers that are now in what will soon become my old office". A murmuring spread through the assembled officers. He continued, "They are the members of my new team. I'm sorry that I couldn't include you all, but it's not that sort of case. So for now, your senior officer will be DCI Tim Clarke, who will be taking over my old duties, until a permanent replacement can be found. Thank you all for the hard work and support over the years we've been together and keep up the good work".

That was it and Jack turned on his heels, walking back into his office. He entered a room filled with conversation, which pleased him, as it was so important that they all got on well together.

"Would you all please return to your old desks and collect your goods and chattels. We'll meet upstairs in room 516 in, what shall we say, an hour's time. That should give you time to say your good-byes and remember, not a word about your new assignment to anyone and I mean anyone" Jack said to them, really emphasizing the last statement.

After they had left, he followed the instructions that he had given to them, collecting together all the bits and pieces that had accumulated over the years. Just before he left it for the final time, he stood in the doorway looking back into the room, as he thought back over the many years that he had occupied it. "Well" he said out loud, "I had to leave it sooner or later and now is as good a time as any".

As Jack organised things in his new office, he realised that he was recreating his old one, but in a new space. Why shouldn't he? After all, he was used to where things would be, 'So why make things difficult, by moving things around' he thought. The amount of space allocated to the team was not vast. but it was adequate for four people. Phones and computers had been installed, as had the all important coffee percolator. They were all pleased to see that they had facilities to make 'proper' coffee, rather than a machine. This small gesture helped to show them the high esteem afforded the team and its investigation.

Jack emerged from his office, which was actually an area that had been partitioned off, to be greeted by the smell of freshly brewed coffee. "What a wonderful smell" he said, "I'm sure that it will help to keep us going, when it gets tough, as I'm sure it will".

They all poured themselves a drink and sat in a group, in what was to become their discussion area. Jack was the first one to speak. "Two things I need to mention. You may have noticed the safe at the back of the room. We will never leave the office without all the paperwork, documents etc being placed in there. I will let you all know the combination and we will be the only ones to know it. So if anything goes missing, it will be one of us. Is that OK?".

They all nodded in acceptance, as it made perfect sense, especially with the security implications of the investigation.

"Secondly" Jack said, "As there are only four of us and as we will be working in very close proximity, for as long as it takes, I propose that we use first names. I would certainly feel more comfortable working that way and I feel that it would help us bond as a team".

Just as the other members of the team were agreeing, the phone started to ring. "At least the phones work" David said, as he reached behind him, across the desk. "Superintendent Hargreaves Team" he answered and then passed the handset to Jack while he said "it's the custody suite, they want to talk to you". "Superintendent Hargreaves, how can I help" Jack replied and then became engrossed in conversation. When he finally put the phone down, he turned to the team. "Something of interest cropped up this afternoon, here in the town centre. They want us to go down to the observation room, while a man is questioned". The paperwork was placed in the safe and the room secured, as they left to go downstairs.

They were ushered into the observation room by a discreet route, so that they were not noticed by any other officers. "You three stay in here, while I go and sit in on the questioning" Jack said, "As I want to ensure that the right questions are asked, as this is our first opportunity for some first hand information". They watched, as Jack entered the interrogation room and sat down beside an officer, who had his back to them.

"This is Superintendent Hargreaves and he would like you to relate this afternoon's events for him," the officer said.

"But I've already been through it a number of times, isn't that enough for you" the man replied.

"I might need to ask some questions that haven't been asked before. So if you wouldn't mind, please tell me what happened, just one more time" Jack said, trying to calm the man down.

"Alright" he said in reply to Jack's request, "But this is the last time. I want to forget the experience, not keep going over it. I was just turning out into Westgate, by John Lewis's, you know, and I wasn't moving very quickly because pedestrians kept darting out in front of me, as if they had the right of way. Anyhow, I had just started to move when I felt this almighty thump, as if I'd hit something. But the road was totally clear, there wasn't anyone in front of me. So I stamped on the brakes and stopped. By then, the usual crowd of nosey-parkers had stopped to see what was going on. I got out of the van and walked round to the front, to see if there was anything there and I swear to you that there wasn't anything there. I turned round to the sightseers that had stopped to gawp and asked them if they had seen anything. They started to point and I turned around, only to see the body of an elderly woman lying there, in front of the van.

At this point, I phoned you lot. I was totally confused, because one moment she wasn't there and then she was. How could I stop, if I couldn't see her" and he started to sob as he said "I don't know what I'm going to do".

The officer turned to Jack and said "A breathalyzer test carried out on site, was clear and we've taken some blood to check for chemicals, but I've a feeling that it will come back clean. I'm glad I'm not one of the lawyers that will have to sort this out". Jack thanked the officer for calling him in and then joined the rest of the team in the observation room.

"Well, what do you think about that man's account?" Jack asked them. "I think it's astounding, he seems really believable" Clive said, adding "If it's all true, something like that could happen to anybody, at any time. I find that really frightening".

They all added their comments, each of them

basically agreeing with all that Clive had said. They then made their way back to room 516 and got themselves settled.

"Now then, down to business" Jack said "Lets start with this incident and find out who this old lady is, or was. Dave you take Sarah and take a trip to the morgue, to get her fingerprints". "Oh God, the morgue. I hate that place" Sarah said.

"I don't think anyone really likes going there, especially the dead ones" Dave answered. "Very funny" she replied.

"Off you go, you two" Jack said, with an authoritative tone to his voice. "Clive, I want you to read the files of incidents that have taken place in our area, that seem to fit our remit. We'll all pool our information when we assemble again. Then we'll see if the finger prints can help us identify our mystery lady".

Just before Dave and Sarah left the office, Clive piped up, "How did the officer in custody know to contact you, Jack". It seemed strange addressing his superior officer by his first name and he felt a little unsure about doing it. Jack picked up on his caution and said, "You'll soon get used to calling me Jack, but don't try being that that familiar with any of the other senior officers. Anyway, in answer to your question. All the senior investigating officers have received a memo from division, asking them to contact me if in the course of their duties they come across anything unusual, something that cannot easily be explained, like what happened to the man downstairs".

"But doesn't that compromise our security?" Dave questioned.

"No, not really. They won't know why I need to be contacted, or what use the information will be to me.

Knowing-most of them, as I do, they'll be glad to get rid of anything out of the ordinary" Jack replied.

The fingerprints of the elderly lady, who had been knocked down and killed, were revelatory. Her name was Linda Bryson and she had gone missing, about seven months before, from a residential home for dementia sufferers in Little Port, which is just north of Ely.

"How she got here, we'll most likely never know" Jack stated.

"Why were her prints on file?" Sarah asked.

Clive, who was sitting at the computer said, "She had a conviction for assault. Apparently, this happened before her dementia was diagnosed, as she lived alone and no-one picked up on it. But one day, while she was in the local Co-Op, she flipped and attacked a member of staff, really beating her up. The woman pressed charges and Miss Bryson was convicted of common assault.

By the time it came to trial, the doctors had diagnosed her condition, so she was bound over to keep the peace and to pay £50 compensation to the injured woman. It goes on to say that following this incident, her condition became more acute as there are reports of the local police being called in when she became abusive and threatening to her neighbours. It was at this point she was placed in the nursing home, for everyone's benefit. That's all there is on file about her" he said.

"So she must have managed to slip out of the home, at some point" Sarah said, "But who knows what happened to her after that."

"I've a theory about that" Jack said, adding to the speculation, "What if the events that causes these people to become invisible, happened to her in the nursing home. Then she could easily slip out, as no-one would be able to see her. It's also very unlikely that she would be aware of her changed condition".

David then entered the conversation with another educated guess. "In the light of what we heard downstairs today, do you all think that it's fair to assume then, that if these invisible people die somehow, they become visible once again. That would certainly link together all that we know about this woman and what happened with the van driver. What do you all think?".

"It certainly links together all the pieces that we have so far, doesn't it" Jack replied and the continued, "I feel that this is the first major step in our understanding of the phenomenon that we're dealing with and that our investigation is now well and truly under way".

***

CHAPTER SEVEN

ACCEPTANCE

Gary finally woke, unsure as to how long the drugs had made him sleep, all he knew was that it was now dark outside. He felt really hungry and thirsty, so he started to call out for a nurse. The surveillance system was obviously working, as a few minutes later, he heard the sound of a key turning in the lock and then the door swung open. The nurse reached inside the door and switched on the light, which really hurt his eyes, until they adjusted to the brightness.

"How long have I been out?" Gary asked.

The nurse looked at her watch and said, "Just over twelve hours. They must have given you a large dose, to make you sleep that long".

"I'd love something to drink" Gary said "and something to eat as well, if possible". "I'll see what I can find" she said, "It will most likely be a sandwich, as the kitchen is closed at this time of night".

"Anything at all, will be gratefully received" Gary replied "and could you see if there's anyone about that has the authority to release me from these restraints. I'm perfectly safe now, the event is well and truly over and I'm back to my normal self. Whatever that is. But you know that I'm not usually any trouble, don't you". "I'll ask the doctor on call and see how they feel about that" she said, "but don't build your hopes up too much, in case you're disappointed".

While she was talking, one of the orderlies arrived

and he remained in the room when the nurse left to do what she could to fulfill Gary's requests. Although he hadn't spoken to an orderly before, he decided to try and engage the man in conversation. By the time the nurse re-appeared, Gary and the orderly, who was called Chris, were actively engaged in a discussion about horse racing, which they both seemed to be enjoying.

"Well, you lads seem to be getting on together" she said, as she placed a tray, carrying Gary's coffee and sandwich, onto his table. "I've spoken to the doctor on call, who feels that it will be alright to remove the restraints while you eat, so long as the orderly stays in here with you. Seeing that the two of you are getting on well, I don't think that it should cause any problems. While I'm gone, the door will be locked, so there's no chance that you can get out. Is that acceptable to you?". "That's fine" Gary replied, as he watched Chris walk across the room, to help the nurse unfasten the straps that held Gary to the bed. "I'm leaving now and as long as you behave, I don't think the restraints will be needed again. It's up to you". "Yes mummy" Gary called out, with a big grin on his face. Machine coffee is never coffee at its best, but to Gary it was like nectar and the sandwich, although not that fresh, was one of the best he had ever tasted. He was grateful that the nurse had got them for him and that he wasn't left to wait for breakfast.

A few hours later, Gary was sitting in Dr Hedley's office, facing her across the desk. He realised that he would have to come clean about the 'see-through.' people. How else was he going to explain his actions of the previous day. He knew the question was coming, so he did the best he could to prepare for it. "Well, Gary" she said, "What was all that about, yesterday? I think that there's something going on that you haven't explained to me. How about letting it all out. You know that you'll feel so much better once it's all out in the open. So, how about it?".

Gary didn't respond. His mind was racing, trying to fathom out what to say. How do you tell somebody that you see people that others can't, without making yourself sound like a nutcase?

"I can see that you're struggling Gary. Just tell me, no matter how silly it may sound".

He was unable to hold it in any longer. His mind was desperate to purge itself of all the troubling information. Just to be able to tell someone, was something he had wished for and now the opportunity had presented itself to him. So he let it all spill out. Starting with the men on the stairs, right up to the young woman in the common room, the previous day.

When he had finished, he started to sob, even though a feeling of relief flooded through him. Dr Hedley didn't say anything for a few moments. She was busy writing her notes, along with her comments, about all that Gary had said.

"I think that we could both use a nice cup of coffee about now. What do you think?", she said to Gary, whose sobbing had quietened down a little.

"I could use a stronger drink than that" Gary replied, "But I suppose that's not allowed".

"If I allowed you to consume some alcohol, it would react with the drugs in your system and we'd be carrying you out of here. Take my word for it" she said.

"I best stick to coffee then" Gary replied in acceptance of her statement.

"I know that this isn't a real substitute for a drink," she said, reaching down into the desk drawer, "But how about a chocolate digestive. I don't know about you, but I really enjoy one, or two, with my coffee".

Gary smiled and reached across the desk towards the proffered packet of biscuits. The two of them sat in silence for a few moments, until it was broken by Gary asking a question. "Do you think that I'll ever be free of these visions? Could drugs or shock therapy clear the problem out of my brain?".

She didn't reply immediately but then said "I'm not really sure at the moment what the best approach will be. But have you considered the possibility that being able to see these people could be a gift that you have."

Gary was about to speak, when she continued, "Just think. If they are real people, who for whatever reason have ended up in that state, don't you think that they would be glad that some-one could see them? Step into their shoes for a minute. If you were one of them, how would you feel?"

"I suppose that I would want to be able to prove to people that I still existed."

"I agree, I certainly would. I would be desperate to let my loved ones know that I was alright and that I was still around, even though they were unable to see me".
"Thinking about it like that does put a different slant on things," Gary replied, "I'll have to think about this some more".

"I'll have you taken back to your room now, so you can have some time on your own, to think this over and then later on, after the evening meal, you can

can return to the common room. Does that suit you?"

"That would be great" Gary replied, "Even though I

don't really know the other occupants of the common room too well, I've missed seeing them all and it will be nice to have the freedom again".

After Gary had left the room, Dr Hedley reached into her handbag for her cigarettes and lighter. She opened the window, one of the old sash types, and leaned out onto the concrete sill, allowing the sunshine to wash all over her. This was the only way she could have a smoke, leaning out of the window, as it wasn't allowed inside the building. This method worked so long as the. wind wasn't blowing towards her, as then the smoke was blown back into the room and as she had already been warned about smoking on the premises, she had to be careful. However, this time she got away with it and felt quite pleased with herself. She really felt that she needed a smoke after hearing Gary's revelations, but if she was honest with herself, she knew that it was just an excuse to carry on her habit. The cigarettes and lighter were placed back in the bag and she fumbled around for her purse. When she found it, she looked through the various sections, until she found where she kept all her cards. The white card, with the number across it, was extracted and she dialled the number.

After a few rings, it was answered, by a male voice this time. After introducing herself, she summarized the meeting with Gary, that had taken place earlier. "No" she said, "I didn't have to drag it out of him. He was in such a wound up state, that he just couldn't stop himself telling me what he was seeing, just so he could get some relief. But it is what we suspected, isn't it? I'll see if I can talk him round to using his ability to help towards solving this situation".

She paused briefly, while listening to the voice on the phone.

"I'm not sure how he will respond. Authority figures don't feature too strongly in his life and I think that he tends to see them as the enemy. So I'll have to tread carefully". The voice on the phone continued speaking for a few moments and then the call was terminated.

Gary enjoyed being back in the common room and his arrival had been greeted by a few welcoming comments. He was able to settle himself in the chair by the window and was enjoying watching the people come and go. He suddenly stood up, so that he could get a better view. He had seen a couple of people that looked very familiar and he was sure that they were a couple of his drinking buddies. After they moved out of his line of sight, he sat back down, unsure if he had been correct. About ten minutes later, an orderly came in through the doors and called out, "Gary. There's a couple of visitors to see you".

He got up and started to walk towards the doors, arriving there just as the two young men he had seen in the car park, entered. He had been right, it was Bill and Dave. They weren't a gregarious group of friends, so they were confused and unsure how to react, when Gary hugged them both.

"Come on" said Gary, enthusiastically, "Let's sit over here by the windows, that's where I usually sit".

Dave opened the conversation by conveying, Nigel's apologies for not being here and then asked, "What on earth did you do to end up here, in the nuthouse?"; "Tactless or what" Bill responded.

"Sorry" Dave said, "But it's what I always called this place".

"Don't worry about it" Gary said, "There are some right nutters in here. But I can assure you both, that I'm not one of them".

"I'm pleased to hear it" Bill replied, "So what happened to you and why did you end up in here? We're dying to know, aren't we Dave".

"To be honest, all of your friends are," Bill said, "You just disappeared one day and it took us quite a while to track you down".

At that moment, another part of Gary's mind kicked into operation, rekindling another part of his memory. "How did Suzy take it?" he asked, "I was sent off to the shops and ended up in here."

"Boy, was she mad," Bill said in reply. "She burst into the Chequers, almost knocking the doors off their hinges, as she was sure that you'd stopped off for a drink. But of course, you hadn't". Dave then took up the account. "She really interrogated us. She was convinced that we would know what you were up to. But we had no more idea than she had".

"It was about this time that we heard the sirens. That's right, isn't it Dave?" Bill asked.

"Oh yes. I'd forgotten about the sirens. I remember saying at the time 'some poor sod's in bother'... ". "...and that was me," Gary said, finishing off his statement. "So come on, what actually happened to you? Suzy thought you'd been in an accident and shot off down the road. None of us have seen her since, but I would think that if you ever come face to face with her, you'll have some explaining to do," Dave said, "So, what happened to you?".

Gary's mind was in overdrive, he couldn't tell them the truth, or they would really think he was mad and that he belonged in the hospital. So he did the next best thing. A little of the truth, mixed in with a little bit of fiction. "I seemed to have had some kind of breakdown and flipped out for a while. I feel that the excessive drinking may well have had something to do with it. I don't really understand it myself but I was well out of things for quite a while and that's all I know".

He was relieved to see that they were willing to accept this explanation and it filled in the gaps for them.

"We knew that you must have been quite bad, as this is the first time that they've let us visit you".

"Have you tried before then?" Gary asked.

Bill took over the conversation. "After we found out where you were, we phoned up to ask about visiting. But we were told that you were too ill at the time and to keep phoning so that we could find out when you were in better health".

"I never knew about any of that" Gary said, but it did answer a question that had been going round in his mind, 'Why hadn't his friends visited him'. He continued speaking, "It would have been nice to know that you were asking about me, who knows, it may have helped in my recovery. But I think the doctors are as mental as the patients, anyway, so who knows how their minds work"

This statement caused them all to break into uncontrolled laughter. This was a beneficial thing for Gary to experience and was one of the best things that had happened to him since his committal. The three old friends were still engaged in animated conversation when they were told that visiting time was over. Gary asked a nurse if it would be alright for him to accompany his friends down to the main entrance.

"You're not planning on making a break for it, are you?" she asked.

"No way" Gary replied, "I know that you'd soon track me down and bring me back. Then I'd never have a chance of getting out of here".

"Go on then" the nurse said, "I'll trust you".

As he prepared himself for bed that night, Gary was feeling quite contented. By now he had become used to the rhythm of life in the hospital and had actually begun to enjoy his new way of living. The time that he had spent with his friends that evening had really given him a boost and he looked forward to further visits from them. He hadn't realised just how sick he had been but the explanation for why they hadn't visited before had brought it all home to him. He wondered how he would cope with life outside, when he was finally released. Although he did appreciate that it would be a strikingly different Gary that exited the front door of the hospital than had arrived in the ambulance all those weeks ago. He had a better understanding of himself now and was coming to terms with his gift, for that is how Dr Hedley had described his condition.

He decided to challenge that description, the next time he saw her and also wondered how his friends would react if he told them. Talking about his condition was obviously the best course of action, as it had proved to be, during that evening with his visitors. Sitting on the edge of his bed, he thumbed through the pages of the magazines that his friends had brought him and also had a quick look at the covers of the paperbacks that they had also brought.

"They're really good mates," he said out loud, "To think enough of me, to bring these things". He was overtaken by a bout of yawning and suddenly realised how tired he was. "I think I'll have to put the record straight in the morning, when I see Dr Hedley" he said as he was getting into bed and fell asleep while he was working out exactly what to say.

Following breakfast the next morning, Gary took one of his magazines and sat in the common room, while he waited to be escorted to Dr Hedley's office. He did not fail to notice that he was conducted there by a nurse on her own, no orderly following behind. This helped him to appreciate how much progress he must have made, that they would trust him enough to not have an orderly present. Gary was delighted to find that the nurse was quite chatty and was rather upset when they arrived at Dr Hedley's office, as that terminated their conversation.

The doctor was on the phone as they entered and she gestured to Gary to sit in his usual chair. She concluded her call and then apologized to Gary, for making him wait. "The call took a little longer than I anticipated" she said, "As there were some points that I needed to clarify, before I saw you this morning".

That comment stirred Gary's interest. Who had she been talking to? How was the person involved and what did she need to clarify? All these thoughts were buzzing around inside his head, as he heard Dr Hedley dismiss the nurse and tell her that she would be called later on when the session with Gary was over. Now, this was unusual. He had never been left on his own before. What was she going to say? The usual cups of coffee were poured out, with Gary just wishing that she would get on with her revelations.

She started with the standard question. "Well Gary, how are you feeling?"

"I just wish that you would get on with it," Gary fired back, never realising that she was just as apprehensive about starting the conversation, as he was about hearing what she had to say. He continued, "I know that you want to explain something about my situation, so let me have it. Both barrels".

"Fair enough," she replied, "But before I do, it is necessary for me to get you to agree that everything I say stays between us. You are not, under any circumstances, to repeat any part of our conversation to any other person". She could see from his expression that he found this restriction a little confusing, but she continued, "If you do, be assured that it will be uncovered and you will be prevented from doing it again".

Gary didn't like the direction that the conversation was taking and felt threatened. "Who's deciding all these restrictions then?" he asked. "I cannot give you a name, but I'm allowed to tell you that this all comes from the Home Office and that there are some powerful people involved".

Gary didn't say a word. He was astounded by her revelations and was unsure how to react. Neither of them spoke for a few minutes and then Dr Hedley finally broke the silence. "Well then Gary, will you be able to keep anything I say to yourself?".

"I don't really have a choice, do I. If I say no, then I'll be locked up in here, forever. So I'll have to agree, won't I".

"Right then" she said, "Let's see how you deal with this. How would you feel if I told you that you were not the only one able to see these invisible people?"

Gary's mind was racing, struggling to comprehend what she had said. "Do you mean that they really exist and aren't created by my mind?".

"That's correct and for the present you will have to accept that for some reason, you are able to see them. Why that is, I don't know. Just as I don't know who these people are". She paused at that point, as she could see that Gary was somewhat disturbed by what she had said. "If you would feel better by having a wander around the room, please do so".

"Thanks" Gary replied and then asked, "Would you mind if I opened the window to get some air, as the room suddenly feels a bit stuffy?".

"Go ahead" Dr Hedley said, "Would you like me to give you something to help you calm down?".

"No thank you" Gary answered, "I've had enough of feeling like a zombie. I just need to get all of this sorted out in my mind. You really mean to tell me that these people exist and I am not alone in being able to see them?"

"I'm sorry if that upsets you, but it's the truth" she replied, "It was thought that you were ready to deal with the information".

"Who thought?" Gary asked.

"As you can perhaps deduce from what I told you earlier, I am not the only doctor who is having to treat a patient with symptoms similar to your own. In fact there are quite a number of you spread all over the country".

Gary was astounded. He had gone from being someone with a problem, to one of an exclusive group, in the space of a few minutes. Dr Hedley could see that he was struggling, as he tried to come to terms with his newly revealed situation. "What about all the stuff you pumped into me and the restraints pinning me to the bed. What was that all about?".

"You were in such a state when you were brought in that tranquilizing you was the only safe course, for you and us. You have to realise that your brain was trying to cope with the trauma you had been through, so putting you into an induced coma was the only way to allow it time to come to terms with the situation. Even now, as you are getting back to your old self, you have still found this all a bit difficult to deal with, haven't you?".

"You can say that again," Gary replied and then said, "I think I would like to go back to my room now if you don't mind".

"Are you sure that you're feeling alright?" she asked and then thinking about his previous reactions, added, "I think I'll have someone sit in with you for a while". Gary's response surprised her, when he said, "Do you know, I think I'd like that".

Gary didn't have any more one-to-one sessions with Dr Hedley for a few days, although he often saw her walking around in the hospital. She always spoke to him when she was passing and a couple of times she had come over to his window seat and had spent a few moments talking to him. But nothing concerned with their last private conversation was ever mentioned. He thought that she was testing him, to see if he would say anything while they were in a public place so he always allowed her to lead the conversation.

Gary found that as the days passed, the revelations that he had heard from Dr Hedley slowly began to become part of the way that he thought about things. He found himself trying to work out who the invisibles could be and where they had come from. He even astounded himself one day when he realised that he was wishing for another encounter with one of these mystery people, just to see how he would react, now that he knew the truth about them. He didn't have long too wait.

A couple of days later, he once again saw the young

woman, that had been the catalyst for his last psychotic episode. This time he surprised himself with his reaction. True, his pulse rate rose, he could hear it thumping in his ears and his hands became clammy as he gripped the arms of the chair. But he never panicked. as he watched her closely. All the things that had caused him to break down before took place but this time he was able to survive it all. As she was about to follow an orderly through the door closest to him she turned, waved and smiled. Instinctively, Gary realised that he was waving in return and then she was gone.

By no stretch of the imagination could you say that Gary was alright, but he had survived through an experience that only a few days before, would have ended up with him being tranquilized and restrained on his bed. After she had left, he felt relieved and elated at the same time. This had been the first really positive thing that had happened to him since all this had started. He called over to a nurse, who was speaking to another patient and asked her to find out if it was possible for him to see Dr Hedley.

'What's going on with me' he thought, 'Here I am asking to see a psychiatrist, perhaps I am really mad after all' and chuckled to himself. The nurse re-appeared a few minutes later.

"Dr Hedley is seeing a patient, at the moment" she said, "But she can give you a few minutes once she has finished. Is that alright?".

Gary thanked her and sank back into his chair, while he looked out of the window and waited for the time to pass by. Over an hour passed, before Gary was sitting in Dr Hedley's office once again. He could even feel the heat from the previous occupant, as he sat down in the chair, so he knew that there had been someone here before him.

"This is unusual" Dr Hedley said, "You asking to see me. Has something happened to warrant this request?". Gary went on to explain what had taken place with the invisible young woman and how well he had reacted.

"Well, that is certainly a big step forward in your progress..Do you think that from now on, each time you have a similar experience, it will become easier to deal with?".

"I hope so," Gary replied, "I really surprised myself today. I never expected to deal with it as well as I did".

"I think that's because you now know the truth about the situation and that has made it easier for your mind to deal with. Do you think that's the case?".

"I certainly wasn't so frightened as I had been during the previous encounters. I think that knowing she was a real person and not a figment of my imagination, really helped me" Gary replied.

"So our last session and the things I revealed to you, really helped then".

"I wasn't too sure at the time," Gary said, "As it all seemed all so fantastic. But now that I've had time to get used to the idea, my mind seems more able to deal with the whole concept".

"Well, I'll see you tomorrow for our regular meeting as I'm afraid that I have another appointment in a few moments. So I'm unable to give you any more time, right now. But really well done, for dealing with the situation as well as you did. You're making some real progress and I'll see you in the morning".

"Thanks for seeing me now," Gary said, "I just wanted to tell you how well I had coped with seeing one of them again especially as I can't tell anyone else, so thank you for giving me the time this afternoon".

On the way back to the common room, Gary was analyzing his actions, as to why he needed to tell Dr Hedley how well he had done. 'It's like a child running to his mother, to tell her how well he's done at school', he thought to himself, 'I was never that way before, not even with my own mother. So why am I acting that way now?'.

He concluded that this was another instance of his mind working in a way that he wasn't used to. 'I wonder if it's the effects of all the meds that they've put in me.' he thought, 'Because I never used to act that way. Oh well, another unexplained mystery'.

The next morning, following breakfast and medication, Gary occupied his usual chair in the common room. He noticed that Benny was making a bee-line for him. Gary was unsettled by his approach as Benny was a large man and he normally didn't have much to say to anyone. Anyway, he settled himself into a chair close to Gary and said, "What's going on between you and Dr Hedley? I heard that the last time you were in there, the nurse was asked to leave. So you were alone with her".

"Nothing's going on" Gary replied.

This obviously didn't satisfy Bennie, who continued, "Are you sure that you're not doing naughties with her? After all, she's a good looking woman. Well. Are you?". "I agree that she's a good looking woman, but I can assure you that nothing of that nature is taking place," Gary replied, "We were alone, because we had to deal with some confidential matters. Does that satisfy you?".

"It all seems very suspect to me," Benny said, "I'm sure that something is going on".

At that point, a nurse arrived and said, "Gary. It's

time for you to see the doctor. Are you ready?".

"More than you'll ever know" Gary replied.

"Just keep an eye on him, nurse. I think he's up to something with the doc," Benny said, as a parting comment.

As they walked down the corridor, the nurse asked, "What was all that about with Benny?".

"He accused me of being up to no good with Dr Hedley as he's found out somehow, that the nurse was asked to leave the last time that I saw her," Gary replied.

"Don't worry about it," the nurse said, "Benny has a bit of a crush on Dr Hedley and I think that his comments are prompted by jealousy. He's actually not too safe around the female members of staff but I shouldn't have told you that, so please don't mention it to anyone".

"I won't" Gary said, smiling to himself. They carried on chatting until they reached the doctor's door and went on in. Gary was surprised to see a man sitting alongside the doctor's desk and also made a mental note that there were a number of folders on her desk.

The nurse left the room and Gary was invited to sit down, something he would normally do without being asked. "We'll call this gentleman Mr Smith, for the duration of our time together this morning".

"So what's all this about then?" Gary asked. He was always wary of official looking people, as in his experience they always ended up causing him trouble in one way or another.

Dr Hedley picked up the conversation, saying "Mr Smith is from the Home Office..."

"I thought as much" Gary said, interrupting her.

"....and he is part of the team that's looking into this

situation with the invisible people. I'll let him explain why he's here and what he hopes to achieve".

Mr Smith started to speak in a very educated voice, which confirmed Gary's suspicions about him. "First of all Gary, I'd like to thank you for letting me speak to you," he said.

Gary thought to himself, 'I don't remember being given a choice'.

"How much do you know about this situation?" He asked.

"Well, the doctor explained to me that I'm not alone in being able to see these invisible people, but apart from that, I don't know much else" Gary explained.

"I didn't know how much more I was to tell him," Dr Hedley said.

"Fair enough, I know how we stand now," Mr Smith replied. "Well Gary, this situation appears to be nation wide and you are one of a small group of people who for some reason are able to see these ones who are invisible to the rest of us. I'm sure you can understand the security implications, if this is happening in less friendly countries as well".

"I'd never even thought about that" Gary said.

"We have actually been investigating this problem for some time now and this is the point where I need to ask for your help".

"My help?" Gary said, with a surprised expression on his face, "How can I help? I can see them admittedly, but know no more than you do, probably less".

"But it is your ability to see them, that makes you invaluable" Mr Smith stated. "I've never thought of myself as invaluable before" Gary replied, while laughing. "Now a big question" Mr Smith said. "How do you feel about the police? Answer truthfully, as I need to know".

"I'm not their greatest fan," Gary said.

"I can see from your record, which I have here, that you've had a few run-ins with the police. But as far as I can see, it's all minor stuff, mainly drink related. Is that correct?".

"Yes, you've got it right" Gary answered, feeling somewhat embarrassed about it for the first time.

"Well, there's nothing here that causes us any concern. How's the drinking now. I know that you haven't had the usual opportunities since you've been in here but do you still crave drink, in the way that you used to?" Mr Smith asked.

"It's strange that you should ask," Gary replied, "It doesn't really bother me now. I must have gone cold turkey while I was unconscious and who knows what side effects the drugs they've given me might have had".

"So, do you think it will cause a problem in the future?" he asked.

"For the first time in many years, I can honestly say that I don't think it will," Gary replied, feeling quite pleased with himself.

"Well then, here comes the big question" Mr Smith said, "How would you feel about working along with the police to try and resolve this mystery?".

Gary was stunned. He had always tried to avoid the police in the past and now he was being asked to work along with them. "It would certainly be a new experience for me" Gary replied.

Mr Smith then clarified his request. "We're only talking about a small team of a few officers, not the whole force. In fact, the majority of them have no knowledge about any of this".

"I've wanted to get one over on the police for years,"

Gary said "and at long last it seems that I have the opportunity. Although I'm not too sure about it at the moment, I certainly would like to find an explanation for all that I've been through". At this point Gary paused, while he thought over his options. After a few minutes he spoke. "OK" he said, "I'll give it a go".

Mr Smith appeared to be relieved when he heard Gary's decision and said, "I'll arrange a discreet meeting, between you and the local team and after speaking with them, you can make your final decision. Does that suit you?".

"That's fine," Gary replied, as he was looking forward to being part of the investigation and also meeting the officers.

That evening, Gary spent a lot of time reviewing the afternoon's events. He

couldn't believe that he was going to be working along with the police and if what he had been told was correct, they would be unable to make any progress without his help. After a while he left the common room, there was too much noise and bustle for him to be able to think straight.

For the first time that he could remember, he appreciated the silence and solitude of his room. Would he really be of use to the police? What about the level of discipline that would be required? But on the other hand, who knows what benefits could come from this in the future. Could it be that his old life, living alone in the flat, surrounded by empty lager cans, would disappear into the past. After all, if they wanted to make use of him, the least they could do was to make sure that he was comfortable and had a presentable appearance.

'Over all' Gary thought, 'This could well work out to

be a nice arrangement for me. I'm sure that I'll get used to working with the police, it all depends on how well they treat me. If they treat me like a second class object, then they can stuff it! But deep down inside, he was somewhat excited by the whole prospect. He was part of an exclusive group who knew about the invisible people, all those around him, had no idea of what was going on and he rather enjoyed being in that situation. Never before had he experienced feelings of superiority, but from this point on, he had a different feeling about himself.

The Gary of old was quickly retreating into the past and a new Gary was emerging. Along with this he had a new outlook on life, not knowing what he could expect in the future. That night, as he drifted into sleep, he had all these possibilities going around in his head. He was feeling positive about the rest of his life, something that he never had reason to feel before.

***

CHAPTER EIGHT

INVESTIGATION

Linda's death had hit the group very hard but none of them suffered as much as Michael did. She had been his whole life. Caring for her had given his life meaning and distracted him from dwelling on his current situation. No-one really said much or did anything apart from the necessities for the first couple of days, but then life started to drift back into what they called normality.

It was Emily, much to everyone's surprise, who first broke the ice concerning Linda's death.

"Do you think the police are investigating the circumstances of her death?" she asked, "As it doesn't seem to have been a normal kind of accident".

Once the dam had been breached the discussion quickly spread through the group. "I never knew where she came from, or even her surname" Michael said, "She, would only say that her name was Linda. So I wonder what the police have turned up?"

At this point, Theo got an idea. "Why don't we go and see for ourselves. We're in a unique situation being able to go where we please without being detected. So let's make our condition work for us and go into the police HQ and have a nose around to see what we can find. How about it? Phil, Michael, are you interested?".

"That's right. Leave the girls out," Emily said.

"I'm sorry" Theo replied, "That wasn't the intention. It's just that Phil and I have been going around together and Michael has a personal interest. No insult intended".

"All right, I'll let you off - this time" she answered.

"Is that OK with you Jennifer?," Theo asked and she nodded her approval.

There was a cough from the edge of the group, followed by a voice. "What about me? Don't I fit in anywhere with you lot?".

"I'm so sorry Frank. We didn't mean to ignore you, but you usually go your own way, so I didn't include you in our plans," Phil said.

"Well, I think it's time that I became more integrated into the group. If that's alright with the rest of you?" Frank said. All the other members of the group signified their approval of his decision. Theo then took centre stage, once again. "Tomorrow morning, we'll split up into teams, so we can do as much digging as possible. Let's see what we can turn up".

"I think that it will do us all good to have a purpose. It will help us to get our minds off recent events," Jennifer added and they all indicated their approval of her comment.

The next day was very windy and the rain was pouring down, so their plans had to be put on hold. This was advisable, as going out in the rain, especially in public places, could cause problems for them. So it was more prudent to avoid the possibility of detection and remain under cover. This actually worked to their advantage as it gave them more time to plan out their enquiries in more detail. Whenever a group of people try to make a decision, it usually takes some time to reach an agreement and this time was no different. Eventually, a solution that satisfied everyone was reached.

As there were two main police stations, one in the city centre and a larger one on the outskirts, two teams were needed to cover them both. It was decided that Jennifer, Emily and Frank would cover the city centre station, leaving Michael, Phil and Theo to travel to the edge of town to look at the larger station.

The group then split into their respective parties, to finalise their own assault procedures. But all this was just speculation at the time, as the rain didn't show any signs of easing up, so a general conversation about what to look for, developed. Of course, this should have happened before the group had split into the two teams, but better late than never. It was a good thing that this happened, as some of them didn't really know what they were looking for.

Eventually, Phil took charge, as he seemed to have a better grasp of police procedures and all associated items. During their discussion, an interesting point was raised when it was asked, "Shouldn't some-one go to the morgue, to see if any information could be gleaned from there. As this was suggested, both women strongly voiced their objections to fulfilling the assignment.

"I don't think anyone particularly relishes the thought of doing it, but it needs to be done. We need to find out all we can about Linda's death and I, for one, would like to know who she was" Michael said, to which Jennifer added, "I know you're right, but I can't deal with the thought of all the bodies, especially if an autopsy was being performed when I was there".

"I'd throw up, there and then," Emily confessed, "and think of the problems that could cause, apart from the cleaning up. To the people in the room, it would appear out of thin air and coupled with the story told by the driver, after he had hit Linda, apologies Michael" -

who nodded his acceptance - "I think it could stir up trouble for us all".

So it was agreed that a volunteer would be given this task. They were surprised when Frank offered to help. "Although it was a long time age, I worked as an ambulance man for a number of years, so I'm quite used to blood and bodies, so it shouldn't effect me adversely. Therefore, I think that I'm the obvious choice for the assignment."

This revelation from Frank, highlighted to them all, that they didn't really know a great deal about one another. So the rest of that rainy day was spent with each person relating a potted history of their life. Of course, the two youngest members, Emily and Theo, didn't have as much to say as did the older members, Jennifer and Frank. They all enjoyed hearing about each other's lives and it did help to pass the time, while they waited for the rain to stop.

They woke the following morning, to be greeted by a gloriously sunny day. The

sunshine stimulated them all into action and with breakfast over, preparations for the day ahead started in earnest. Phil organised them all, impressing on them the need to find out everything they could and if anything else of interest came along, to follow it to see where it would lead. So they ended up in these configurations. Jennifer and Emily would go to the town police station, Frank would go to the hospital, where the morgue was situated, leaving Phil, Michael and Theo to travel to the outskirts of the town, to the main police station. As they arrived in the town centre, they peeled off in turn, each heading for their respective assignments. They were all quite excited by the prospect of what lay ahead. They had never done anything like this before and even though they had the advantage of being invisible, making detection almost impossible; the thought of being discovered added to the excitement, even though there was a serious side to their quest. They wanted to find out what had happened to their friend and compatriot, along with some information about her, if possible. So with expectant hearts, they set off to fulfill their assignments.

Jennifer and Emily were the first team to reach their goal. After surveying the building for a while, they came to a conclusion. The public access entrance was not the best way in for them, as their way would be blocked by the desk and the chance that some-one might open the hatch, was quite slim. So it made more sense to go to the back of the building, where the police cars came in, as they felt that they would stand a better chance of entering the building that way.

This proved to be a correct assumption and they were soon inside the building. They were both old hands at moving around in occupied spaces, allowing people to open doors for them to gain access. It was soon obvious to them that this was not the main centre of police activities, although the traffic wardens were based there. They split up, to facilitate a quicker coverage of the buildings four floors. The ground floor included the public entrance and the custody suite, along with the cells. The custody suite was accessed from the rear entrance, so the prisoners could be brought in by police car and swiftly transferred into the building. There was, of course, the locker rooms and showers for the officers and ancillary staff.

Emily had started at the top of the building and hoped to collect some information from the offices situated there. It was unfortunate that they were unable to open folders and filing cabinets, but in a way, this limitation protected them. For it only needed someone to notice a folder apparently opening on its own, or a filing cabinet drawer to suddenly slide open, to raise suspicions that all was not well. So they were limited to whatever was open on desks, or on the sheets of paper that were laying around. But the most effective way, was to listen in on conversations.

So when the two of them met up in the stairwell, near the second floor, they decided that the best place to listen to gossip was the canteen, so that's where they headed. At that time of morning it was almost deserted, but they decided to wait until some more people drifted in. For the traffic wardens there was a set meal break, but for many of the police officers the day was split up in a number of ways, so they often found themselves eating at strange times of the day, or even the night. The two of them settled themselves in, enjoying the warmth and the smell of the cooked food and coffee.

As various groups of people came in, made their purchases from the counter and sat down, either Jennifer or Emily swooped in on them, to overhear their conversation. But after spending most of the day there, they were no further forward in their hunt for information. The only important thing they did pick up, was that the traffic police were based at the out-of-town station, where Phil and Theo were headed, so they stood the best chance of overhearing something. Linda's accident was mentioned by a female traffic warden, who happened to be nearby when it happened, but she only said that it was a strange affair and was glad to pass it over to the traffic police. That was the sum total of their day's investigation although actually they had enjoyed listening to all the joking and banter that took place.

Fortunately for Frank, the hospital had plenty of direction signs, so he was able to find his way to the morgue without too much trouble. His next problem was waiting for the door to open, so that he could get in. As would be expected, such a sensitive area was protected by a key pad lock, ensuring that only those authorized could gain entry. Eventually, he heard the key pad being operated on the inside of the door and when it opened, he was able to slip inside. He realised at this point, that he had to ensure he didn't get trapped in there for the night, so he kept a close eye on the time and the personnel.

The smell hit him straight away, bringing back memories from long ago. He took some time to survey the rooms, to ascertain the best place for information gathering. Although there were plenty of files in the area, his limitations stopped him being able to gain access to their contents. For the first time, he was frustrated by his condition, even though it had made it possible for him to be there. He was just about to leave the office, when his attention was drawn by a file that was laying on it's own. The name on the label was Linda Bryson and the date of birth seemed to fit in with Linda's apparent age. His heart skipped a beat, as he realised that he may well have found the solution to one of the questions that they had all set out to answer. But there was more to his discovery. A

note was held to the cover by a paper clip. It said 'To be passed on to Superintendent J Hargreaves, along with your comments'.

'So' thought Frank, the police are involved in some way. Maybe they're looking into all of this and who knows, they might even find a solution'. The note convinced Frank that he had been successful in uncovering Linda's surname and was pleased that he had confirmed the involvement of the police. He wasn't paying too much attention to where he was going and found himself looking down on to an autopsy that was taking place. He wasn't prepared for the sight of a body in that condition and much to his surprise, he felt his stomach knot itself up and a wave of nausea washed over him. He had to get away from there as quickly as possible and was relieved when he found the corridor that led to the exit. Enjoying the cool air, he waited for the door to be opened, so that he could escape. His insides were beginning to settle down by now and he was feeling. a lot better although he couldn't wait to get back into the outside world and then return to the group, to report his findings.

It had become normal practice, by now, for Phil, Michael and Theo to move through public places, holding their own conversations, with little regard to those around them who were oblivious to their presence. They had discussed, at times, how things would change if the people were aware of them and had frightened themselves with some of the possibilities. But for now, they were safe, invisible to people and free from their prejudices. Gaining access to the police station was easy for people in their condition and it wasn't long before they were inside. Without realising it, they followed a similar pattern to the one followed by the girls earlier. They also decided to meet up in the canteen and see if they were able to pick up anything from the conversations. The building was extensive and they found that they were unable to gain access to the majority of rooms. It was possible that what they were looking for was hidden away behind one of the closed doors, but it was unlikely that they would ever know.

About an hour later, Michael was the first one to arrive at the canteen and looked around for a likely source of information. A group of young police women discussing boyfriends and some policemen debating the previous night's football match, was all that was going on at the time. After a few minutes, a sergeant walked in and chased these young officers out, returning them to their duties. He then got himself a mug of tea and sat down with a couple of older officers, who were sitting near the windows.

'Right' Michael thought, 'This might be interesting' and moved closer to overhear them, but unfortunately nothing of interest came up. Just more general chatter, no doubt important to them, but not to Michael.

Within the next twenty minutes, all three members of the team were united. They compared notes and realised that their sum total of information was zero. Disappointed, they decided to stay on in the canteen for a while, on the off chance that they would overhear something that might help them. Groups of people drifted in and out, each unaware that one of the trio sat nearby to listen to their conversation. Both Phil and Theo were getting to the point where they had had enough, when they saw Michael beckoning to them from the other side of the room. He had obviously heard something useful, so they moved over to join him. There were five people sitting around the table, two of them in plain clothes and three in uniform. They appeared to be discussing what someone called 'Jack' was up to. One of them said that this Jack had gathered together a small team and was obviously looking into something, but nobody seemed able to find out what it was. They continued to speculate about the purpose of this secretive team's investigation, but were unable to reach a definitive conclusion.

"Well" said Michael, "What do you think? Could this be what we're looking for?". Both Phil and Theo agreed that it could well be something of interest to them, but they needed to find out more.

"I did hear it mentioned that they had tucked themselves away on the fifth floor, but I don't know where," Michael explained.

After hearing this, they all thought that a trip up to the fifth floor was in order, to see if they could pick up on something. The doors on the fifth floor were not amenable to giving away their secrets. A few doors had names on them, but there wasn't a Jack, or J among them and the remainder of the doors were just numbered. So they split up again to spend some time watching the lifts and the stairways. They had to take the chance that the right person would come along, who would unlock the mystery for them. But even if that did happen, the chances that it would be of any interest to them, was slight. After all, the police have to investigate many things the need to be done under a cloak of secrecy. They waited and waited, but nothing happened to get them out of their quandary. Eventually, as it started to get dark, they all agreed that they had had enough for one day and decided to call it a day. But that was not to be the end of it, as they could well be onto something, so until it was resolved they could not give up.

Michael, Phil and Theo were the last to return to base, which is not surprising as they had the furthest to travel. A general feeling of optimism spread

through their ranks, each eagerly waiting to see what the others had found out. Frank was the first one to speak. "Ladies first, let's hear what you two got up to during your expedition". They all listened intently as Jennifer and Emily related their experiences, which tended to differ at times, as they had spent quite a lot of the time individually searching for information. The others were a little disappointed that nothing was uncovered, but realised that it could have easily have happened to them.

"Thank-you for all your hard work girls," Frank said with a smile, as he didn't want them to feel downhearted. He then said, "Right Phil, how did your group fare?". Phil related the day's events, allowing both Michael and Theo to relate their individual parts. He concluded with the details of the conversation overheard in the canteen. This certainly raised the interest level in the group and a few minutes were spent trying to work out the implications of their discovery.

This discussion really lifted the mood within the group and was interrupted by Theo, who said, "Hang on, we haven't heard from Frank yet, he may well have unearthed something even more important".

"Well, I think that I possibly did discover two pieces of information that will be of use to us all" Frank stated.

He then revealed to them all that he had found out. When he told them about Linda's name, Michael stood up and started to shout at the top of his voice. "Hallelujah, Hallelujah. Thank you so much Frank" he said, "You just cannot appreciate what that means to me. I now know Linda's full name, which is something I have wanted to know for so long and now you have brought me the answer. Thank-you, Thank-you".

They all noticed the tears in Michael's eyes and nobody said a word when he walked away from them all. They realised that he wanted to be alone with his thoughts while the good news sunk in. For the rest of them, that was not the end of it. Frank then told them about the note attached to Linda's file and it's contents. It didn't take them long to realise that the Superintendent J Hargreaves mentioned on the label and the secretive Jack mentioned in the police canteen, were one and the same person. Now they had a name, which would help them track this man down, the next time they returned to the police HQ. It was also decided, that the whole team would go together next time as they could then cover the ground more efficiently. Now that they knew a name and the floor he was based on, they could concentrate their efforts in the one area. They then spent the rest of the evening making their plans.

While the group went about their business, they were unaware that eyes were watching them. Well, not them exactly, as they were invisible, but the results of their actions. To a normal person, things seemed to be moving about on their own. Pieces of wood were throwing themselves onto the fire and cans tipped themselves up, as if someone was drinking from them. It was the fire that had attracted his attention and now he couldn't believe his eyes. He turned his head away, rubbed his eyes and then turned back again, only to be confronted by the same scene. A state of panic overtook him and he started to run.

In his haste, he didn't worry about knocking things over and old boxes and pieces of wood went flying in all directions. This sudden explosion of noise, caught the group's attention and they stopped in their tracks. No-one wanted to say it, but the chance that they were discovered had always been a possibility and it now appeared that someone had stumbled across them.

They decided to put the fire out, collect together their bits and pieces and get away from there as quickly as possible. There was a good chance that whoever it had been would soon come back, maybe with other people and although they couldn't be seen, evidence of their activity could start people thinking.

He didn't see the fire being extinguished, he just wanted to get away from there. Running as fast as he could go, he headed for the city centre and wasn't really looking where he was going. At one point, he ran straight out into a road and was clipped by a passing police patrol car. Fortunately he wasn't hurt and the officers took no time in checking him over. When they ascertained that he was unhurt, they put him in the back of the car and then asked him why he was running. They thought that he was being chased by a gang, or someone that he'd upset. When they heard his story, a breathalyzer bag was produced even though they couldn't smell alcohol on his breath. They wanted to make sure. The indicator stayed firmly in the green, proving that he wasn't drunk and further checks convinced the officers that he hadn't taken any drugs.

"C'mon then" said one officer, "You'd better show us where these things were flying through the air".

"I don't want to go back there" the man said, "It was too weird for me. You have a look and prove that I'm not going round the bend".

It took some time for the officers to locate the exact spot, but as the fire that had acted like a beacon to the man had been extinguished, it proved to be difficult. The officers probed the darkness with their torches and finally found the still smoldering pile of ashes. "Well, some-one washere and they obviously left in a hurry, by the look of things" he said while probing the ashes with a piece of wood. Neither of them found any evidence to back up the man's story, so as they were well out of earshot, they decided what to do with him. They concluded that the best course of action, so that there wasn't any come-back, was to take the man back to the station and arrange for him to be handed over to Psych Services. When they returned to the car, they told the man that they were taking him back to the station so that he could be seen by a doctor, as he had been hit by their car. He was amenable to this, but strangely, he never asked the officers if they had found anything.

The custody officer was a little bemused when the man related his experience

to him and struggled not to laugh, even though he was an experienced officer and had been told many fantastic stories in his time. The man was the most peaceful person in custody that night and was fully compliant when the FME checked him over for physical injuries. It was explained to him that he would have to stay with them over night and that he would be seeing a different doctor the next day. He did query the need for this, but when it was explained to him why it was felt necessary, he accepted it.

At the booking desk the custody officer was talking to the two officers, before they went back out on patrol, and stated that they seemed to be getting some really weird reports of late from all sorts of people. "Do you remember that man we found hiding between some rubbish bins, behind some shops? He was another one similar to the one you brought in tonight. I think he's still in the funny farm." "Best place for him, one of the officers said and then left along with his companion to go up to the canteen, to get a mug of tea.

It was fortunate that the group didn't have too many material possessions, so the relocation didn't take very long. "It was bound to happen sooner or later" Jennifer said, "We're lucky that we got away with it for so long. Anyway, no harm done". Michael was thinking about how difficult the move would have been had Linda still been with them. She wouldn't have understood what was happening and could be surprisingly strong when she set her mind to it. So it was fortunate that she had avoided this incident. He was now free to face the future without having to think about her all the time and could now be more useful to the group. At times in the past, his lack of involvement had bothered him. But there wasn't anyone else qualified to care for Linda, so her care had to be his primary concern.

They quickly settled into their new location and life returned to normal, or as normal as it could ever be for them. Before the disruption, they had been making plans for their infiltration of the police HQ and decided that it would be advantageous to get there first thing in the morning. At that time of day, when everyone was arriving, they would stand the best chance of locating their target and those he worked with, before they became involved in the day's activities. They all accepted this as the most sensible approach and they were looking forward to the next day's activities.

By eight the next morning, they had all managed to get to the police HQ, which was to be the centre of their investigation. Michael and Jennifer decided to scan the canteen, as it was a possibility that the ones they were looking for might well call in there, before starting their day's work. The rest of them spread themselves around the fifth floor, giving them the best possible chance of success. So they waited.

The canteen saw a steady flow of people at various stages of their daily routine. Some just starting their shifts, others eating during their lunch break and those who were writing up their notes at the end of their shift. But it was those in plain clothes, not uniforms, that were the main focus of the group's attention. They had reached the point where they felt ready to take a break, when Jennifer suddenly heard a snatch of conversation, between two young plain clothes officers, that caught her attention.

"I wonder what Jack's got lined up for us today?". This prompted a comment from a uniformed officer, who was behind them in the queue at the counter. "What is it that you lot are doing? Come on, you know you can tell me". She turned to face him and said, "You know I can't tell you anything. Stop bothering me and concentrate on doing your job properly, for once".

"Stroppy," he replied and with a big grin on his face, he turned to his mates and said, "Must be that time of the month", which caused them to start laughing and making comments. She paid for her purchases and along with her male companion, moved towards the doors. Jennifer called out to Michael, who was on the other side of the room and said, "These two. I think they're the ones we want". So Michael moved over to intercept them before they left and along with Jennifer, followed them along the corridor and into the lift. When they saw her press the button for the fifth floor, Michael raised his thumb and said, "I think we're onto a winner here".

Those already on the fifth floor, were getting a bit fed up. They hadn't exactly been over-run with people to check out and like Jennifer and Michael in the canteen, were about ready to take a break for a while. So they didn't pay much attention when the lift stopped on their floor and the doors opened. A young man and young woman exited, closely followed by Jennifer and Michael, who said, "These two are involved, let's follow them". The group members were called in from the various parts of the fifth floor, where they had been keeping watch and they all followed the two plain clothes officers. They followed them along the corridor and round a corner, into an annexe and finally into room 516, which was a bit out of the way. It was as if they didn't want to be found, which was exactly right. What these two officers would have felt if they knew that they were being closely followed by half a dozen of the invisible people they were investigating, is open to speculation, but it would have been quite a shock to them that their quarry was so close.

The group looked around the room and saw that it was fitted out just the way they would have expected. Nothing was out of the ordinary, apart from one thing. Unlike any ordinary office, there weren't any papers or folders about, anywhere. Neither was there any way of identifying the officers who worked there. Even the small private office, that was separated from the rest of the room by glass partitions, didn't have a name on its door. There was an air of secrecy about the whole set-up, which all of the group picked up on. It was a good thing that they were able to speak and move about without being noticed by 'normal' people, as the six of them going unnoticed in a quiet room, would have been an impossibility. They noticed that the two officers they followed in didn't sit down at any of the desks or start any work, not even switching the computers on. It appeared that they were waiting for instructions before they started the day's activities. Phil pointed out the safe and speculated that they were waiting for it to be opened, not knowing that the officers could have opened it themselves. The whole operation had an unusual feel about it, especially as at that time, the group didn't realise that they were the subjects under investigation. Had they known this, they would have been able to understand why everything had an air of secrecy about it.

They didn't have to wait too long, before the door opened and two more men entered the room. The usual morning greetings were exchanged and from this they were able to connect a face to Jack's name, for the first time. It was obvious that he was in charge of this little band, not only by his superiority in years, but in his manner as well. He was obviously some-one who was used to being in charge and his actions confirmed this. He came across like a kindly grandfather, but at the same time, he managed to get things done. He was the kind of person you were willing to put yourself out for, knowing that if you did a good job, it would be appreciated. He carried a briefcase in his left hand and from it he lifted a number of files. None of the group had ever seen files like it before, as each one had a red line diagonally across the cover. At this point they all realised that they had stumbled upon something really serious, although they were still unaware of the investigation's purpose. This situation was not going to remain for very much longer, as they realised, when Jack outlined their proposed course of action.

"We have two main avenues of enquiry to follow. So I'm going to split us into two teams, as we don't need to go everywhere together. Dave, you take Clive with you and I want you to go to the Fairview Hospital, it's not too far, just on the outskirts of town".

"So they've found out about you two at last, have they" Sarah joked. "Very funny" Clive said to her and then asked, "But why do you want us to go there, of all places Jack?".

"Well, I've spoken at length with one of the doctors there and she feels that one of her patients could be of help to us. The idea has been put to him and he says that he's willing to give it a try" Jack explained.

"But how on earth could a psychiatric patient be of any use to us?" Dave asked, "Anyway, I've heard that they're usually drugged up to the eyeballs in that place". "Well, this man's a little bit different" Jack explained "He's able to see these invisible people that we're investigating". A shock wave swept through the invisible group. They now understood why everything was so secret. They were the cause of all this secrecy. They quickly returned their attention to the conversation, which had been continuing, while they were distracted. "......so he says that he's willing to work along-with us to help us pinpoint these people and possibly find out what has caused them to be the way they are".

Then Sarah chipped in. "So what's the point of the whole exercise, I mean why go to all this bother?"

Jack then explained the sole purpose..:,"We don't want to persecute these people in any way..." The group were relieved to hear that. "....we want to locate them and, with the help of the top scientists, try to reverse their condition. They all had normal lives before it happened to them. I'm sure that their current condition has certain advantages, but I'm sure that if we could ask them, they would want to return to their previous lives".

Jack never knew it, but the majority of the invisible

group, standing alongside him, agreed wholeheartedly.

"This brings me to the second prong of our investigation" Jack said, "Sarah, I want you to accompany me to a government research centre that's tucked away in deepest Lincolnshire, a little place called Kirkby Green, or thereabouts. They've been doing some research into making soldiers invisible for behind-the-lines activities. I'm sure you can see the advantages such soldiers would have, as invisibility is the best camouflage you could have. Apart from that, I don't know much more, they were reluctant to tell me too much, especially on the phone. You know what government departments can be like.

"Dave and Clive, I've made arrangements for you to see our friend at the hospital tomorrow and Sarah, we'll make our trip at the same time. Do those plans suit everyone?"

They all voiced their agreement and started to make their arrangements. Although everything that Jack had just said was typical police work, the group of six were stunned by all that they had heard. None of them said anything, as there were so many thoughts going round in their minds. They realised that it was time to leave and waited for a chance to make their move, when the door was opened.

Back at base that evening, the group had to decide their course of action and how they could explore the latest lines of enquiry. They all agreed, that the more they knew, the better it would be for them, especially after the day's revelations.

"Fore-warned is fore-armed," Frank said, "If they are after us, the more we know about their plans, the better".

Nobody disagreed with this comment. Both Jennifer

and Emily said that they had had enough of police and police stations over the previous two days and asked if they could be excused from these latest assignments. Frank then jumped in and stated that as one of the oldest in the group, he would use his age as an excuse and asked to be excused as well. That left three of them and they decided that Phil and Michael would accompany the police to the research centre, as there was bound to be more than one person could cover in a place like that.

Theo was thus designated to go to the hospital, after all, the two officers were only going to interview one patient and his invisibility gave him the chance to gather any other information he considered relevant. There arrangements were given the seal of approval and while some of them spent the remainder of the evening. feeling relieved that they had been excused, others were excited by the prospects that the day ahead held for them.

***

CHAPTER NINE

CONVERGENCE

Jack was happy. He always enjoyed getting the weekend off and this current case made that possible. So many times during his career he had to forgo his weekends because he was working on something that required the perpetrator to be apprehended as quickly as possible. At times like that, weekends off were not a possibility. But this morning he could wallow in the bed a little longer while he planned his day out. Joyce, on the other hand, had adapted to Jack's erratic hours quite early on in their marriage. Some wives and girlfriends found it too much to take and sadly, many relationships did not last the course. They had always considered themselves fortunate that they had been able to adapt to the unusual hours required of a policeman and had learned, to work around the problems that this caused. So when conditions allowed Jack to take the weekend off 'they really enjoyed it and used their time wisely!

Jack's reflections were interrupted by Joyce entering the bedroom, "Come on, get up. You can't lie-around in bed all day," she said, "I'm sure that you haven't forgotten that we're going shopping this morning".

Jack had forgotten, but he had promised to give her a hand so he was committed. They had a larger than normal shop to do that week as their daughter and her family were coming for Sunday lunch. Now, that was something he was looking forward to. He enjoyed seeing his daughter and her husband, but it was the youthful exuberance of his grandchildren that he really enjoyed. He found it difficult to keep up with them, even though he was in pretty good shape, and often found himself out of breath.

Breakfast was quickly dispatched and he mentally prepared himself for the task ahead. He had come across some pretty bad drivers in his time but the ladies with their shopping trolleys were a thing to behold. The concept that they weren't the only ones in the shop seemed to elude them. It was usual for Jack to return home from these expeditions with battle scars on his ankles caused by the numerous collisions with shopping trolleys, whose owners were looking one way while travelling in the opposite direction. But what astonished him most was the look on the woman's face following an assault on his ankles. You would think that it was his fault for being there and an apology was a rarity. Occasionally an apology was given and when it came accompanied with a nice smile, it seemed to deaden the pain.

So Jack was quite relieved when they arrived home with the shopping completed. After helping Joyce to unload it all from the car, the next task was to get it all put away. They had been doing this for so long that they each instinctively knew where the items went, so the job was soon completed. While Joyce made them some tea, Jack sat at the kitchen table, removed his shoes and socks and examined his ankles for damage.

"Don't do that in here," Joyce said, "There's food about".

"What's the matter, I'm not contagious. Just look at

that." he said, pointing to an area where the skin had been sliced off, "That'll hurt for days now".

"Don't be such a baby. Go up to the bathroom, put some cream on it and cover it with a plaster. You won't even remember it's there in a couple of hours".

So, huffing and puffing, Jack left the kitchen to tend to his damaged flesh.

"Don't be too long, the tea will be ready in a minute". Joyce never heard Jack's reply, as he was halfway up the stairs by this time and maybe it's better that she didn't.

On those occasions when Jack managed to get the weekend off, Joyce always left him to sleep on a Sunday morning. 'After all' she thought, 'The poor old soul needs it, at his age' and laughed to herself.

By the time he finally appeared, the kitchen was already a flurry of activity, as Joyce prepared the roast lunch. Her daughter was always telling her not to go to all the bother but Joyce was of an age to remember that Sunday lunch meant a roast dinner, so she always felt that it was the proper thing to do.

After he had had his breakfast and a quick scan of the paper, Jack thanked her and went to prepare himself for their visitors. " ..... and put something nice on" Joyce said.

"Don't I always" Jack replied.

"You know what I mean, a nice clean shirt, not one of your tatty old tee-shirts".

"I don't own any tatty old tee-shirts, they're all rather exceptional" Jack answered. The two of them started laughing and hugged each other. A half hour later, he re-appeared. "How's this then. Shall I do a twirl?".

"Go on then" Joyce replied. "Very nice. Now come

over here and give me a hand. Remember, I've got to get myself ready yet".

They knew each other so well after all the years they had been together, that they could mess about and joke with one another, without any offence ever being taken. They had been through this sequence so many times before, that they instinctively knew what was required of them, so the dinner was cooked and the house prepared on time.

They always knew when the grandchildren had arrived, as each of them took turns to see who could make the loudest noise with the door knocker. Jack always answered their call and was overwhelmed by the children as they swept through the house like a tornado, heading for the kitchen, to see what was for dinner. Laura was next in and she greeted her dad with a kiss and a hug, and bringing up the rear, loaded down with all the bits and bobs a family seems to need, was Justin.

Setting a roast dinner in front of two hungry children and they were hungry, as they were never allowed any snacks when they were going to grandma's for dinner, could be likened to inviting a plague of locusts into your home. Jack often wondered how they could pack so much food into their small frames, but there always seemed to be room for another helping of pudding.

It was a tradition, that after dinner Jack and Justin would take the children for a walk, allowing Laura to have some time alone with her mum. When they returned, everyone pitched in to do the washing up and start the preparations for tea-time. The children were always told, "If you don't help to clear up after dinner, you won't get any tea."

This seemed to spur them on to greater activity, as the promise of more food, was a great enticement. No sooner had the day started than it was time for the family to leave, the children had to be ready for another week at school and they needed to be in bed before it got too late.

After they had left, Joyce and Jack were sitting together on the settee and he said, "Do you ever wonder why we do that to ourselves?".

"Just think how it would be, if we didn't" Joyce replied "We should be grateful that our children and grandchildren want to come and see us. So many people our age are totally ignored by their families. We should count it a blessing that our offspring haven't turned out like that".

"You're right, as usual dear. I see so many officers, at the station, young and old, whose families have no time for one another, that's if they still have a family, as so many of them don't. So we should be really thankful that our's still love us". They just sat there in the subdued light, holding hands, each of them thinking how much the other one meant to them.

The car turned into the drive that lead to the Fairview Hospital, both Dave and Clive made a few tasteless jokes, but that could be put down to nerves. Neither of them had ever been to a Psychiatric Hospital before and they were a little unsure about what they might encounter.

They pulled into a car parking space and both got out. They had never realised what an extensive place it was, as they had only seen it from the main road before and as it was set a long way back, it's size was deceptive.

"Right then, here we go" Dave said, as they walked towards the imposing wooden doors, that formed the main entrance. It wasn't until you got up close to the doors, that you could appreciate the amount of work that had gone in to making them. There were some quite intricate carvings making up the frames and these were repeated on both sides, so when the doors were closed, they matched up perfectly. Clive stopped for a moment so he could get a closer look at the workmanship.

"What are you looking at?" Dave asked him.

"I'm appreciating the skill that went into making the carvings on these doors" Clive replied, "My father was a cabinet maker and although I never had the ability to follow in his footsteps, he did teach me to appreciate good workmanship".

They moved into a large impressive entrance hall and it was obvious that in the past, this had been a house of some note, before it became a hospital. Looking around, Dave located the reception desk and called Clive over. They presented themselves and informed the receptionist that they had an appointment to see a Dr Hedley. She asked them to take a seat for a moment and told them that someone would be along in a few minutes.

As they walked over to the waiting area, she picked up a phone, to inform Dr Hedley of their arrival. About ten minutes later, a young nurse in a white uniform walked over to them. "Are you the gentlemen here to see Dr Hedley?" she asked. Dave told her they they were and she then said, "Would you please follow me". "I'd follow you anywhere," Clive said, under his breath. Whether she heard his comment, or not, he wasn't sure, but she looked back over her shoulder and smiled at him.

It was fortunate that they hadn't been left to find their own way, as the place was quite a maze. This often proves to be the case in old houses, that have been converted into hospitals or rest homes. They eventually arrived at an ornate wooden door, that bore the name Dr Marion Hedley.

The nurse knocked on the door and was summoned in. "These are the two gentlemen to see you, Doctor" she announced.

The woman behind the desk looked up and said "Come on in gentlemen and thank you Sally". The nurse then left, giving Clive another glance on the way and closed the door behind her.

"Good morning Doctor, I'm DI David Grantham and this is DS Clive Barron," he said, "I believe that you've spoken to our superior, Superintendent Hargreaves?". "That's correct" she replied, "We were put in contact with one another by those who are overseeing this situation".

For the first time, the real scope of the investigation was brought home to them. "So, what can you, or are you allowed, to tell us about the man we've come to see?" Dave asked.

"Well, I have to tread a fine line between patient confidentiality and helping you. But with the guidelines I've been given, as well as the patient's permission, I don't think that there should be any problems" she explained. "His name is Gary and had only come to terms with the reality of his condition, in the past few weeks. Before that, he was in quite a sorry state but we were slowly able to bring him out of it. I'm not sure how we would have coped if we hadn't been prepared, by being part of this enquiry. I don't know how much you know about it, but it is country wide and is overseen by a hush-hush department in London. All I have, is a number to phone when required and of course, they're able to contact me, which is what they did, to inform me about your team".

"You don't seem to know any more than we do. But I hope that we will all get a clearer understanding, eventually" Dave said. "I thought that it would be best if you met up with Gary here in my office, as he's used to being here and should feel more relaxed. Also, there's less chance that our conversation will be overheard in here and if he starts to get upset by it all, I'll be here to oversee the situation" she said and then picked up the phone. "Could you please bring Gary to my office now, thank you".

While they waited, she offered them some coffee, which they readily accepted. "That's lovely" Clive said, "Much better than the stuff we get at the station".

"I bring my own in," the doctor replied, "If you'd tasted the coffee I was originally given, you would understand why".

It was while she was saying this, that there was a knock on the door and Gary was ushered in.

Gary cautiously entered the room, unsure as to what he might expect. "Come on over Gary" the doctor said to him, "There's nothing to be apprehensive about, They're not here to arrest you, or anything like that, they need your help. Just as we talked about. Do you remember?" Gary nodded and walked towards the centre of the room.

Dave stood up, offered his hand and said "Hello Gary. I'm Dave and this is Clive." This was something new for Gary, a policeman wanting to shake his hand. "Morning," he said, "But what about the other man.

Aren't you going to introduce him as well?".

They all looked around the room, although they knew there wasn't anyone else there. "The young man sitting in the chair just behind you" Gary insisted. A look of panic passed across the young man's face, what would they do now, as this was the last thing any of them expected. Dr Hedley broke the tension by saying, "Are you telling us that one of these invisible people is actually sitting in the room with us right now?".

"That's right" Gary replied, "As I just told you, he's sitting right there".

"Am I right in presuming that he can hear us?" asked Clive, to which Gary replied, "He's nodding his head, so we can take that as correct".

"Is it possible, in any way, for him to tell us his name?" Dave asked. Gary had now pulled his chair round, so that he could easily see all those present in the room and asked Dave how he expected the young man to do this. Nobody spoke for a few minutes, until Gary suddenly broke the silence, saying "He's solved the problem himself, by spelling out his name, letter by letter in the air".

"Well, what is it?" Dr Hedley said, expectantly.

"Hang on a minute," Gary replied, "He's starting it again. T   H   E   0. What sort of name is that?"

"Actually, it's quite a common name," Clive said, cutting in, "I know a couple of people, who have similar names".

"So then, his name is Theo" Dr Hedley concluded. As she said this, Theo raised his thumb into the air, this movement being conveyed by Gary, to the rest of them. "This is a real breakthrough" Dave exclaimed, "We came here to see you Gary, to find out whether you would be willing to help us locate these people. A question you have more than answered by your actions. But along with that success, we have actually met, as far as it is possible to do so, one of the invisible people and even learnt his name. I call that real progress".

They all agreed with his statement, but the whole situation did highlight to them, how easily these invisible people could infiltrate their lives, without them having the slightest notion of their presence. It also highlighted the important role that a person with abilities like Gary's would be able to play in the investigation.

"I would like to ask Theo a question, if that's alright" Dave said and in response, Theo raised his thumb, once again, "and that is, Does he, along with his friends, feel threatened by our investigation into their condition?" and after thinking about it, he added, "I do realise that questions will have to be constructed so that you can answer either yes or no. So I'll ask again. Do you feel threatened?".

Theo gave that question the thumbs down but he felt frustrated that he couldn't convey to them that he was so happy that someone was working to try and resolve their situation.

The remainder of the time they spent together was taken up with this simple question-and-answer format. For Dave and Clive, it was their first opportunity to gather information about the mysterious invisible people, even though the simple approach they were forced to take did limit the extent of their enquiries.

Theo, on the other hand, did not reveal everything about his group, because like Gary, he didn't fully trust the police. But for the moment they seemed like his best option if he ever wanted to find a solution to his problem. So he thought it was best to go along with them, but only so far, as he didn't want to jeopardise the safety of the group. Eventually, the meeting wound to a halt, Dave and Clive pleased with their discoveries, Theo happy that he had at last been able to make contact and Gary was feeling surprisingly satisfied with himself, for being of use to all of them.

As for Dr Hedley, she kept in the background, while mentally noting everything that was taking place. Knowing that the meeting that had just taken place, would have to be reported, via the phone number on the white card. A nurse was called, to take Dave and Clive back to reception, with Theo tagging along behind. As the door closed behind them, Dr Hedley asked, "Gary, can you assure me that we're alone in the room?". "Yes" he replied, "Theo left along with the two policemen". "That's good" she said, "I'll always feel a little unsure from now on, never knowing if I'm really alone, or whether I've picked up an invisible guest along the way". "You better be careful Doc," Gary said laughing, "You're beginning to sound like me. You'll get locked up, if you start talking like that". He saw a look change her face, one he hadn't seen before, not realising that his comment had unsettled her. "Can I ask you something?" Gary said. "Yes. Go ahead" she replied. "Some time ago, you told me that I wasn't the only one with my problem, here in the hospital. What happened to this other patient?".

"It's rather sad" Dr Hedley replied, "They didn't respond as well as you did, remaining in a psychotic state and continuing to go downhill. They got so bad, that they've had to be put in a room where they can't hurt themselves".

An expression of shock appeared on Gary's face.

"That's terrible," he said, "So, that could have happened to me".

"Very easily" she replied, "But something deep inside you wanted to fight it and get you back to normal. I think it was this natural drive that helped you to come to terms with the situation and learn to use it for your advantage. You're a lucky young man".

"It seems that I am" Gary said, reflectively.

The sound of a car horn, told Jack that Sarah had arrived to collect him and to confirm it, Joyce peeked through the curtains. While Jack was collecting his bits and pieces, there was a knock at the door. "I'll get that" Joyce called out, wanting to get a closer look at the young woman her husband was to spend the day with. "I'm sorry for knocking" Sarah said, "But I wanted to make sure that you'd heard me. I'll go and wait in the car".

Joyce watched her, as she walked down the drive and Sarah was sure that she could feel Joyce's eyes looking her up and down. Jack arrived in the hallway. "Have you got everything?" Joyce asked him.

"I think so. I don't have much to take anyway," Jack replied. "Just you make sure that you behave yourself with that young woman" Joyce said, with a grin on her face.

"You know me" Jack answered.

"That's the problem" Joyce said, "I know you too well".

"Don't worry Joyce" Jack said, "You know I always behave myself".

"Just make sure you do" Joyce replied, feeling a little jealous, that Jack was going to spend the whole day with such an attractive young woman. They hugged and

Joyce added, "Just you remember what I said", then they parted with a good-bye kiss.

Unbeknown to them all, another pair of eyes, had been following this activity. They belonged to Phil, who was supposed to be accompanied by Michael. But he had woken up that morning feeling very sick, so it was thought best if he remained behind. Phil entered the car, when Sarah got back in, as he wanted to learn as much as they did. Then, upon his return, he could relate all that he'd learned to the group.

"Morning" Jack said, as he got in the car. "Good-morning Sir" Sarah said, instinctively. "Oh, I'm sorry. I mean Jack". She still couldn't get used to calling a superior officer by his first name.

"Don't worry about it," he replied and then said, "Have you got our route all worked out?". "Yes. We'll head towards Sleaford and Kirkby Green is about eight miles further north. So it shouldn't take us too long". "That's good. I'm going to sit back and enjoy the ride".

It was a treat for Jack, not having to drive, for when he was out with Joyce he didn't have a choice, as she had never learned. Sarah was a smooth driver, which made the journey even more comfortable and Jack soon dozed off. He was brought back to the land of the living by Sarah tapping him on the arm.

"Do you have an address, or even a map of exactly where this research centre is?" she asked.

"No. Kirkby Green was the only information I was given" Jack replied, "You know what these places are like. They're not keen on making their presence too obvious".

Eventually, they found some-one to ask. "Use all your feminine charms" Jack said, grinning.

"I don't have to try" Sarah said, while laughing, "It

just comes naturally".

Returning to the car, she said "He told me that the place with the scientists is just up the road. We go along here for a little way and then take the only turn left". "Let's go then" Jack said, "and see if we can track these scientists down". She followed the man's directions and eventually arrived at a gate, bearing a sign that read 'MOD property - No unauthorised Access'. Phil was interested to see what would happen. He hadn't ever been in a situation like this before and was worried that someone would have the means to detect his presence. As it was, he would have no cause for concern.

They pulled up to the gate and were surprised when a couple of Military Policemen appeared. They never did work out where they had hidden themselves. "This is private property. What do you want?" he said curtly. Jack wound his window down and called one of them over. As they both displayed their warrant cards, Jack said "I'm Superintendent Hargreaves and this is Detective Sergeant Mitchell. We have an appointment to see Professor Taylor and Dr Haart".

"Just a moment" he replied and spoke into his radio. A few moments later, a message came back. "That's fine" he said, "You can go on up. Just follow the driveway and you'll be met at the other end". Although he had no cause for worry, Phil felt relieved that he had passed this first test.

As they travelled along the drive, Jack kept an eye on the mileage, just to see how long the drive was and was surprised that it was well over a half mile. Jack was unsure what to expect and was greeted by a collection of 1950s buildings, that at one time had formed part of an RAF base.

They both kept their eyes alert as they got out of the car and Sarah pointed to a feed from some power lines that passed nearby. There were two people to meet them, both wearing traditional scientists white coats.

"I'm Dr Yvonne Haart and I'm a Physicist" and "I'm Professor Phil Taylor, I deal with all the electronics around here".

"A good morning to you both" Phil said, even though he knew nobody could hear him. Jack introduced Sarah and himself and they were led inside, where the 1950s look disappeared, to be replaced with a more modern setting.

They were guided into a room that was obviously used for meetings. The room contained a large table with chairs spaced all around it and a writing pad and pencil at each position.

Dr Haart then invited them to "Help yourselves to coffee and something to eat", pointing over to a table in the corner of the room. Both Sarah and Jack were ready for a drink after their journey and Jack was pleased to find a plate of Danish pastries for them to enjoy. Of course Sarah chose not to indulge, as she was watching her weight. Once they had obtained their refreshments, they all took their seats around the table.

"What is it that you are researching here?" Jack asked and then said, "I presume it's alright for me to ask, as I was told that complete disclosure had been arranged".

"We were also informed that we had clearance to discuss our work with you and that you were cleared to tell us the reason why you're here," said Prof Taylor in response.

"Well, I'd better break the ice by telling you what it is that we're investigating" Jack replied and then told them about the appearance of the invisible people. He noticed that as he explained what had been happening, the two scientists looked at one-another indicating to Jack that what they were doing was along similar lines.

He had arranged with Sarah beforehand to act as his secretary and take notes of the proceedings. So when it was time for the scientists to reveal all, he asked them if it was alright for Sarah to continue taking notes, which they agreed to. "After all," Dr Haart said,"You're working under as much security as we are, so there's little chance of anything leaking out". She then went on to explain the purpose of their research. "It's been known for a long time that all things vibrate at specific frequencies and if an item, somehow, has its frequency altered, it was thought that it could become invisible to us, as it's out of phase with normality. From what you've told us, it seems that we've been beaten to it by people who it's happened to, purely by chance. We're trying to achieve it and they want to undo it".

Prof Taylor then picked up the conversation, "The MOD feel that if soldiers could somehow be put out of sync with the rest of us, they would become invisible and you can appreciate the strategic advantage that this would give us. But so far, despite our best efforts, we haven't been very successful".

The discussion continued for some time, each side trying to pick up tips from the other. Some time later, Dr Haart announced, "It's almost lunch time now, I'm sure that the two of you must be ready to eat. Although we're only a fairly small establishment, we've been provided with excellent restaurant facilities",

"It's surprising how accommodating officials can be when they want something from you," Prof Taylor said, with a smile on his face. The moment food was mentioned Phil began to feel hungry. The problem was, that he was unable to do anything about it but he decided to follow them anyway. Perhaps an opportunity would present itself, where he could get something for himself. 'Why should I miss out,' he thought as he watched them gather all their papers together, before they left.

This caused Prof Taylor to say "I see the security aspects of your work have become second nature to you, it wouldn't do if any of this got out. Would it".

The walk to the restaurant led them down a number of corridors, allowing Jack and Sarah to get a more complete idea of the layout of the facility. As they walked along, Sarah turned to Jack and told him that she felt a great deal of money had been spent on the place.

"I agree" Jack replied, "As Prof Taylor said a while ago, the better they are treated, the harder they will work, increasing the possibilities of a positive result from their work". T

They knew they were getting close to the restaurant, well before they reached it and were impressed with what they smelt. As they entered, they were greeted by a scene reminiscent of any classy restaurant. They also saw a number of other people, who were already seated and enjoying their meals. Although the menu was not too extensive, which was wise seeing as they didn't have to feed too many people, it provided for most tastes.

After collecting their meals, they all sat around a table together and continued their previous conversation although Jack and Sarah could not be too forthcoming about their work, as they didn't want to be overheard by anyone sitting close-by. As they completed their puddings, Prof Taylor asked them if they would like to see around the laboratories. "That would be great" Sarah said and then Jack added, "Anything that we could pick up that would help us in our enquiries, will be of great benefit to us. We might not understand all the science involved, but if we can get a basic understanding of the principles, it could help us in the future". "That's exactly what I thought" Sarah said, agreeing with him.

As they approached the main laboratory, they didn't know what to expect. But what they saw took their breath away. It was as if they had entered a film set of a mad professor's laboratory. The light in the room was subdued, in fact it was almost dark, the gloom only being penetrated by individual lights and desk lamps. One side of the room appeared to be taken up with what they assumed was, computer equipment, complete with sequentially flashing lights. As their eyes adjusted to the light level, they saw that some of the benches were covered with the 'statutory' chemical test tubes, beakers and glass tubes, in a variety of shapes and, of course, Bunsen burners. The back of the room, which was facing them, was fitted out with some kind of glass paneled cubicle with what looked like an operating table in its centre and a lighting gantry above it.

"Well. What do you think?" Prof Taylor asked. Almost at the same instant, both Jack and Sarah said, "It's incredible". Jack then said "I never thought that these buildings would contain something like this".

"As we've both got some other necessary business to take care of, we'll leave you in the capable hands of our Head Technician, Robin Pitt," said Dr Haart and then both she and Prof Taylor turned to leave. As they did, Robin put down the piece of equipment he was dealing with and turned to speak to Jack and Sarah. "Hello, I'm Robin and I believe that you would like a quick run through of what we're trying to do here?".

"That would be excellent" Jack replied.

"Are we allowed to ask questions?" Sarah asked.

"Of course" Robin replied, "It's a treat to have someone new to talk to. As I'm sure you've found out in your job, always having to keep things secret and hidden away, gets to be a pain after a while"

"While we're working on our current case, we've really had that brought to our attention. We can't afford a single piece of paper to be out of place" Jack explained.

"At least you don't have members of the secret service always checking up on you. Making sure that you don't say of do anything out of place. In fact, you two are the first outsiders I've ever known to be let in here" Robin stated.

"Do you mean that you actually get the spooks coming here?" Sarah said. "That's really exciting, but I suppose it has its serious side. I hate to think what would happen to anyone they thought was out of line".

"Anyway, let's forget about all of that. Over here, as you have most likely guessed, is the computer equipment. Please don't ask me about all the programming, as I leave that to my assistant, who is a complete and utter computer wiz. This is her, Rebecca the genius" Robin said.

Rebecca swung around on her chair and greeted the visitors with a hello and big smile. "Have you been introduced to the rest of the team of lowly technicians?" she asked.

"No, not yet" Sarah replied.

"Typical man" Rebecca said, looking straight at

Robin. "Right. Over there, on that bench, there's Susan and Trevor."

At the sound of their names, they turned and waved. Rebecca continued, "And the one over there doing something with a soldering iron, is Brian. That's it, we're a small family, but we all get on well together".

"Thank you mother" Robin said sarcastically. "Right then. Let's continue the tour around our little world".

So they followed Robin around the lab as he explained the functions of the various areas and also speaking to the other technicians, as they met them. Finally, they arrived at the glass cubicle, with the operating table in the centre, as this was the focus point of the whole operation.

"Have you actually had anyone on this table, in an attempt to get them out of phase?" Jack asked, trying to sound technically competent, which he really. wasn't.

"All those that have been here, have been volunteers from the army and so far, there's only been five. But we haven't been that successful up to now. Although these last two attempts were the best so far. We did actually make them invisible, but the effect disappeared the moment the equipment was switched off" Robin explained.

"What effect did it have on the soldiers?" Sarah asked.

"I was hoping that you wouldn't ask that" Robin replied, "The first two that we ever tested, actually died from heart failure. Apparently, the experiment placed too much of a strain on their system, and unfortunately their hearts couldn't cope and gave up. Number three survived, but was not physically well afterward and as for the last two, as I said earlier, these gave us our best results so far. But those two were also very poorly afterward. Their condition was considered serious enough, that these last three volunteers had to be medically discharged from the army." "Not exactly the result you were looking for then" Jack said.

"That's why the powers that be were so interested in the situation that you are investigating. It seems that, once again, nature has beaten the scientists to the finish line, achieving what we have failed to do," Robin explained.

"But the people that we're into, also have their limitations" Sarah added, "So even nature hasn't totally succeeded".

Dr Haart returned to the lab at this point. "Has this motley crew been helpful and fully explained our purpose to you?" she asked.

"They've been really helpful," Jack replied, "We couldn't have asked for better". This comment brought smiles to the faces of all the technicians in the lab.

"See Doc" Rebecca said, "We're worth every penny you pay us".

"So you say" Dr Haart replied and turning to Jack and Sarah, said "Is there anything else you would like to have explained?".

"No thank you," Jack replied, "We've had a comprehensive explanation to all of your goals here".

"Maybe you'd like another drink before you leave then?" she asked.

"I'm fine" Jack said and turning to Sarah, he asked, "What about you?". "No thanks, I don't need a drink at the moment" she replied "and I think it's about time that we made a move anyway".

A few moments later, they were saying their good-byes to Dr Haart and Prof Taylor. They then walked over to their car and as Sarah was unlocking the doors, an army truck drove up to the front door of the building. A group of young soldiers were called out of the truck and led into the entrance through which Jack and Sarah had left just minutes before.

As they were sitting in the car, Jack said "I thought that we were ushered out of there pretty quickly. Now we know why. Another batch of volunteers, poor souls. I wonder if they realise what's in store for them".

"How long do you think it will be, before they start experimenting on them?" Sarah asked.

"I don't think it will be very long" Jack replied, "Let's get out of here". She started the car and pulled away from the buildings. As she turned into the drive, Jack asked her, "Do you feel that this trip today has been of any real help to us?". "Well, to be honest, although I found it all very interesting, I don't think that any of their work has any real bearing on our problem," Sarah replied.

"I agree" Jack said, "C'mon, let's go home and leave them to their experiments". Phil was also glad to get away. He too had been impressed by the laboratory, but he was overwhelmingly worried about being discovered while there. He had kept well away from the glass cubicle for fear that he might show up on some piece of equipment. He didn't feel comfortable while he was there and agreed with Jack's sentiments, as the car drove away.

That evening, Jack was in the sitting room with Joyce, who was watching one of her 'soaps', while Jack read the newspaper. He was looking forward to the following morning and finding out how Dave and Clive had got on at the hospital. He hoped that their day had proved more profitable than his and Sarah's had been. Allowing his thoughts to drift, he wasn't paying too much attention to what was on the television. Suddenly, his attention was grasped by an advert that shook him to the core, causing him to drop his paper in amazement. The serious sounding voice over said,

"They are among us. You can't see them, but they're all around you. Read this exclusive story only in this week's Sunday News". Jack felt the color drain from his face. "Are you alright, love" Joyce asked. Jack didn't reply. He was too stunned and then the phone began to ring.

***

CHAPTER TEN

COMPUTATION

Theo had been back with the group for almost two hours before Phil arrived. He had wanted to wait until Phil's return before relating his experiences, but they had pressured him to the point where he caved in and told them what had happened. He explained how he managed to follow the two police officers from when they arrived at the hospital, until they were in the doctor's office. But it was his account of the meeting with Gary, that had brought gasps from his audience. When he explained how he had been able to convey information via him, he shocked them all into silence.

This was an immense breakthrough, as he had managed to bridge the barrier between them and the 'normals'. A flood of questions followed, which he tried to answer, although at times he had to speculate the implications for them all.

"So, is this Gary going to work along with the police as an interpreter, or go-between?" Jennifer asked.

"That's the feeling I got," Theo replied, "So, what way this will pan out, I don't know, but I got the impression that a great deal of work is going on into trying to resolve our situation".

"Do you think that someone is trying to work out a way of changing us back?" Emily asked, "It would be wonderful to be able to return to my real life".

Theo hadn't seen them all so positive about the future ever before and realised that he'd had the privilege of bringing hope into their lives. He thought about his own life, if he was able to change back. Would he return to working in a supermarket or would his unique status open up new avenues to him.

Knowing that such thoughts were just speculation for now, he realised that they all had a long way to go before having to cope with such decisions. He also noticed that Frank didn't seem so animated as the rest of the group and wondered how he would react, if the opportunity to revert to normal, was offered him.

While all of this was happening, Phil arrived. He was out of breath as he had been running, wanting to get back to the group as quickly as possible. He was immediately bombarded with questions and comments about all that Theo had achieved.

"Just let me get my breath," he said. Once he had settled himself and was given a hot drink he said, "From what you've all been saying, Theo seems to have had a much more successful day than I did".

His lack of success put a bit of a damper on the group and quietened them all down. "I'm not saying that I wasted my time, but I didn't uncover anything that's of any practical use to us. I couldn't estimate the cost of all the equipment they've got there, but they haven't been successful in achieving what we all did by accident. In fact, their first two test subjects died, as a result of the experiments," Phil stated.

"That's terrible," Michael said, "and did they carry on with their experiments?". "Oh yes" Phil replied, "In fact some more young soldiers arrived just as we were leaving. Anyway, have you ever known the MOD to be put off by a few deaths, if they help it to achieve its aims. But on a lighter note, Theo, tell me what you achieved today, as you seem to have been much more successful".

So Theo told Phil what had happened with various group members interjecting questions and personal assumptions. Eventually he manager to get to the end and said "Well Phil, what do you make of that?".

"I think that we should make sure that we're in a position to be able to interact with Gary again as he's our only link to the outside world".

The group thought that it was a sensible suggestion and they went on to discuss how this could happen.

When he arrived at the police station, that morning, Jack went straight to DCS Richmond's office. It was an arrangement that had been made the previous evening, following the transmission of the advert that seemed to undo all of their security arrangements.

"Come on in Jack" he said, as he knocked on the door.

"Well, what do you make of it all then, Jack?".

"I must admit that it shook me," Jack replied, "I wasn't sure what to make of it". "Let me tell you. Since that advert was transmitted last night the phones haven't stopped ringing."

"What's going to be done about it?" Jack asked. "The editor of the paper is to be interviewed under the guise of public disorder and he will be told that headlines of that sort could start some people panicking etc, you know the kind of thing".

"Are they going to try and trace the source of the material. The area where it originated and if any particular individual was involved, because I'm sure that an editor would not be willing to part with that kind of information".

"Yes, that's the intent but we know what editors are

like so we're playing it down. We don't want him to realise that he's stumbled onto the story of the century. If we can find out the area of origin we can then discover which force is involved. So it's best if none of you go anywhere today until we get this sorted out".

"That's alright," Jack said, "We have our reports of yesterday's activities to get written up and we will want to discuss them between ourselves. So I'll wait until I hear from you".

"That's fine, Jack. I'll speak to you as soon as I find anything out".

As Jack entered room 516, all eyes were fixed on him.

"What's happening,Sir," Sarah asked.

"Just let me get a drink and then I'll bring you all up to speed with the situation," Jack replied. He then related to them the conversation he had with DCS Richmond and then said "I'm sure that none of you have slipped up, so I'm not worrying. Anyway, someone's in line for a good dressing down from their superiors. But let's forget about all that for the moment and discuss what was achieved yesterday, Go on Sarah, you start by telling them what happened to us". She went on to relate all that had occurred at the Research Centre and that they didn't learn anything of benefit to them. "In fact I found the whole set-up a bit creepy. I also found it quite frightening that they were being supplied with young soldiers to experiment on" Sarah said and it was possible to notice a slight tremor in her voice. "In fact, a new batch of soldiers arrived there, just as we were leaving and even though we were given a cordial reception, I think they would have prefered it if we hadn't seen them arrive" she concluded.

Jack then took charge of the conversation, "We felt

that we were rushed out rather suddenly at the end as if they were expecting something to happen, which must have been the arrival of the soldiers. But I must agree with Sarah, when I say that I wasn't sorry to get out of there. Anyway, enough of our experiences. How did you two get on at the hospital?".

"Well, I don't want to brag, but we got on rather well," Dave said, with a smug grin on his face.

"Typical male show-off," Sarah said and then added, "Sorry. Only joking, really". "Ignoring that sarky comment, I'll let Clive explain what took place and the final outcome" was Dave's response.

Clive stood up, folder in his hand and was about to address them when Jack stopped him in his tracks. "Sit down lad, you're not giving evidence in court" he said. The other two found Jack's comment hilarious and started to laugh, while Clive turned a delicate shade of red. After sitting down and re-arranging himself, he related what had happened in Dr Hedley's office, the previous day. He also highlighted the shock they all received when Gary told them that one of the invisible people was in the room with them.

"What? Do you mean to tell me, that one of these people had followed you into the doctor's office?" Jack asked. "Yes, and with Gary's assistance, we even managed to learn his name, Theo" Clive answered.

"Did you run a check on him, in the missing persons data-base, to see if he popped up?" Jack asked. At this point Dave joined the conversation and said that they had carried out a search the previous day. One person cropped up, that matched the name and description given to us by Gary. The name was Theo Brown, a young man in his early twenties, who has been missing for just over two months.

"So we now know that he isn't really missing at all, he's just slipped out of normality" Sarah said and then continued, "It's such a pity that we can't put his family's mind at rest. But how could we explain his present condition and I suppose that if we told them it would be a breach of security".

"You've got that right" Jack replied "and I'm glad that you realise it".

Jack now turned to the team and asked them, "Well, you bright young things, what do you think would be the best move to take now?".

After a few moments of silence, Clive was the first to speak. "I think that it would be a good idea to try and arrange some kind of get together between ourselves, Gary and the remainder of the invisible people, or their representatives".

"Any other thoughts?" Jack asked.

Both Sarah and Dave said that they were thinking along similar lines to Clive. "Our first task, is to make sure that we can rely on Gary's help and secondly, try to find some way that we can contact the invisible ones. We now know that they get all over the place, which highlights the government's concerns and we have to realise that it's possible that one of them is listening to us right now, but without Gary's help, we would never know. So I need your thoughts on how we achieve this" Jack asked them. He then answered his own enquiry, saying, "I think, if the hospital allows it, that it would be best if we accompanied Gary into the town centre and use his experience to see if he could pick any of them out. Anybody have any other suggestions?".

Sarah responded by saying, "I don't see any other way of contacting them. Say, for instance, that there was one of them in the room with us now. How would we know? How could they contact us? They couldn't. So I agree that Gary's help is imperative".

"How about you two?" Jack said, addressing Dave and Clive, "Can either of you think of a better solution to our problem?".

They both agreed that Jack's suggestion was the only practical route open to them and thought it best if they contacted Dr Hedley to arrange a trip into town for Gary. They didn't have any idea of the kind of response they would receive, or if she would even be willing to allow Gary out of the hospital.

"Well, the only way we will find out, is to ask" Jack said, "I'll go and phone her now and see what I can arrange".

While he was sitting in his office, Jack realised that it had been a couple of days since he had reported to whoever it was that answered the phone number on the white card. This time his call was answered by a man's voice and Jack determined that he was quite mature. So he related the activity of the past few

days, holding back the best to last. The account concerning Gary and his interaction with Gary was very well received. Jack was told that this was the first time that such interaction had been known to take place. After talking for a few more moments the call was terminated, leaving Jack feeling rather proud that it had been his team that had made such an important breakthrough.

Next, the phone call to Dr Hedley had to be made. He explained the plan to her and explained the necessity for Gary's involvement, which she accepted. She

suggested that he came to the hospital the following

morning and ask Gary if he was willing to participate, also explaining to him, that he was the key to the success of the whole operation. Jack agreed that it was a sensible suggestion, as Gary's willing participation was paramount to the success of the venture. So it was arranged for Jack to be there for ten, the next morning.

As he emerged from his office, although he didn't realise it, he must have had a smile on his face, because Dave asked, "What are you looking so happy about?". "What do you mean?" Jack replied, prompting Sarah to say, "Well, something must have caused that smile on your face. Have you been phoning your girl friend?".

"Now, that's something I'd never considered," Dave said, "Jack with a girlfriend". "And why not?" Jack replied, "What's the matter with me?". Jack's answer resulted in a burst of laughter from them all. When they had all calmed down, Jack told them about the contents of his call to Dr Hedley and that he was going to try and arrange, with Gary's help, a trip into the town centre as quickly as possible. He then told them, "You can take it a bit easy this afternoon, while you get your reports of yesterday's activities written up. Remember, don't leave anything out, however trivial it may seem, as it may well fit in with other information, that's gathered by someone else.

"Hopefully, by tomorrow, the panic caused by the TV advert last night should have been dealt with and we can get back to normal. If for some reason it isn't, I'm afraid that we're all confined to barracks; But I'm going to work on the assumption that we will have had the all-clear by then. But before you all start on your reports, I'd like to spend a little time explaining a job that the three of you can do tomorrow. An article in a ladies magazine has been brought to my attention, as it may well come under our remit. Although we have to keep in mind, that these stories are often sensationalised to increase the potency of the account.

"What magazine is it?" Sarah asked and after Jack had told her, she said, "I'll pop out and get a copy during my lunch break. Then we can see what it says and if there's any sense in following it up".

That's what she did and when Dave and Clive returned from the canteen, Sarah was reading the magazine.

"Well," said Clive, "Do you think it's of interest to us?". Just then Jack returned from his lunch with DCS Richmond, which was also used to update him with the team's progress.

"Well timed" Dave said, "We were just about to get Sarah to relate this magazine article to us".

"It will be interesting to see how closely their account ties in with the official one" Jack said, holding up a file, with the usual bright red strip running from corner to corner.

"Here goes" Sarah said. "It concerns a small hospital, not too far from here, where a lady was brought in following a road accident. She wasn't too badly hurt, apart from a nasty wound on her head. The police were involved as a blood test had shown high levels of alcohol in her system. They were able to put her in a small side room, away from prying eyes and making it easier for the police to keep an eye on her. They were hoping that she would be able to answer some questions about the accident and clarify why she left the road before ploughing into a tree.

"The nursing staff had closed the door to give her

some peace and making it easier for the police to make sure that she didn't wander off. Due to her condition, the doctor had asked the nurses to make regular checks on her in case she deteriorated. A nurse had entered the room, to perform the required checks, only to find that the room was empty. The nurse stood in the doorway and called out, "Where is she?". The policeman who had been left to watch over her, leapt up from his chair and peered into the room, from over the nurse's shoulder. True enough, the room was empty and no trace of her could be found, anywhere in the hospital. The only theory that made any sense, was that she had regained consciousness and had somehow managed to sneak out of the hospital, as she wanted to avoid the repercussions from the accident.

"But it wasn't only the hospital that she had disappeared from, she seemed to disappear totally. She didn't turn up at her home, neither did she contact any of her friends or withdraw any money from her bank acccount. It was as if she had ceased to exist."

"What do you make of that then?" Sarah asked. Nobody answered her, until Jack, who had been thumbing through the pages of the folder, said "It's not too far removed from the official report. So let me ask you all, Does any part of that account sound familiar to you?".

The three of them all agreed that it was, to them, a very familiar story. Of course, they couldn't let anyone know that, as it could start people thinking, especially with the recent showing of the TV advert. It was decided that on the following day, while Jack visited the Psychiatric Hospital, the remaining members of the team would visit the hospital were the report of the disappearing woman had originated from, to see if they were able to add some flesh to the bones of the story.

Consistent with the rest of his team, Jack had never been inside the Fairview hospital before. He'd seen it plenty of times, as he had driven past on the main road and he considered himself fortunate that he had never been in the position of having to visit either a friend, or family member that had ended up in there. So it was with a little trepidation that he turned into the car-park. He found himself speculating about the number of people that must have travelled this way before him, realising that it could so easily have been himself that arrived there as a patient.

Putting such morbid thoughts behind him, he walked from his car to the imposing main doors. Something, possibly an instinct, made him look up and saw a man watching him from a third floor window. He noticed the bars that were fitted on all the windows and reasoned that he must have been one of the patients. Was it Gary? It wouldn't be long before he found out. Jack had always enjoyed exploring old buildings and ancient houses and was pleasantly surprised as he walked in through the large wooden doors. The reception area was very impressive and did not try to hide that it had once been the entrance hall of a stately home. A home that reveled in it's quality woodwork and architecture. The receptionist saw Jack surveying the panelled work around the walls and called over to him. "Oh, I'm sorry" Jack said, "I've never been in here before and I never knew what a lovely building it was. I suppose you would like to know who I am and why I'm here?". "It would make things easier" the woman said, "Do you have an appointment with someone?".

"Yes I do. I'm Superintendent Hargreaves and I have an appointment with Dr Hedley at 10 o'clock".

"Thank-you" she replied, "Take a seat over there and I'll let the doctor know that you're here".

Jack sat down in the reception area and continued admiring the architecture. He was so engrossed in his examination, that he failed to notice a nurse walk up to him.

"Excuse me" she said, "I believe you're here to see Dr Hedley?". Once again Jack had to apologise and then said, "I was just admiring this fine old building". He felt a little embarrassed that this was the second time, since he'd been there, he had to apologise and determined to keep his wit's about him for the rest of his visit. As they walked down, what seemed to Jack like a maze of corridors, the nurse asked him, "Are you anything to do with the other two, who came here a few days ago?". "Yes I am" Jack replied, "I'm their boss. I hope they behaved themselves and didn't say anything out of place". "Oh no, nothing like that" the nurse said, "It's just that the younger one was a bit cheeky, but in a nice way. I actually thought he was quite nice".

"I'll convey your feeling's to him when I get back and I'm sure that you'd like to know that he's called Clive".

"Thank-you" she replied, "That's very kind of you. But I wasn't prying, just making a comment. Anyway, we've arrived".

Jack saw that they'd stopped in front of an impressive wooden door, bearing a plaque that stated a Dr Marion Hedley resided within. The nurse knocked on the door and a voice from within called out, "Come in". The nurse opened the door and Jack allowed her to enter first. "Superintendent Hargreaves to see you Doctor".

"Thank you," the doctor replied. "Come on in Superintendent and take a seat."

"I would feel more at ease if you called me Jack" he said. "That's fine by me" she replied "and I'm Marion and although we've never met before, I've been kept up to date with your progress by those that answer the magic phone number. Do you have any idea who it is, or where they are?".

"I'm as much in the dark as you are. I was just given this," he said producing the familiar white card from his wallet.

"Snap," Marion replied.

Jack then said, "Putting all that intrigue to one side, I'd like to discuss a new plan that the team has devised as it would help us take the next step forward in the investigation".

"Could you explain what the plan involves" Marion asked, "As I presume that Gary would be the lynch-pin of any such endeavour and I presume that's the reason why you're here, not one of your underlings". Thinking over what she had just said, she added "I'm sorry. That didn't come out the way I intended. What I meant to …… " She stopped in mid sentence, as the alarms started to ring. Then her personal bleeper went off. She unclasped it from her waistband and read the display. "Don't worry, it's not the fire alarm. There's a problem with one of the patients" she said, "I'll be back as quickly as I can. Help yourself to a drink while...."

Her final words were lost in the noise emanating from the corridor, as she disappeared through the door. The alarms continued to sound for a few moments more and then suddenly stopped. Allowing an eerie silence to descend on the room.

Jack was seriously considering pouring himself a second cup of coffee, when Dr Hedley returned. "What was the problem. Nothing serious I hope?" Jack asked, as she settled herself behind her desk once again. He noticed that her eyes were red-rimmed, as if she'd been crying.

"Would you like me to pour you a cup of coffee?" Jack enquired. "That would be very nice, thank-you" she replied and then said "It's a good job that I wasn't seeing a patient when this happened. Just look at the state of me. I must apologise for my appearance, but there's been a serious incident".

"Do you want to talk about it?" Jack asked.

"I should follow the advice I give to others on a regular basis, shouldn't I".

"It's been known to help" Jack replied, trying to be helpful. He noticed that tears welled up in her eyes as she thought about what she was going to say.

"One of our younger female patients had a set-to with some-one else, which tends to occur, as they're all crammed in together every day. But this particular girl got really upset over something that either happened, or was said, causing her to return to her room and she hanged herself. Nobody realised what had happened until it was too late. We cut her down and tried to resuscitate her, but we weren't there quickly enough".

As these final words escaped from her lips the tears started in earnest and Jack pushed a box of tissues across the desk towards her. He didn't say anything, but he eventually felt that he should speak. So he asked if she would like him to leave, so she could sort herself out.

"Please don't go," she said through the tears, "I really need your company at the moment. I don't know why this has affected me so badly, she wasn't even a patient of mine. I think it was her youth that's hit me so hard. How she was willing to discard all the possibilities that her life could have held. Now, because of a stupid argument, or something, that's all lost. I think it's that, that's got to me".

"I'm quite happy to stay, if you feel it. helps" Jack replied and continued to discuss the situation with her.

Eventually, she calmed down enough for the original conversation to be re-star   ted. "Right then. What do you intend to do with Gary?" she asked.

Jack then related the plan to use Gary to help them pin-point one of the invisibles, so that they could instigate a more comprehensive dialogue with any of Theo's friends that were willing to get involved. "It certainly was quite remarkable to see a similar situation to what you plan to take place right here, in this office, when the other two officers were here. None of us thought for as instant that one of these, 'invisibles' I think you called them, was right here in the room with us. We had no idea, until Gary pointed him out".

"Who knows if we're alone now," Jack stated, "That's why we need Gary's help. We're not going to be able to make any further progress, until we can make and then sustain contact with these people". Dr Hedley adjusted herself in her chair, while she thought over what Jack had said, her usual controlled appearance slowly returning.

"I think the best thing that we could do now is to bring Gary here and see how he feels about taking part in your plan. Don't you agree?".

"I most certainly do," Jack replied, "If we don't have Gary's whole hearted support for this scheme, we will be wasting our time".

She picked up the phone, dialled a number and after identifying herself, asked if Gary could be brought to her office. Neither of them said very much while they were waiting for Gary to arrive. She was feeling a little embarrassed that she had broken down in front of a stranger, but accepted that her emotions had overwhelmed her. Fortunately, he had been a man that was empathetic towards her suffering and had done what he could to calm her down and for that she was grateful. While all these thoughts were going through her mind, a knock came at the door and a nurse lead Gary into the room.

"Gary, this is Superintendent Hargreaves and he has come here this morning to put a proposal to you. I'll let him explain it in a minute, but remember, you're free to say yes or no. So don't feel pressured in any way".

"Good morning Gary. It's nice to meet you" said Jack as he walked across to Gary's chair, to shake his hand, a move that impressed Gary greatly. "You now know who I am and, if you're allow me, I'd like to explain our plan to you. As Dr Hedley says, you're at total liberty to refuse to participate, if you so desire. Is that acceptable to you?" to which Gary nodded. Jack noticed that Gary was looking all around the room and asked him if he was looking for unseen visitors and he replied that he was. So Jack told Gary the plan and the purpose of it and then sat back in his chair, to allow Gary to think over all that he had said. Gary said that he understood the plan and the need for his involvement, understanding that without him it was impossible. This gave him a sense of power over those around him. For the first time in his life, he had a purpose and a really important one at that. He quickly realised another advantage to all of this, which was that he would get a day out, away from the hospital. He appreciated that he would have to return at the end of the day, but he was happy about that, as he felt safe and secure when he came in through those big doors.

"Will I get my dinner at a restaurant?" he asked. "I don't see why not" Jack replied.

"Remember" Dr Hedley added "No alcohol. As it will react with your medication and you don't want to go back down that road, do you?".

"I don't have any intentions to do anything like that" Gary replied, "I just fancy a meal out, that's all".

"That's OK then," the doctor said. There was silence for a few moments, while Gary was allowed to think it all over. Gary then sat himself bolt upright in his chair and said "OK. I'll do it".

"That's great" the other two said almost instantaneously. "Just remember" Jack added, "I think that it would be best if we waited for a nice sunny day, as I feel that we would stand a better chance of finding what we want, when the weather is good. None of us really likes going out when it's wet and windy, do we".

"That makes sense" Dr Hedley agreed and then said to Jack, "Will you contact me as soon as you decide when it's to happen".

"Definitely" Jack replied, "But just remember, that it's all dependent upon the weather. Is that alright with you, Gary?".

"Yes and I do understand your reasoning" he answered. As he was being guided back to the reception area, Jack once again took the opportunity to examine the old building.

As he walked along, he wondered about the things that had happened in those corridors in the previous centuries and decided to spend some time looking into the history of the place. Then, almost before he was ready, he was back in the reception area. He turned and thanked the nurse and walked out through the impressive wooden doors, stopping for a moment so he could admire the work that had gone into them.

'Yes' he thought to himself, 'This building deserves some further investigation. I'm so glad that I had the opportunity to see it's beauty' and this strengthened his resolve to further investigate it's history.

When he returned to his office, Jack did something that was very unusual for him. He accessed the internet, for something personal. He switched on his computer and instigated a search, looking for details about the history of the Fairview Hospital. This provided him with some material about the history and

the previous occupants of the house, before it became a hospital. After waiting while the printer made copies of the information, he switched off the computer and looked around, making sure that no-one had seen him, even though he knew that the office was empty.

In those few moments, Jack was whisked back to his childhood and the many times that he had done something he knew that he shouldn't and had looked around to see if anyone was watching him. He was still reliving these memories, when the phone started to ring. This abruptly returned him to the present. He placed his note book and the printouts into his pocket and responded to the insistent ringing of the phone. It was DCS Richmond's secretary and she said, "Could you come up right away as he would like to see you for a moment".

An invitation like that, was one that didn't include the option of refusal, so he replied, "Tell him I'll be there in a minute. I have something to complete first". "That's fine," she replied, "I'll let him know".

Jack sat there, trying to get his wits around him. 'I wonder what this is all about' he thought, 'I'm sure that none of my team will have done anything wrong, so what is there to worry about'.

Having regrouped, he was ready and on his way out he made sure that all papers were secure. Then, as he left the room, he ensured that the door was firmly locked. As he walked along the corridor, towards the lifts, he wondered what rumours were circulating about what went on in room 516. He would have to get his team to do some eavesdropping, especially in the canteen. 'I'm sure that we can get some amusement out of the various stories,' he thought, as he walked past the lifts, around the corner and onto the stairs.

"Come on in Jack," the DCS said,"Get yourself a coffee and sit down".

Jack willingly accepted the invitation. He always liked having a drink in the DCS's office, as he had such good coffee. With drink in hand, he pulled up a chair and sat down in front of the desk that dominated the room.

"I'm sure you remember the TV advert that really put the cat among the pigeons." In answer Jack nodded.

"Well, investigations were made by some of our more shadowy compatriots and the outcome is that the source of the leak had been tracked down and identified. As I always expected, none of your team were implicated, which I'm sure you knew all along. A reporter happened to overhear two officers talking in a pub down in Exeter and then did some digging around. The officers concerned have been dealt with but the whole thing has left us with a problem. A hint about what is taking place is now at large in the public domain".

"But will the public believe it?" Jack asked, "After

all, the newspaper concerned doesn't have a very good reputation for accuracy, in fact it's always been a bit sensationalist".

"That may well be the case" the DCS replied, "But the public, in general, lap such things up. There are always rumours of cover-ups doing the rounds and this will just add to the canon. If the government were to make a statement concerning this report, trying to discredit it, that would only make more people willing to believe it. So silence is, in this case, golden".

"I can understand that line of thought," Jack replied. "So I presume that's the official policy. We say nothing and carry on our investigations as we did before. Some people may well have their suspicions, but they won't be able to prove them. We'll just carry on as normal then."

The DCS indicated to Jack that he was correct and then Jack went on to explain to him about the plan involving Gary. He also highlighted the one possible problem that could occur, which was the onset of inclement weather, but that they hoped to implement the plan as soon as they could.

"Please make sure that you keep me up to date with your progress Jack," the DCS requested.

"I always do, don't I" Jack replied, as he turned to leave. As he moved towards the door, a thought came into his mind. 'I wonder if he was given one of those white cards with the phone number on it?' he thought, as he left the room, closing the door behind him. If Jack had the ability to see through walls, he would have been able to answer his question. For at that moment, the DCS was using his card to phone in his report, concerning the status of the investigation.

After he had returned to his office, Jack was

enjoying a moment's silent reflection, when suddenly the peace was shattered by the team's return from their field trip. Bags and personal items were dumped on their desks, before the dash for the coffee pot commenced.

"You're a noisy crowd" Jack said as he emerged from his office. "Well, how did it all go? Did you learn anything new?" he asked.

Dave, being the senior officer, related the day's events. "The account was pretty well the same as we had read in the official report" he said.

"As we would have expected," Jack stated, interrupting him.

Dave then continued. "There was one interesting development, that wasn't in the report. A couple of days later following the woman's disappearing act from the side room, a nurse discovered her body, laying on the floor, beside the bed, on the side that was hidden from the door".

"The intriguing thing was that all of the staff, swore that she wasn't there earlier in the day'" Sarah said, who also interrupted Dave mid flow.

"If you don't mind Sarah, I'll continue," Dave said.

"Sorry" Sarah replied.

"A post mortem discovered that she had a bleed in her brain, that had gone undetected and it killed her. But no-one could explain where she had been during the interim period of time. To them, it was a complete mystery. Of course, we were not able to add our knowledge to their speculations but I only think it would have muddied the waters further. So that's the whole story".

"We interviewed everyone, starting with the ward Sister and finishing up with the cleaners. No-one had a suggestion that would totally explain what had happened" Clive added. "Well, thank you all for your efforts" Jack said, "I think we can wrap this one up now, as there isn't any more that we can do. We'll just have to leave them to speculate. At least the family has a body to bury so that must be a relief to them. They must have been very confused during their daughter's disappearance. I'm sure that they must be relieved that it's all over. Anyway, changing the subject. You will be pleased to learn that my trip to the hospital was successful. Gary says that he's willing to help us out, by pointing out any of the 'invisibles' that we may encounter in the town centre. In fact, I think that he's grateful just to get a day out, but we must remember that he's our only link with these people, so we'll have to be tolerant with him.

"It's all set up so that it can happen in the next few days, dependent upon the weather. So let's pray for good sunny days and then we can possibly move onto the next stage of our investigation. Making contact with the invisible people will be a major step forward, no-one else has got closer than we have to this goal, so let's hope it all goes to plan."

***

CHAPTER ELEVEN

POSSIBILITIES

The following morning, Gary was back in Dr Hedley's office, once again, "I've called you in this morning," she said; "Concerning the conversation We had yesterday, about your helping the police to identify these invisible people. I want to make sure how you feel about it, without the presence of Superintendent Hargreaves, just in case you felt pressured, at the time, into accepting the proposal. Please be honest with me. How do you feel about it?"

A few moments of silence passed and then Gary answered her by saying, "I don't have any reservations, in fact I think it will be an interesting project and, for the first time, give my life some meaning and purpose".

"Well that's all right then. I was worried that you'd felt pressured into agreeing," she replied.

Then Gary continued to speak. "As I said at the time, well I think I did, it will be nice to get out for a while. But I'll always have this place and your support to fall back on if required".

Dr Hedley was watching him all the time that he was speaking. Trying to read his body language and see if his words matched his true feelings. When he had finished speaking, she explained that she wasn't trying to stop him helping the police. "My basic concern is for your mental well being. You don't know, at the moment, how your mind will be able to cope with the demands that will be placed on it and what will happen if it all turns out to be too much for you to deal with" she explained and then continued, "I was wondering if it might be advisable for a nurse to be with you, as well as someone from the police. Just so she's there if you happen to need some support and can provide what's required. How do you feel about that suggestion?".

"I hadn't thought about that aspect at all" Gary replied, "Actually, the more I think about it, the better the idea seems".

"Also you mustn't forget that at any time you can say you've had enough and return to the hospital, where you feel safe. On the other hand, if you emerge from the experience without any problems, it may be time to think about you returning home. Maybe, just for a week-end to start with, just to see how you get on," she said.

That comment worried Gary, he hadn't even thought about returning to his flat, in fact the life he had before the hospital was lost somewhere in the back of his mind. That was an alien way of being, compared to the Gary that now existed, which had been formed by the trauma he had been through and the care that the hospital had provided. This was the first time, that life outside of the hospital had forced its way into his consciousness, but he realised that the time would come, when he would be considered well enough to leave and that time seemed to be rapidly approaching. He had been sitting there, consumed by his thoughts for some time, before Dr Hedley broke the silence.

"What are you thinking about?" she asked.

"Just how my life has changed and will continue to change from now on. You may think that this is a funny thing to say, but being admitted was the best thing that could have happened to me. I've been taught to accept, what you called my gift and I feel that I have become a better person in the process. All thanks to you and your staff".

"Well. That's very kind of you Gary. I'm glad you feel that way. It's getting close to lunch time now, if you would like to leave. I'll contact Superintendent Hargreaves and let him know that a nurse will accompany you when you make your trip into the outside world".

"Thanks Doc" Gary said, as he left the room, shutting the heavy wooden door behind him.

Gary really enjoyed his lunch that day. He couldn't work out why that was, as he had eaten that combination of food items dozens of times before. But for some unknown reason, they tasted really good this time. He eventually put it down to the fact that he was actually beginning to enjoy being alive. He realised that in all his years, he had never really been alive before, he'd just been existing and drifting along. After the meal was over, he settled himself into what had become known as 'Gary's chair' and after a while he started to doze off.

He was brought back to the here-and-now by a nurse shaking his shoulder and he slowly began to decipher what she was saying. "Gary, you've got some visitors".

'Just when I thought the day couldn't get any better,' he thought to himself and looked across the room to see Bill, Nigel and Suzy walking towards him. He struggled to see if he could work out how Suzy was feeling, before she got up close to him and was half expecting a slap across the face. But he needn't have worried, as she explained, after giving him a kiss. "Your trusty trio of friends sat me down and explained what had happened to you and where you had disappeared to," she said, "So I now feel very guilty about the things I said about you and called you, even though you never heard them".

"Perhaps it's a good thing that I didn't" Gary replied, then they hugged and kissed again and Gary suggested that they sit down, which they both did.

"I'm sorry that I haven't been in before" Nigel said, "But I've been pretty busy in the afternoons, it's only lazy buggers like Bill that can come and go as they please".

Gary smiled, as he watched Bill and Nigel follow a young nurse with their eyes, as she walked through the room. He was also aware that Suzy was watching him closely, just so she could determine where his eyes were.

"Do you have any dealings with young nurses like that?" Suzy asked, "Think carefully before you answer, as you know that I can read your mind".

"Well, I have to be honest," Gary replied, "I often have dealings with the nurses. But they're not all young, in fact some of them could be my mother, or even my grandmother. What's most important in here, is how they treat you".

"A very well thought out answer," Suzy said and they all had a good laugh about it. Gary hadn't laughed like that for such a long time and it felt good.

"You're looking a lot better, compared with what you were like when I saw you last time," Bill said, "Do you remember. The time I came with Dave?".

Gary indicated that he did remember and then Bill added, "But more importantly, do you feel better?"

"Yes I do," Gary replied, "In fact it was only this morning that my doctor mentioned the possibility of my returning home for the weekend, just to see how I cope." They all said that it would be a big step forward and that they hoped it would happen soon. Gary had to fight really hard to stop himself telling them about all the other developments, but he knew that he couldn't because of the resultant consequences if he breached the trust that had been placed in him. That doesn't mean that he enjoyed keeping such a major part of his life hidden from his friends, in fact he hated doing it. But he had no other choice.

While all of this was taking place, Dr Hedley walked through the common room and smiled when she saw how animated Gary was with his friends. Gary didn't notice her as he was too wrapped up in the conversation and anyway, she wasn't in his line of sight. The friends laughed and joked together, until the visiting period was over and once again, Gary was allowed to walk down to the main entrance with his guests.

Bill and Nigel said good-bye first to allow Gary and Suzy to have a couple of minutes alone before they had to part. Gary really felt pangs of regret as his three friends walked away across the car park but he knew that if everything worked out the way he hoped he would soon be able to join them. As they drove past, the car's horn was sounded, causing everyone to turn and look, and good-bye's were shouted through the open windows until they reached the end of the car park. Then they turned into the driveway and soon disappeared from sight. Gary turned, planning to return to the common room, but he felt happy, as he thought about what a good day it had turned out to be.

Following a phone call from Dr Hedley, Jack informed the team about the decision that had been reached. He told the team that when Gary was allowed to visit the town centre, he would be accompanied by a nurse, just in case anything adverse was to occur.

"I'm pleased to hear that" Dave said, "As I was a little concerned about the possibility of Gary not being able to cope with the demands that were being put on him. Now it seems that possibility has been removed, so I feel a lot happier about the situation".

"I hadn't even thought about that" Sarah said.

"Neither had I" Clive responded.

"So it's a good thing that it all doesn't depend on us then" Jack said, "and there's something else we should consider. That is, I don't think we should go mob handed, when we accompany Gary into town. If just one of us attends, I think that will suffice".

"Does that mean you want us to take turns?" Dave asked.

"Well, it does make sense to do it that way," Jack replied, "I'll leave myself out, as I'm often needed here, as you know. How do the three of you feel about taking part? Anyone not want to do it?".

It was this kind of approach that the officers who worked with Jack appreciated. He never forced anyone into anything as he felt that an officer forced into a task, would not perform as well, as one that had chosen to do it. This did not imply that Jack's subordinates were in charge, far from it, as those who had crossed him in the past had found, to their cost. The dog may well have been old, but he still had a loud bark and sharp teeth.

So it was agreed, that Dave, Sarah and Clive would accompany Gary and his nurse, on the expeditions into town. The two younger officers, Sarah and Clive, were quite looking forward to wandering around town, frequenting cafes and eating out, all on expenses. Jack showed that he was able to determine the way they were thinking, when he said, "I know that you'll be on expenses, but you'll have to get the claims past me before they're paid out, so keep that in mind".

"I wouldn't think of taking advantage," Sarah said, with a chuckle in her voice. "Just make sure that you don't" Jack replied and then retired to his office, to phone the DCS and inform him of the latest plans.

The next few days were drizzly, along with quite a chilly wind for the time of year. Hardly the best time to be wandering around the town centre. A discussion developed as to whether those they were looking for would themselves want to venture out in such weather. It was impossible for them to arrive at a definitive conclusion, the only way they would ever find out, was to ask one of them. That in itself raised some problems. Without Gary's help, how could they even know if one of these people was in the vicinity?

So there was a great deal of speculation, but under the circumstances, speculate was all they could do. At the same time, although they weren't able to reach any definitive conclusions, it did help them all to understand the problems that living in an invisible state could cause. Without knowing it, the things they discussed were along the same lines that Theo had asked on the night that his change had taken place.

Although he was in his office, the door being slightly open, allowed Jack to overhear the team's conversation and from its content he felt that they had come to grips with what the whole case was about. They had begun to speak of the 'invisibles' as real people, in fact, people just like themselves, but with a different set of problems and challenges to face. Jack had always found that treating the focus of an investigation as a real person, not just a target, added a sense of reality to them. It didn't matter how terrible their crime was, the chances are, that it could only take a specific set of circumstances for anyone to end up in the same position.

Even though Jack had met some very unpleasant characters in his time, underneath they were still human, but only just, in some cases. Jack had always felt that the key to the offender was to understand their motivation. If you could find that key, you could unlock their mind. But, of course, the ones they were looking for now were not criminals, far from it, they had been put in an unusual situation without their consent and no doubt had found it very difficult to come to terms with. So hearing the team reach that conclusion by themselves, by effectively placing themselves in their situation, had humanised them. Now, when it came to the time to deal with them, they would do so with a more compassionate frame of mind.

The three of them were still talking as Jack emerged from his office and into the room.

"How about one of you using your very expensive computers to try to determine the weather for the next few days" he said.

Dave, Sarah and Clive looked at each other, waiting to see which of them would move first. "Well. Come on," Jack said sharply, "Let's get moving".

The three of them jumped into action, their limbs a little stiff as they had been sitting on the edges of their desks for some time. The wonder that is the internet, soon provided the answer. After consulting a number of different weather services, the overall opinion was that the cool drizzly conditions, that had plagued them for the past few days, were about to be replaced with warmer, dry weather for a little while.

"Right" Jack said, "That's it then. We'll plan on starting our search tomorrow. I'll phone the hospital and make the necessary arrangements for Gary and you three can sort out the order that you want to take."

Dr Hedley didn't have too much trouble in locating Gary. He was occupying his usual chair in the common room. She walked over to him, pulled up a chair and sat down. She saw a worried look appear on his face, when he saw her.

"Don't worry." she said, "I'm here to let you know that, weather permitting, you'll be making your first trip out tomorrow. How do you feel about that?".

"I was beginning to think that that the whole thing had been cancelled. Then I realised that if it had you would have told me" he replied and then said, "Do you think that I'll be able to cope with it?".

"I'm sure you will. Under normal circumstances, I would give you something to calm you down but you will need your wits about you. So I feel that we should give that a miss. How's that strike you?" she asked.

"If you feel that I'll function better as myself, without anything, then I'll accept that. You see, I think that you know my mind and the way it works better than I do. So I'll trust your judgement. Anyway, I don't have to worry, as you've told me that there's going to be a nurse there".

"The nurse will stay with you and in case things get too much, she will have the appropriate medication with her. So, there's nothing for you to worry about. Enjoy your time out and I hope that your search will prove successful" she said reassuringly.

After she had left, Gary's mind kicked into overdrive. He was wondering about how he would cope with all the people, the noise, the bustle, but then he realised that this is what he had been looking forward to for such a long time, so he best get out there and enjoy it. He then began to appreciate that another great change had to take place.

After he had first discovered that he was able to see the invisible people, he had done all that he could to avoid them. But now the opposite was required of him. He was going to have to look for these people and develop the skill of noticing them in among the crowds. Learning how they moved and how to pick them out in a group of people. 'What a reversal of my situation' he thought, 'When I was brought in here, I couldn't handle seeing one of them but I'm now going out looking for them' and he started to feel quite pleased with himself.

At the same time, he really appreciated, for the first time, the wonder that Dr Hedley had performed with him, without him even being aware that it was taking place. This tended to soften his attitude towards doctors, as he had never thought very highly of them, always treating them with suspicion. But his treatment and care while he had been in the hospital, had helped him to get over his problems, in a way he never thought possible.

He wondered why such good care had been taken with him, after all, at the time they didn't know about the gift that he had. Then he looked around the common room, examining his fellow patients and began to realise that they were not the best that society could offer. In fact, most of them were the ones often rejected by society and not counted worthy of any care or attention. But here in the hospital, they had all been treated with care and respect, which for many of them was for the first time in their troubled lives. So Gary began to understand the overall purpose of the hospital. Not only to cure, to the extent possible, although some would never be cured, but to give them hope and a safe environment to live in, which would not be possible for them in the world outside.

As he prepared for bed, that night, Gary felt more positive than he had ever done before. He appreciated, that in the past he was just existing from day to day, but now he had a purpose in life. He felt useful for the first time and indirectly was going to help other people. Something he would never concerned himself with in his old life. With these pleasant thoughts circulating in his mind, he slowly drifted off to sleep, while he looked forward to the day ahead.

As forecast, the following day turned out bright and sunny. Clive pulled up in the hospital car park, just after nine in the morning. He walked into reception and asked the lady to inform Dr Hedley that he was there, then he took a seat in the waiting area.

He knew that it was a possibility that he would have to wait for a while, as the doctor would have to collect Gary and ensure that he was still happy to help them out. Then, with the assigned nurse in tow, they would be ready to come down to the reception area.

So he settled in and got himself a drink, then he sifted through the selection of magazines, until he chanced upon one that caught his attention. He chose a motoring magazine, a subject he was keen on and participated in as a member of a local rally club. He was so engrossed in his magazine, that he failed to notice the doctor and her charges arrive, so they all walked over to him. Their sudden appearance in his line of sight, shocked him so much that he dropped the magazine on the floor and almost knocked his drink flying.

The sight of this flustered young police officer, with arms and legs going in all directions, started them all laughing, which in turn made Clive turn bright red. "I'm so sorry" he said, "I must look a right idiot".

"Don't worry about it," Dr Hedley replied, "At least it's brought some light relief to what could have been a tense situation".

"Well, I'm glad someone benefited from my carelessness," said Clive.

"This is Gary," Dr Hedley said, "Whom you may remember you met during your last visit." The two of them shook hands and the doctor continued. "And this is the nurse who will be coming with you, Carol".

"Good morning Carol, I'm Clive".

"Good morning Clive." Carol replied.

"Right, that's all the formalities over and done with," the doctor said, "Time for the final checks. Gary, are you still feeling alright about this?".

"Yes, I'm fine, in fact I'm rather looking forward to it."

"That's good and Carol, have you got everything that you need?".

"Yes. I've double checked everything and I charged my phone up last night, just in case it's needed". Then she opened her small handbag and showed the contents to Dr Hedley. It was done this way, so that Gary wouldn't see the syringes and tablets she had stashed away, just in case of emergency.

"Right then boys and girl, I think you're ready for the off, so you might as well get going. Good hunting and I hope you have some positive results".

Off the three of them went, with Dr Hedley watching them from the door, like a worried parent. Although she had every confidence that it would be alright and knew that provisions were in place, on the off chance that something didn't go to plan.

Clive parked in the shopping centre car park, as he felt that large crowds of people would be a good place to start looking. But he had failed to take Gary's situation into account, forgetting that he was not used to being in large crowds and that could have ended the trip before it started. Gary was a little embarrassed and didn't know what to say, without causing offence.

Carol realised what had happened and explained it to Clive. For the second time that morning, Clive found himself in a position where he was having to apologise. "I'm so sorry Gary" he said, "I just didn't think about it. I failed to appreciate the effect that a large crowd would have on you, forgetting that you're not used to such large numbers of people".

Gary was relieved, "Thank you for being so understanding," he said. Neither of them realised that all of this was strengthening the bond between them and would serve to make things easier in the future. Carol was astute enough to see this taking place, after all, she was trained to watch people's emotions and see how they were coping with the situations they had to face. She was rather pleased that this had arisen as it had made Gary start to deal with someone he didn't really know and this would, in turn, help him to become a more complete person.

"As we're already parked here, there's no sense in moving. But I think I have a way round this problem," Clive said. "If we leave by the side exit and walk around the bus station we can walk down to the other end of the city centre without meeting many people. Then, as it's still quite early, we can start walking through the shops and the amount of people you will have to confront will slowly increase, rather than you having to deal with crowds right from the start. How does that seem, will you be able to cope with it?" Clive asked.

"I think it's a great idea" Gary replied, "and it's what I had thought of, but I was a little unsure about suggesting it".

"You don't have to be scared of me" Clive said, "Today, I'm just an ordinary bloke, out with his friends and having a wander around the shops. If you want to say something, you go ahead, regardless of whether you think I'll like it or not. Is that OK?".

"That's great," Gary replied, now feeling more at ease. Carol didn't get involved in any of this, as it was developing the way Dr Hedley hoped it would, with the two young men getting to know one-another. Then they started walking and Gary was surprised by the amount of change that had taken place, while he had been in the hospital. But his greatest shock came when they turned into Bridge Street. They had only just turned the corner, when Gary exclaimed, "What's happened to Woolworth's".

Clive and Carol explained the situation to him and the knock-on effects that had caused problems for some other well known shops. Gary was astounded by it all, but it demonstrated to him just how fragile the whole system is. "How are your legs coping?" Carol asked, "As you haven't walked this far for a long time".

"Well, I must admit that I am getting a little tired" Gary replied.

"There's a cafe just along here, that does some

excellent French pastries. How about popping in there for a drink and something to eat?" Carol suggested.

"I know the place," Clive said, "and I agree that they do some good stuff".

"Do you know, I think I can remember the place you're talking about" Gary said, "But I never went in there. Thought it was too posh and anyway, I never had the money. You have to remember, that in the past, the old Gary spent all his money on drink and smokes. So fancy French pastries didn't really feature in my life". They all had a bit of a laugh about Gary's comment, but they all agreed to give it a try, even a reluctant Gary.

They spent the rest of the morning wandering around the shops, with Gary constantly looking around to try and locate one of the 'invisibles', if he was fortunate enough to be looking in the right direction at the right time.

"What exactly are you looking for?" Clive asked Gary, who replied, "It's the way that they act, when they're among people. They don't have to move out of the way of others, as we do, because they are able to walk straight through them. For instance, that man in front of us stepped off the pavement, to allow a lady with a buggy to get by. If he were one of our invisible friends, he wouldn't have to do that, he could keep on walking and the lady would be none the wiser".

"I'd never thought about any of that, but it all makes sense. So you are looking for someone who doesn't have to obey the normal pattens of movement within a crowd of people. But doesn't that mean that you have to be looking in their direction to catch them out?" Clive asked. "You've just identified the main shortcoming of our plan. I could easily miss something that would identify one of the people we're looking for and it's quite possible that I have already done so. I think it might be easier if I watch from a stationary position for a while and it will give me a chance to rest my legs, as they're beginning to ache now" Gary replied. So they sat down on one of the many benches, that are scattered around the town centre. After a while, they began to get fed up with just sitting there and were quickly up on their feet when Carol suggested getting some lunch. Fortunately, they were not limited in their choice of food, but Gary said that he really fancied some fish and chips as he hadn't tasted the real thing for so long.

With a smile on her face, Carol turned to Gary and said, "Is that comment a dig at the hospital food?" she said, "They do the best they can, you .know".

"It's not that at all" Gary replied, "It's just that the taste of fish and chips straight out of the fryer is unique and cannot be copied".

They walked away from the town centre, heading towards the market place and on the way, located the chip shop. Gary's face lit up like a small boy let loose in a sweet shop and took no time getting into the queue. Some five minutes later, they were all sitting on a bench, eating their lunch with their fingers.

Carol realised that she hadn't done this since she was a young girl, when she used to go shopping with her mother. Gary had finished his meal before the others were half way through theirs and topped the meal off with an almighty belch. "That was great" he said. The other two couldn't help laughing, even though their mouths were full of food.

The afternoon passed uneventfully, except when they had a break for a coffee and another bun and were able to enjoy the comfort of padded seats. By the late afternoon, they were all ready to call it a day, their sore feet no doubt having an influence on their decision. As they arrived back at the car, Gary was full of apologies for his lack of success.

"Don't worry about it" Clive said, "There could have been dozens of them, but as you explained earlier, if you weren't in the right place at the right time, you wouldn't have seen them"

At this point, Carol joined the conversation, saying "In the past, I've arranged to meet up with someone in town and still missed them. Even under normal circumstances it's very easy to miss someone in among all those people. Let alone under the difficult restrictions you have to face."

Gary appreciated their comments, they made him feel a bit better, as he was feeling guilty for letting them down.

"Never mind, don't you worry about it," Clive said, "There's always tomorrow". But he was thankful that he wasn't going to be the one doing it. He had started the day looking forward to it, but found the novelty had quickly worn off and he was glad he didn't have to face it again, for a couple of days at least.

When they returned to the hospital, the receptionist told them that Dr Hedley wished to see them all, to ascertain how the day had gone. So Carol led them through the corridors, finally reaching the doctor's office. First of all she asked Gary how he was feeling and was pleased that he had been able to cope with it all. Then came the big question.

"Was your search successful?" she asked. After hearing that it wasn't, she said "Well, don't worry. If you think you can manage it Gary, we'll make arrangements to try again tomorrow".

"I'm up for it," Gary replied, "When I didn't want to see these people, they were everywhere but now that I'm looking for them, they're not going to escape me". His positive attitude really pleased Dr Hedley, as it demonstrated how far he'd come in his recovery.

"I'll make the same arrangements for tomorrow, but if you don't feel up to it in the morning, I'll cancel it", and then turning to Clive she asked, "Who will be coming from your team tomorrow?". Clive said that he wasn't sure, but he thought it would be Sarah.

"There you are Gary," Dr Medley said "You'll have two young ladies to take you out tomorrow. What do you think of that?".

"I think I'm very lucky" he replied "I just hope that it won't be a waste of time, like today".

"I wouldn't say it was a waste of time" Carol said, "We all had a good time together, didn't we?"

They all agreed that they'd enjoyed the time spent together and hoped that the following-day might prove more successful. At the evening meal, Gary didn't eat as well as he normally did, not because he was unwell, but because he had eaten so well while he was out. In the evening, Gary would have normally spent some time in the common room, but he was too tired and went straight to his room after the meal. His system wasn't used to expending so much energy and he now felt desperately tired. Gary didn't have any problems getting off to sleep that night, the old adage about being asleep the moment your head touched the pillow, really applied to Gary that night and he slept like a baby.

As predicted by Clive, it was Sarah who arrived to collect Gary the next morning. Following the introductions, they walked over to the car. While they walked, Sarah asked about the areas they had covered, on the previous trip and suggested that they park on the opposite side of town. The others agreed and they parked in the multi-story by the market place and started their search from there.

As they walked past the fish and chip shop, Gary started to compliment the quality of the lunch they'd enjoyed there the previous day. "Please tell me that you sat inside, using a knife and fork, not outside using your fingers?" Sarah asked, with a pleading expression in her voice. "We sat outside in the fresh air, fingers covered in grease and it was great," Gary replied.

"I was a little hesitant, at first" Carol added, "as I haven't eaten fish and chips with my fingers since I was a little girl, but I must admit that I quite enjoyed it".

"You're both disgusting," Sarah said, in response to their comments. "Today, we'll eat in a more civilised fashion". "

Very good m'lady," Gary said, imitating Parker from Thunderbirds, upon which they all broke out in laughter. Later that morning, Gary caught something out of the corner of his eye, that really grabbed his attention. He was quite sure that he had seen one of the 'invisibles' and they went dashing off in the general direction of the main shops As the street was quite crowded, he lost sight of the woman that had caught his attention. He stopped, looking around him but she was nowhere to be seen and he explained what had happened to his companions. Sarah told him not to worry, as the woman could have gone into one of the shops, or turned into one of the side streets. Anyway, that close call was the closest they had come so far and Gary then went on to tell them that he had only come face to face with one of these people, since his recovery, the one called Theo that he had met in Dr Hedley's office.

As he stood there, talking to his companions, a worrying thought suddenly shot through hid mind. What if he was seen out with these two young women and it was reported to Suzy. 'Then I'd be in line for a good tongue lashing', he thought, 'I know what I'll do. I'll say that the trip out was part of my therapy and that they both were nurses'. "Yes, that's what I'll tell her".

"You'll tell her what?" Sarah asked. Then Gary realised that he'd said the last comment out loud, so he had to explain to them, the whole process that had been going through his mind. The girls found this quite amusing and tried to imagine how they would feel in Suzy's place. Unfortunately, the glimpse that Gary had earlier, was the only sighting of the day and they returned to the hospital mission unaccomplished, once again.

"I'll try once more tomorrow, then I'll have to give it a rest for a few days" Gary said, "As I don't think my legs can stand much more. I'm not used to all this exercise, so I'm going to need a few days rest. Then we can try again, if anyone wants to".

They all agreed that Gary's decision was a sensible one and that they'd try for one more day then they'd leave it for a while. Sarah told them that Dave Grantham would be with them on the following day and that was the end of day two. Once again, without any success.

Dave was a bit older than Sarah and Clive and that slightly altered the feel of the trio. But it wasn't too long before they were all getting along. The day fell into roughly the same patten as had the previous two and Dave allowed Gary to direct operations as he felt that he was the newcomer and after all, it was Gary's ability that was being put to the test, so it was only fair to give him the freedom to use it in the way he thought best.

Carol noticed the differing choices made by the three officers, which were no doubt dictated by their own personal taste. So the mid-morning break was held in another new café, but that added to the variety of the experience. As the morning wore on, they made the decision where to have lunch that day, Dave's choice being the one chosen, as neither of the others had ever eaten there. They were walking across the large open space in the town centre, when Gary couldn't believe his eyes.

Carol and Dave quickly realised that something was happening, as Gary stopped in his tracks and was obviously watching something that had caught his attention. "What's happening Gary?" Dave asked. "I can't believe it" Gary replied, "I'm sure that's Theo and a young woman walking straight towards us".

"Isn't that the man you met in Dr Hedley's office?" Dave enquired. "That's the one, look, he's coming straight towards us" Gary said. To him, Theo's presence was obvious, but Carol and Dave couldn't see anything, which Gary forgot, because to him Theo appeared as a normal person. Dave realised that this was exactly what they had been searching for and at this point, he could be of no use what so ever, he would have to leave it all in Gary's hand's.

"Theo, Theo" Gary called out, the other two assuming that he must be close by. "They've both stopped" Gary said, so I'm going to find out the young lady's name. Dave and Carol moved in closer, so that Gary didn't look as if he was talking to himself.

"If we're encroaching on their space, please tell us, will you Gary?" Gary replied that he would and then

Dave said, "I feel that although we cannot see or touch them, we should respect their personal space, as we would with anyone else". "They're both smiling, after hearing that," Gary said and then asked the young woman to say her name, so that he could tell Carol and Dave. As far as Emily was concerned, she was saying her name out loud, but Gary had to read her lips and it took a few attempts, with Dave and Carol listening to what Gary was saying. Then, all of a sudden, Carol blurted out, "Is it Emily?"

"She's given you the thumbs up for that Carol, well done. You've beaten me to it" Gary said.

Both Dave and Carol then introduced themselves and told Theo and Emily why they had been trying to contact one of their group. It was somewhat easier for Dave to tell them his information than it was for them to give him an answer, but Gary was becoming quite adept at lip-reading and so that tended to speed things up.

Then Carol came up with a brilliant idea. She asked Theo and Emily if they were able to touch paper, books etc. and after they replied that they could, she suggested sign language as a way for them to converse with Gary, if he was willing to learn it as well. Gary said that he hadn't tried to learn anything new since he'd left school, but he was willing to have a go and a similar response was given by Theo.

So an arrangement was made for them to meet up again a couple of days later and in the meantime Carol would obtain a couple of copies of a basic sign-language book, one for Gary and one for Theo. They then bade each other farewell, Emily and Theo returning to their activities and Dave, Gary and Carol went to get themselves some lunch.

As they were eating their meals, Dave commented on Carol's suggestion to use sign-language. "That was a stroke of genius" Dave said, "I never would have thought about that as a solution to the communication problem" and he thought it was rather sweet, when he saw Carol blush slightly. "Well, I just thought about how we deal with deaf patients," she said, "and it just came into my mind, as this is a similar situation". "Well I think you deserve a pat on the back" Dave said and Carol's cheek's flushed again, but inwardly she felt rather pleased with herself. "What do you think about it Gary?" Dave asked, "As you're the one who has to learn it all".

"I was a little bit daunted when I thought about what I'd agreed to, but now having had time to think about it, I think it will be rather interesting" Gary replied. Their conversation continued during the meal, as they speculated on the possibilities that were opening up and what it could all lead to in the future. Of course, when they returned to the hospital and told Dr Hedley what had taken place, she was thrilled and congratulated them all on their achievement.

"It's all down to Gary" Dave said, "He's was instrumental in making it all happen and it was Carol who suggested the use of sign-language. So they're the ones that deserve the praise".

As they were leaving her office, Dr Hedley asked Gary if he could stay for a few minutes and asked Carol to escort Dave back to the main entrance, which she did. After they had left the room, Dr Hedley turned to Gary and asked him, "Well, how are you feeling, after your day out?".

"Tired, although I'm feeling quite pleased with myself," he replied.

"I'm glad to hear it," Dr Hedley said, "You should feel pleased with yourself, because you've done exceptionally well. Now, if it's alright with you, I'll make arrangements for you to have a crash course in sign-language. Is that acceptable?".

"That's great. I'm really looking forward to it, now that I've become used to the idea," Gary replied. "I hope that you appreciate that this skill will be of great use to you, when all of this is over. You will have a skill that the majority of people don't have, so it is possible that it could provide you with a source of income. Did you realise that?".

"No I didn't," Gary answered, "But that's too far in the future for me to worry about for now".

"Very wise" she replied, "Let's deal with one thing at a time. That's the best way".

Even with all his years of experience, Dave was bubbling over with excitement as he returned to room 516. When he entered the room, all eyes turned towards him. "What's this" Jack said, "Only working part days now?".

"Let me get myself sorted out and I'll tell you why I'm back," Dave said. After getting himself settled, he related the morning's events to them. As he finished, they spontaneously started to applaud. "

Well done," Jack said, "That's a result, for sure. I normally phone in a report at the end of the day, but with news like this, I think the sooner they know the better" and he started walking towards his office at the end of the room. He seemed to be on the phone forever, but when he finally emerged, he had a subtle smile on his face. "They were as pleased with your result, as I was, but they gave me some new information that you all will find very interesting" Jack told them and then he paused.

"Come on Sir. Don't keep us in suspense," Sarah blurted out, causing the other two to laugh at her use of 'Sir' once again.

"Very well" Jack said, responding to her plea. "They told me that one of the Home Office boffins has come up with a theoretical process that could return the 'invisibles' to normality". A murmur went round the office and then Jack continued, "But what is more incredible, is that the theory is based on information we already have. In fact, one of the reports that we submitted, was the catalyst that helped in the development of the theory. We must have discussed it at some time and written a report, without ever realising its significance. I find that amazing".

"Let me get this straight," Clive said,

"You're saying that we had the answer, but never knew it?"

"That's it exactly," Jack replied and then went on to say, "So I'm as intrigued, as I'm sure you are, to find out what it was that we..... I was going to say 'missed,' but that's not really the case. We just didn't realise the significance of the information, we had gathered. I'm sure that it won't be long before we find out all about it. I, for one can't wait".

***

CHAPTER TWELVE

RESOLUTION

When Theo and Emily returned to the group, the expressions on their faces conveyed to the others that something important had taken place.

Jennifer was the first one to ask. "Come on you two. Tell us what you are looking so pleased about?"

The rest of the group gathered round to make sure they didn't miss anything, while Theo and Emily told them about their meeting in the city centre. This information had a dramatic effect on them all causing some gasps along with barely audible comments. " ..... and that's what happened. We finished by arranging a meeting in a couple of days to give us the instruction book. That's all folks," Theo said, with a mischievous glint in his eyes.

Emily elbowed him in the ribs and then chastised him, saying, "Don't mess about. This has serious implications for all of us".

"I know" Theo replied, "I don't know why I said it. It just seemed appropriate at the time".

"It doesn't matter" Jennifer said, "What's more important is how you all feel about this development?".

Phil was the first one to respond to Jennifer's question. "I personally feel that the use of sign-language was a master stroke and I'm all for it. By the way. Who was it that made the suggestion?".

"It was Carol, the nurse who was there to keep an eye on Gary, you know, the one that can see us. Don't you remember, I told you about him," Theo said. Emily's voice then joined the conversation with an observation. "I notice that it was a woman who came up with this brilliant idea. No surprise there, then".

That comment really put the cat among the pigeons and a light hearted argument about the various attributes of the sexes quickly developed. Eventually, Jennifer calmed them all down enough to ask Michael and Frank for their feelings.

Michael was the first one to reply. "I should have spoken up before, but I was a little unsure how I was going to put this".

"Don't worry," Phil said, "We're all buddies here".

"OK then," Michael replied and then said, "Well, as you know, I used to work as a nurse in a care home and some of the residents were either hard of hearing of deaf. So I learned the basics of sign-language, so that I was able to communicate with them".

"What's so terrible about that?" Jennifer asked.

"I didn't want you to think that I was being too pushy," Michael replied.

"That wasn't pushy, I'm glad you already have the ability," Theo said, "and I'm quite happy if Michael becomes our 'sign' spokesman. What do the rest of you think?"

They were in agreement, except for the one person, who hadn't involved himself in the discussion in any way. "Well Frank. What about you?" Phil asked and all eyes turned in Frank's direction, waiting for his answer.

"I'm not sure that you all realise what you're doing," he said, "The lives that we are now living may not be conventional, but we've all adapted and currently have a pretty good standard of life. I admit that there are emotional restrictions inherent in the way we live, but that is the only down-side as far as I can see. I can't say that I'm totally opposed to the course of action you're proposing, but I would advise caution. Do any of you know what their intentions are? Do they plan to eradicate us? Please be careful and don't get involved in something you'll later regret".

Frank's comments tended to put a damper on the group's enthusiasm, but at the same time, they couldn't find fault in anything he'd said. Had they thought about this enough? Did they know the normal's intentions? It was decided to play along, for the moment anyway and see where it would all lead.

"No Gary. You extend your fingers like this," the nurse said.

"I'm never going to come to grips with this signing," he replied.

"Yes you will. It's just a matter of practice. Think back to your first days in school," she said. "When you were learning to read, what was the first thing you had to learn?".

Gary puzzled over this for a few moments and then replied, "I suppose we started with the alphabet. In fact I seem to remember it being up on the classroom wall. A long multi-coloured poster".

"That's what you have to do now. Learn the signing alphabet and then you can begin to put words together, just the way you did when you learned to read."

"You make it sound so easy," Gary said, "But I'll do the best I can".

"Now, I can't spend all my time teaching you, as I have other responsibilities, so Dr Hedley has arranged for you to have a TV in your room. This model has a built in DVD player and I have a sign-language teaching disc for you to use. Your progress will be directly linked to the amount of effort you're willing to put into it" she explained.

'A TV is a benefit I never expected' Gary thought to himself, 'It's worth my while to do the best I can with this, who knows what else could come my way'.

"I don't know why all this effort is being put into teaching you sign, but I'll do what I can to help," the nurse said, as they arranged to meet the following morning at the same time. "I'll be interested to see if you've learned anything in the meantime" she said, as they were leaving the room.

"I'll do my best" Gary replied, "But I'm only going to need to be able to read sign, although I realise that using it myself is the best way to learn".

Later, Gary was in the common room, dozing in his chair, when he saw through his half closed eyes, Benny making his way towards him. Gary was sure that he felt the floor shake, as Benny landed in the chair almost opposite him. "I'm totally convinced now" Benny stated.

Gary knew that escape wasn't possible from this encounter, so he asked, "Convinced of what?". "I'm convinced that something is going on between you and Dr Hedley. I've voiced my suspicions to you before, but following today's developments, they're no longer suspicions".

Gary was getting annoyed, he just wanted to sleep his dinner off before returning to the signing lessons. However, it was obvious that Benny had no intentions of allowing that to happen, so he decided it was best to try and get it over with as quickly as possible.

"What developments are you on about?" Gary asked.

"It's widely known that the Doc has put a TV in your

room. No-one else is allowed to have their own personal TV, so why you? I think you're having an affair with her and she's showering gifts on you now. You've often had preferential treatment before, but this is a new step. Well. Are you going to defend yourself?".

"I have been given the TV because I'm having to learn something special," Gary said, "and using a DVD in my own time is one of the best ways to learn. I'll tell you again and you can pass this on to the other gossip mongers. There isn't anything going on between Dr Hedley and myself. The TV is part of the help that I need for a specific project, you could call it an experiment that I'm taking part in. Now, does that satisfy you?".

"You're a smooth talker Gary, but I'm not totally convinced. Sooner, or later it will all come out. You mark my words," Benny said and then hauled himself off the chair that he had occupied and wandered off, muttering to himself.

The day arrived for the pre-arranged meeting, which was to take place in a small park-like area, beside a small road called Gravel Walk. This pleasant area was far enough away from the city centre, that it wasn't frequented by too many people, although there was a constant stream of traffic passing by. Jack decided that he should attend this meeting, as he felt that as the man in charge of the investigation, he should introduce himself to whoever attended the meeting, on behalf of the 'invisibles'.

It had been cleared the day before, for Gary to be collected from the hospital, along with Carol, as she was used to the situation. At the pre-arranged time, Jack arrived in the hospital's reception area. Everything took place in the same way as on the previous occasions when Gary had been going out, except that it was Jack who introduced himself to Gary and Carol.

"So you're the boss man, are you?" Gary asked.

"I've been called many things over the years, but you're the first one to call me 'the boss man'. Congratulations" Jack replied. It was this kind of light-hearted answer that Gary had been hoping for. If Jack had replied that his title was Superintendent, it would have put quite a damper on things. But Gary felt that he could get on with Jack so the day started with a relaxed feel to it. Fortunately, there was an extensive car-park just across the road from their destination, so there wasn't a long walk involved. This pleased Gary, as his legs were still sore, from wandering round the town centre.

"I'll have to rely on you to tell me if someone arrives" Jack said, "They should be here in a few minutes". While they waited, Jack used the time to try and learn what he could about Gary. He asked him how he felt about what he was doing. Whether he felt a sense of importance, because of the gift he had and other questions along similar lines. When Jack started talking to him, Gary was worried that it would turn into an interrogation. His concern was based on his previous contact with the police, forgetting that these times were after he had been detained in relation to some incident. But Jack's kindly, pleasant manner soon won him over. He didn't feel that he was being talked down to, as Jack treated him like an equal, which made him feel at ease.

"Can you see those two men," Gary asked, "Oh, that's alright, you don't have to answer, as I recognise one of them as Theo, but I don't know the other one".

Gary was impressed when Jack stood up to make room for the two men to join them on the bench.

"I'm going to ask Theo to introduce his companion to me, by using what ever means he can". He watched aghast, as Michael spelled out his name using sign-language. Gary didn't find it too difficult to read Michael's hands and determine his name.

"You'll never believe this," he said to Jack, "The other man is using sign already and he says his name is Michael". This had been the first operational use of Gary's newly acquired signing skills and he was pleased that he had come through it successfully.

Jack watched Gary as he slowly used his hands to thank them both for coming, although it wasn't necessary as they were able to hear him speak. He used signing to show them that he was also putting effort into establishing good communications between the two groups.

Jack introduced himself to Theo and Michael and then produced the sign-language instruction book out of his pocket. "I suppose this isn't really needed, if Michael can already sign" he said.

"Michael is going to answer you, so it will take me a little while to read his hands" Gary said, fixing his eyes on a space, that to Jack and Carol seemed unoccupied. Eventually, Gary turned back to Jack and said that Michael would appreciate the book as it had been some time since he'd used his signing skills to any extent and it would help him brush up on some of the finer points. Jack held the book out in the direction that Gary had been looking and was taken aback, when he felt it grasped by an unseen hand. To Gary, it all looked quite normal, as Jack offered the book and Michael took it, placing it inside his coat. Jack and Carol were mesmerized by what they saw. As Michael placed the book inside his coat, it progressively disappeared.

Jack realised that he had just experienced the first physical interaction between a 'normal' and one of the 'invisibles', appreciating that an important step forward had just been made. "Before we part" Jack said,"I've something to tell you two, that I feel both you and others like you, will find very interesting"

Jack went on to relate what he had been told about the Home Office theory. "That seems to have shocked them" Gary said, "and Michael says 'Thank you' for letting them know".

As they were about to go their separate ways, it was arranged that if Jack needed to contact them, he would leave a message. Gary then said that Michael had asked how he intended to do so

"I've done a lot of thinking about this" Jack said, "But before I unleash my cunning plan, I need to ask you something, your answer will determine if this plan will work. Are you able to touch brick?". Gary said that Theo thought he could, but Michael wasn't sure. "Come with me" Jack said and they all walked over to an extensive brick wall, that formed the boundary of the small park area. "We'll use what spies call a 'dead letter drop'. If I wiggle this brick out" he said, using his pen-knife to start the brick moving, "I can place a. message, written on a piece of paper, behind it. If you arrange to check every odd day of the month, then if we need to meet, I can let you know. Does that suit you?".

Gary looked over to the space where Theo and Michael were and said that they both liked the plan and Michael says that he likes the idea of playing spies. Just before they parted, both Theo and Michael ensured that they were able to move the brick and ended up, pushing it back into place. That concluded their first real meeting on a light-hearted note and they parted on good terms.

Gary and Carol were returned to the hospital and Jack remained there for a while, informing Dr Hedley about what had taken place. When everything had been covered and he'd answered all her questions, he made the return journey to police HQ..

Once he was settled, with a hot drink in his hand, he phoned in his report. He then joined his team, who were dying to know what had happened and related the whole account to them. Overall, it was felt that real progress had been made and the use of sign-language had made interaction much smoother. It seemed that everyone ended the day on a positive note, with the 'invisibles' discussing it all, long into the night.

Even Jack's wife, Joyce, noticed that he seemed more relaxed that evening, although she appreciated that he was unable to tell her the reason for this. Regardless of this limitation, she was pleased that his case was working out, as she had become worried about Jack in recent days, because he seemed to be under a great deal of pressure.

"How I long to have a discussion, like we used to have," Jack said, "But you know I can't talk about it."

"Don't worry, love," Joyce replied, "It just pleases me to see you a little more at ease tonight".

"That's because I'm beginning to see some light at the end of the tunnel" Jack said to her. The two of them spent the evening together, sitting on the sofa, holding hands, as they had done so many years ago, when they were courting.

Jack was late getting in the following morning as a

broken down bus had caused some traffic problems. But when he finally got there, Sarah told him that the DCS wanted to see him. "Called to the headmaster's office," Jack said, "I wonder what I've done now" and left room 516, for the DSS's office.

As had become the usual practice of late, he was ushered straight in.

"I've had a call from the Home Office" the DCS said, "To tell me that your team has been chosen to oversee the first attempts at reversing the invisibility problem. It will be conducted by a Dr Roberts. This was decided because of your team's outstanding progress made in developing communication with the 'invisibles', Are you pleased with their decision?".

"That's quite a privilege" Jack replied, "When do we meet up with this doctor?". "No hanging about" the DCS said, "You're all to be at the local hospital, for ten thirty this morning. When you get there, go to reception, introduce yourself and you will be taken to the appropriate destination. As I've just mentioned, your whole team is to attend, as they've all worked hard for this".

When he returned to room 516, he told the team to get themselves ready.

"Why couldn't we meet up here?" Clive asked.

"Just think about it" Jack replied, "You know what this place is like for gossip. In the hospital, a new doctor won't seem out of place and as visitors, we will just blend in. So if you think about it, it makes more sense to hold the meeting there". "I get it," Clive said, "It's obvious when you think about it like that".

"That's the problem," Sarah replied and started to laugh, "Because you need a brain to think".

"Children, behave yourselves," Jack said, as he

opened the door, to herd them all out into the corridor. A few minutes later, they were all in the car, starting their journey to the hospital and their meeting with Dr Roberts.

Getting to the hospital was easy enough, but once they had arrived, the problem was finding somewhere to park. After driving around for about fifteen minutes, they managed to pull into a space just after the previous occupant had left.

Jack looked at his watch and said, "We'd better get a move on, we're supposed to be there in five minutes."

A speedy walk brought them to the main entrance and the automatic doors opened to grant them access. As they entered they tried to dodge the smoke from the smokers, that had to go outside the hospital, for their fix. As Jack had frequented the hospital many times, the sight of patients standing outside in their dressing gowns, some even with a drip in their arm, so they could have a smoke, didn't surprise him at all. The other three couldn't believe their eyes, when they caught sight of the collection of smokers.

"Is that quite normal?" Sarah asked Jack. "I'm afraid it is," Jack replied, "and you'll even find them out there, in the dead of winter."

"That's incredible," Sarah said, "That they're that desperate for a smoke."

"That's the power of nicotine for you," Dave responded.

They caught up with Jack at the reception desk, just as he was speaking to the security guard. "Superintendent Hargreaves and companions, to see Dr Roberts. You should be expecting us."

The guard looked down his list, until he finally found them. "Here you are. That's fine. 'Before I phone through to let the doctor know that you're here, there's something that I've been asked to pass on to you. You should have been sent this access card for the consultant's car park, but you know what offices are like, everyone thinking that someone else had sent it to you and in the end, no-one did".

"We could have done with that this morning," Jack said, as the guard dialled a number on his phone. He waited for a few moments, until it was answered and then he said, "Dr Roberts, good morning it's reception. I've Superintendent Hargreaves and his party here to see you." He paused, while he listened to the answer and then replaced the phone on its holder.

"The doctor's assistant is coming to collect you, in a few minutes. In the meantime, could you put on these visitor badges, just in case your presence in the hospital is challenged".

As he was saying this, he handed the badges round. Jack thanked him and they sat down on a row of seats, that backed on to the hospital shop. After ten minutes, or so, a young man in a long white coat approached the reception desk and after asking a question, was directed over to Jack and the team.

The young man walked over to them and spoke to Jack, assuming that as he was the oldest, he was in charge.

"Good morning," he said, "Am I correct in assuming that you're Superintendent Hargreaves?".

"Yes I am," Jack replied, "Well deduced, maybe you should be part of my team." The young man seemed unsure how to respond to Jack's comment, but then he saw the grin on his face and realised that he was joking.

"I'm sorry about my reaction," he said, "It's because I

constantly work with serious people who rarely joke, so your comment caught me off guard. I hope you're not offended".

"Of course not," Jack replied, "If we didn't joke we'd all go mad. Just ask this lot" he said, pointing to the team"

"Would you please follow me" the assistant requested, "I'm afraid it's quite a way, but due to the nature of our work, it was thought best if we were tucked away from the normal flow of traffic".

He lead them out of the reception area, past the stairs that went up to the wards, past the lifts and out into the corridor that ran the full length of the hospital. From the A & E department at one end to the children's wards at the other.

As they turned into the corridor and started walking, Clive suddenly said, "Corridors, corridors. Where-ever I go these days, I always end up walking endless corridors".

"Do stop moaning, you're like a little child" Sarah retorted.

Jack turned round to look at them both. They knew that look and quickly decided to keep quiet.

"I never knew what a maze this place was," Jack said, as they went down a flight of stairs.

"It surprised me when I first came here," the assistant said, "Most people think that the hospital consists of the wards and that's it, because that's all they normally see. But there's a great deal more that they never see and you are entering that world, where the pubic are never allowed, even though a vast amount of work goes on here".

As they carried on walking they all kept looking around, astounded by the number of rooms and workers that they encountered.

"I can see why we were required to wear these identification badges," Jack said, "If we weren't wearing them, I don't think we would have got this far, would we?". "You're correct. You would have been challenged long before now and the security guards would have been called. You would have been interrogated to find out why you were in this part of the hospital and if you were not considered to be a threat, you would be escorted out of the building. But if there was any doubt about you, you would be handed over to the police, for them to check up on you".

"The public don't know any of that, even though I suspected it would be that way" Jack replied.

They were walking past a row of anonymous doors, when the assistant suddenly stopped and produced a key from his pocket. The door was unlocked and he invited them in. As they entered the room they were stunned by the sight that confronted them. Making Jack and Sarah think back to what they had seen at the research centre. It could be likened to seeing a film set based on Dr Frankenstein's laboratory. A vast array of chemical and medical equipment was spread out before them and from in among this array, emerged Dr Roberts.

They had all expected to be meeting a man, but it was obvious that Dr Roberts was no man. She was in her mid thirties with jet black hair that was swept back into a loose pony-tail.

"From your expressions, you were expecting a man, weren't you?," she said. "I know I'm supposed to be a man in my fifties, pipe in my mouth and thick rimmed glasses on my nose. That's what people expect, so I'm sorry to disappoint you all".

"I'm in no way disappointed," Dave said.

"Down boy" Jack replied and they all started laughing.

"I'm glad to see that you've got a sense of humour. I feel it's so necessary to have a laugh now and then, especially when you are dealing with serious problems. Anyway, shall we do the introductions? I'm Joanne".

Starting with Jack they all introduced themselves in turn and then Joanne's assistant introduced himself as Andrew.

"I don't know about all of you, but Andrew and I have been working together for some years now and we prefer to use our first names, how do you feel about doing the same?" she asked.

"We find that it reduces tension when we use our first names, so we're in agreement there," Jack replied.

"I'm glad about that, as I find it a bit stuffy when we use titles," Joanne said. "Anyway, now we've got that sorted, let's get down to business. I suppose you've tried to work out how one of your reports helped me to formulate my idea. Yours wasn't the only one, of course, There were similar reports from other parts of the country. This means that I had to read through countless reports, before this commonality became apparent. This is the report that you sent in," she said, holding up a sheaf of papers. "You may not remember it, but it's contents are significant. A van driver felt his van hit something, although when he got out and looked around, he couldn't see anything. Turning to the people standing on the pavement, he asked them if they knew what was going on. You hit her, they said. Turning back, he was shocked to see the body of an elderly woman under the front of his van and she was dead".

"I remember that one," Dave said, "We all had a good chat about it and didn't you take part in questioning the driver, Jack?".

"Do you know, you're right," Jack replied, "I remember it now. It caused quite a stir at the time, because the driver insisted on sticking to his story. Where as, if he said that she just walked out in front of him, it would have been easier for him. But he didn't".

"I'm glad that you remember it so clearly," Joanne said, "It saves me having to go through all this paper work. Anyway, that report, along with some others like it, started me thinking".

At that point Jack interrupted her and said "I think I can see where you're heading".

"Let's see if you're right" she replied and then continued by saying, "There seemed to be one common aspect to all of these reports. That when one of these 'invisibles', I believe that's what you call them, when one of them dies, they become visible again. Dying seems to allow their body to revert back to it's normal condition. Is that what you were thinking, Jack?".

"That's it exactly. I can't see why I didn't pick up on it before."

Sarah was considering a humorous comment at this point, but wisely decided against it.

Jack then said "I think that we were involved in so many different aspects of our investigation, that it managed to slip by us".

"Don't feel guilty," Joanne said, "I didn't see it for a while either and there are many more people involved in this whole operation that read the reports. They never picked up on it. So I'll excuse you all. She chuckled as she said this.

"What do you intend to do?" Dave asked, "You can't

just kill them off, can you?". "In a way, it's exactly what I intend to do. But I plan to bring them back to life again".

"This is ridiculous," Clive said, "She can't be for real".

"Just hang on a minute," Jack said, "I think I understand what Joanne means. Correct me if I'm wrong".

"OK" she said.

"You intend to simulate death, by some means and then reverse whatever process it is that you use, once the subject has become visible again. Is that it?"

Pretty well right on the mark," she replied.

"Could you run that past me once again?". Clive asked. "Just so that I can get it straight in my mind."

"What I intend to do," Joanne said, "Is to give an injection that will stop the heatrt, wait until they are visible again and then use the defibulator to restart their heart. They'll feel a little unwell after such a dramatic procedure but it is the only practical method so far discussed."

"Right, I Understand now," said Clive. "Thank you for going over it again. I'm sure we all benefited."

"There is one aspect of all this that still has to be sorted out," Joanne said.

"And what's that?" Jack asked.

"Well, if I'm right, the 'invisibles' can only touch certain items?"

"Yes, that seems to be right," Jack replied.

Joanne then said, "As I described earlier about the procedure, it all starts with an injection. So it is necessary to find out the type of syringe they can feel and I'll need one of them to give the initial injection. I might be a good doctor but even I can't give an injection to a patient I can't see."

"I'll arrange for a meeting with them and tell them your requirements," said Jack. Then we'll get them in here to find out what they can or can't feel. We'll also have to see what we can do about the injection. Don't worry, I'm sure we will get it all sorted out."

"There are some other points for their consideration," Joanne said. "And that is that it will be best if the first couple of attempts are performed on younger people who are in good health."

"I can understand that," Jack said. "Anything else?"

"Yes. One final point and that is that they shouldn't worry as the procedure will be refined as we move along to make it a little less traumatic for them."

"I'll convey all these comments to them," Jack said in answer to her. "And I'll get things moving along as quickly as I can."

Gary was sitting in the comon room enjoying the morning sun. He was dozing, feeling warm and comfortable. In his mind he was turning over recent events and the way his life had changed. What a change from his old life, realising that he was little more than a lagar-swilling yob. If someone had told him that he would end up working with the police he would have told them to stop talking rubbish. Yet here he was and he felt good about it.

He felt a tap on his shoulder and partly opened his eyes to see who it was . Even though his eyes had not properly focused he could make out the familiar white uniform of a nurse.

His time at the hospital had taught him that when one of the nurses wanted you, it was best to respond. He adjusted himself in his chair while he was trying to clear his mind.

"Dr Hedley would like to see you in her office" the nurse said, "You should know the way by now, so you can go on your own."

'This is a step forward,' Gary thought and it demonstrated to him, the level of trust that he'd earned. Just as he was opening the door, to leave the common room, the last person he wanted to see was just entering.

"I don't have to ask where you're going, do I?" Benny said, "Make sure that you leave her in a good mood".

Gary had decided that it was best to ignore such comments and hoped that he'd stop making them when he didn't get a reaction. Ignoring Benny, he pushed his way through the door and walked off down the corridor. He didn't turn to look, but he was sure that he could feel Benny's eyes burning two points into his back as he walked away.

"You've obviously proved your worth" Dr Hedley said, "As you're services are required again tomorrow morning".

"I don't mind" Gary replied, "In fact I rather enjoy the whole thing. After all, I'm actively involved in something that the majority of people know nothing about and that makes me feel rather special".

"It's nice to hear you speaking so positively" she said, "But how do you feel within yourself? What about when you're 'face to face' with these 'invisible' people, although they're not invisible to you of course.".

"I've become used to it all," Gary replied, "Although looking back, I can understand my initial panic. If you remember, I lived my life through an alcoholic haze, so when I started to see these people, I thought that my mind wouldn't be able to cope with it and would shut down."

"That's not too far from what actually happened" she replied, "You were in a pretty bad way, when you were first brought in here. But look at you now".

"I certainly feel better than I can ever remember," Gary stated, "and thank you for trusting me to come on my own today"

"It's only fair that your hard work and the progress you've made, is rewarded" she said, "Anyway, back to the arrangements for tomorrow. You'll be collected from reception at ten tomorrow morning. Do you think that you can get yourself sorted out in time for that?".

"No problem" Gary replied. "Just before you go," she said, "I feel that you should be kept up to date with the way this is all panning out".

"I'd appreciate that," he said. "It seems that there is a theoretical process to help these people to return to their original state and the first trials of this process, are close to taking place. As it's pretty sure that you will be involved, I thought that I should prepare you, so that it doesn't come as a shock."

"Thank you for that," Gary said, "I've been expecting something like that, from the way that it's all going".

Mid-morning the following day, Dave and Gary were sitting on a bench in the small park area. They hadn't been sitting there very long when Gary said,

"Here come Theo and Michael now. I recognise them from last time".

Gary translated while the greetings took place and then Dave took over, explaining to them about what had happened during their meeting with Dr Roberts. To start with, he felt stupid talking to people he couldn't see. After all, he only had Gary's word that they existed at all. However, he told them everything he could about the reversion process. When he finished, he turned to Gary and said, "What do they make of that, then?".

"I think they're in a state of shock at the moment" Gary replied and then said, "They're talking to each other, at the moment and I can't lip read that quickly. We'll have to wait until they're ready to speak to us".

"Fair enough," Dave said. Eventually, they started a conversation with Gary and he relayed what they were saying to Dave, so he could join in. "I think it's quite reasonable that you want to talk it over with the other members of your group" Dave said, "It's a momentous step for you all to take and I agree that it isn't something to be entered onto lightly".

"Michael says that he is able to help, as far as the injections are concerned," Gary said, "As he was trained as a nurse and has administered injections on many occasions".

"That's great," Dave replied, "Dr Roberts was a little concerned about that aspect of the procedure. So if you are going to be the one doing it, it's best that you form part of the delegation that comes to the hospital and you can then chose the best syringe for you to use. Otherwise something totally unsuitable could be chosen. Would you be willing to do that?".

Gary's head turned towards the empty space, where Dave presumed Theo and Michael were sitting. "Both of them said that they would be willing to take part in doing that," Gary said on their behalf.

"If you discuss all of this with the rest of your group tonight and then we can meet here again at the same time tomorrow. Then you can tell us how they all felt about it and we can go to the hospital, to select the equipment that you're happy to use" Dave said.

With the arrangements made and plenty to talk

about, they parted company until the following day.

When Theo and Michael returned to base, only Jennifer and Frank were there. "Where are Emily and Phil?" Theo asked, with a tone of annoyance in his voice. He didn't like the idea of Emily being on her own with Phil.

"Don't worry," Jennifer said, noticing Theo's concern, "Emily loves you, so you've nothing to worry about. Alright?"

Theo was a little embarrassed by his jealously. "I suppose so," he replied.

When the other two returned, it was obvious that they had been collecting supplies. Theo felt uncomfortable about harbouring the thoughts that he had, but now Emily had returned he felt better and when she ran over to him, throwing her arms around his neck, all the previous thoughts and feelings disappeared.

As they sat in a circle, enjoying the food, Jennifer said, "I think we should thank Emily and Phil for such a lovely spread".

They all started to applaud, Theo adding some 'whoops and hollers'. After all, his Emily was involved, so why shouldn't he express himself.

Jennifer had become the matriarch of the group, without her realising that it was happening. But now the role had become part of her, an integral part of her being. So she took centre stage, asking Theo and Michael to report on the meeting that had taken place earlier that morning.

"You're the medical man," Theo said to Michael, "So you do the honours, OK?".

"Thank you kindly," Michael said, bowing slightly as

a ripple of applause ran round the group.

"I've something astounding to tell you all and it's going to require each one of you to make a decision, one that will affect your future. A Dr Roberts has devised a method, that will return us to our original state". He paused there, to allow the significance of what he'd said to sink in.

"How does the doctor intend to do it?" Frank asked.

"Right. I'll explain the procedure to you," Michael said and went on to describe it to them, as Dave had told him at the meeting. As he finished, he asked them all, "How do you feel about it?". Silence.

Phil was the first one to speak. "Although it sounds pretty frightening, I'm willing to give it a go". Eventually, they all responded, one at a time, with some expressing some doubts about it. They realised that one voice was missing. All eyes turned to look at Frank.

"Well Frank. How do you feel about it?".

"I'm not going to do I,t" he said.

"Why not?" Michael asked, "It's a chance to get back to normal".

"That's just the point," Frank replied, "I've nothing to go back to. You all have lives and relationships to return to and re-establish. The old world has nothing for me and I've grown used to living this way. I will be able to live out my life in peace and quiet, just the way I want to. Not having to live the way, that others expect. I hope you all can understand my decision and will respect it". T

hey were all taken aback by Frank's statement, but they all agreed to respect his decision.

"Frank. Can I ask you one thing?" Michael said.

"Of course. Go ahead" Frank replied.

"Would you be willing to give the final injection to

me?" Michael asked. "I'll do it for all the others, but it would be easier for me, if you could administer it".

"Of course I will Michael. Just because I don't want to do it myself, it doesn't mean that I won't help any of you, in any way needed" Frank replied.

"I've been thinking about another request made by Dr Roberts," Michael said, "and that is for the first couple of patients to be younger people, in good health. The only two that seem to fit the bill, are Emily and Theo."

The others agreed with his reasoning and, turning to the young couple, he said, "Well. How do you two feel about being the guinea pigs?".

Emily and Theo turned to look at each other and smiled.

"We'll do it" Theo said, "But there is one thing I must insist on and that is that I go first. That way, if anything goes wrong, then it can be corrected before it's Emily's turn. Is that acceptable to you all?"

They all agreed and Emily, tears running down her cheeks, hugged Theo and said "You'll be alright. You wait and see."

It made Dave feel good, having a pass for the consultants car park and he received a few strange looks as he drove in. Andrew was waiting at the entrance for them.

"I wasn't sure that you'd be able to remember the convoluted route through the hospital, so I thought it best to come and meet you," he said.

They all voiced their thanks and Dave replied, "I'm glad you're here, because I was unsure about remembering the way".

As they followed Andrew, Dave paid a great deal

more attention than he had done on the previous visit. As they reached the door, Andrew turned to him and said, "Do you think that you'd be able to make your way here unescorted now?".

"It's possible that I'd make a couple of mistakes, but I think I could manage it now" Dave replied.

They all entered the room and Dave was surprised at the way he felt, when he saw Dr Roberts again. He had found her very pleasing to the eye, from the moment he saw her, but this time he felt something more. He quickly realised that for the moment, such feelings had to be put to the back of his mind, they had more important things to deal with at the moment. Looking around the room, he saw that a display of syringes had been laid out on a work top. He had never seen so many before, in fact he found it difficult to believe that so many different types existed. He began to feel a little queasy, not being too fond of needles, the large display was a little difficult to take.

Dr Roberts then began to speak. "Even though I've been involved with this project for quite a while, I've never had the privilege of meeting any invisible people and I would be grateful if they could be introduced, so I know who I'm talking to".

That was Gary's cue and he took one step forward. Pointing to an apparently empty space he said, "This is Michael and over here," he said moving his hand, "This is Theo".

"Good morning gentlemen," she said, "I'm Joanne Roberts".

"Michael is the one who will be using the syringe," Gary said, "and if it's alright with you, he'd like to test the syringes out. To find the one that's easiest for him to use".

"That's fine by me," she replied, "Help yourself".

So Gary accompanied Michael and Theo as they walked over to the display. "That's incredible" Joanne said, as the syringes started to move about, apparently by themselves. For Dave, this was the confirmation that he had needed. All the time that he had been involved in this investigation, he'd held suspicions that it was all a con job and Gary was taking them for a ride. But now he had concrete evidence, the proof was right there in front of him. For the first time, he was totally convinced, all the doubts had been washed away.

Joanne walked over and stood beside him. He took a deep breath, as he smelt her perfume and was worried in case his cheeks had flushed. "Have you ever seen anything like that before?" she asked. At that moment, she seemed like an astonished child, rather than a highly qualified doctor.

"Unbelievable" Dave replied, "Yet it's happening right in front of me".

The spell was broken when Gary turned round and said to her, "They would like to know what is going to be put in the syringe and injected into them?".

"Good question and as the stuff's going to be put in you, it's only fair that you know what it is. I'll try to explain, without being too technical," she replied. "My starting point was Potassium Chloride, which can be used to stop the heart. But it was too drastic and long lasting, for what I wanted.

"So over time and with a great deal of experimentation, a potion was developed that would do the job and then quickly dissipate. Otherwise, when the defibrillator is used to re-start the heart, it would be fighting against the effects of the chemical. Does that make sense to you all?".

Everybody was happy with her explanation. Even Gary was able to grasp what she was saying and that really surprised him. He knew that the old Gary wouldn't have been able to make any sense of it, it would have been total gibberish as far as he was concerned. Once again, the amount of progress that he'd made, was starkly brought home to him.

"Now Michael, what about a syringe. Have you found one that feels right for you and you feel that you could use?" she asked. A syringe lifted itself off the bench and moved over towards Joanne. As she took hold of it, she could feel the effect of another hand on it, although she was unable to see anyone.

"That's a strange experience," she said, "Taking something from some-one I can't see".

"There's one more thing to decide, before we part," Dave said, "When is the attempt to reverse their condition to take place. Now, it's not up to me, or my colleagues. The decision has to be made by Theo, Michael, the rest of your people and you, Dr Roberts. You are the ones that have to decide.

"First of all, a question," Joanne said, "How many people am I going to be dealing with? It helps me to know so I can ensure that the correct amount of equipment is available".

Gary looked over to Theo and Michael to get their answer. "They say that five people of varying ages will be involved. In harmony with your previous request, the two youngest members of their group will be first. Theo and his girlfriend Emily have volunteered. Michael will be administering the injections and then one member, who doesn't want to take part, will administer it to him. Is that all acceptable?".

"That's fine" she replied, "How about if we say a

week today. That will give me time to get everything together and allow your group to make sure that they are happy with all the arrangements. Any questions?".

A short period of silence followed, until it was broken by Dave's voice. "That's it then. We'll all meet back here the same time next week, for the world premiere of Dr Robert's procedure. I've only one thing left to say and that is, Good luck to you all".

***

CHAPTER THIRTEEN

CONCLUSION

For Jack and the team the next week went by rather quickly. Although for Dave, the time seemed to drag by, as he was longing to return to the hospital and see Dr Roberts once again. He realised that he had become quite fond of her and as the days passed by, his longing grew even stronger.

As the investigation was in its final throes, there was a great deal of tidying up to do. There were files to be brought up to date, checked and then signed off etc. Their personal computers had to be cleared of any pertinent information and if necessary, the hard drive sanitized. For Jack, it meant a lot of meetings in the DCS's office. One of the most unusual meetings was with two 'suits', who were rather reluctant to divulge any information about themselves and the department they represented. But Jack was required to run through the whole thing with them and answer any questions raised along the way, even though he often couldn't see the relevance of them.

As the days passed by, it became more real to Jack, that this was going to be the very last time he ran an investigation. Regardless of any incentives that were offered, to persuade him to stay, he had decided that he'd done enough. He felt that this was a good case to end on, a nice final entry into his service record before it concluded. He'd enjoyed this one. It was nice to be investigating a situation where people were not determined to be unpleasant and downright vicious to one another.

He had discussed his retirement at length with Joyce and they had both agreed that it was time to call it a day. So that's what he had determined to do and intended to inform the DCS, so he could put his papers in, after the procedures at the hospital were concluded.

Once the 'invisibles' had been returned to their former lives, the case was officially over. He knew that having worked on this investigation would certainly boost the careers of the other members of the team and he intended to do all that he could to make sure that they were well looked after.

For Theo and his group, the week seemed to drag by. They all wanted to get it over and done with. Jennifer accurately voiced their feelings when she said that it was like having to do something you're worried about and you know it's getting closer and closer and you just want it over with. But the days were passing by and even though they'd become used to their way of life, they hoped that it would soon be over.

One evening, while they were having their meal, Phil said, "I wonder what we'll all be doing this time next week?" A conversation ensued, where each of them listed the aspects of life they'd missed, while in their invisible state. Later that evening, Emily and Theo went for a walk together. "What do you think will happen to us?" she asked. "In what way do you mean?" Theo replied.

"About about the relationship we've developed," she said.

"I don't see why anything should change. Why? Is this your subtle way of dumping me, so you can return to an old boyfriend?" Theo asked.

"What I was asking about, is whether you intend to do that to me. So you can return to your old girlfriend," Emily replied.

"I don't want anything to change between us," Theo said, "You know that I love you and hope that you'll still feel the same way about me, after we're back to normal".

"I'm so relieved," Emily replied. "I was so scared that once we'd got back to normal, our relationship would come to an end. You know that I love you and I don't want anything to come between us".

They slowly walked back to the group, to be greeted by Jennifer who said, "The young lovers return."

"You're only jealous." Emily replied.

"You're right there," Jennifer said, "It seems so long ago, that I had a young love like yours".

"Who knows how any of us will fare and what the future holds for us, once we're back to normal," Michael said.

Each of them had their own private thoughts on that subject, but they all had hopes that the future would be good to them.

Time continually marches on and finally the morning of the procedures arrived. Both groups made their way to the hospital with all of them holding a similar hope: that it would all turn out well. Jack's team were also looking forward to being able to see what Theo and his friends looked like.

Jack felt like royalty, as he sat in the back of the car and was whisked into the consultant's car park. Dave had gone over the route to Dr Roberts' room in his mind, a hundred times or more. This was something he had to get right, otherwise he'd never hear the end of it.

As they turned into the corridor of many doors, they

were stopped by a security guard. From his manner, it was obvious that he was very good at what he did and wasn't the kind of person you'd want to tangle with. "Superintendent Hargreaves and team" Jack said.

"I'm sorry sir, but I'll have to ask each of you to show me your warrant cards, if you don't mind" the guard said. Each of them responded to his request and then Jack pointed towards Gary and said, "He's with us".

"And you are, sir?" the guard asked Gary, who told him his name. The guard checked a list he had, on a clip board and then allowed them access. As he heard voices outside, Andrew stepped out into the corridor, to greet them. As they entered the room, Dr Roberts called out a greeting to them and said, "Leave the door open, it will make access easier for our friends". She said this just in time, as Clive had started to close the door behind them.

Jack turned to Gary and asked him,"Are they here yet?". "Not yet" Gary replied. "I hope they haven't got cold feet and decided not to go through with it" Jack said.

"I think if they'd made such a decision, at least one of them would turn up to tell you face to face," Gary said, "But they can't do that, can they?".

"Do what?" Jack replied.

"Speak to anyone face to face, except for me, at the moment," Gary said in answer. Voices could be heard in the corridor, getting louder as they got closer to the door. "Why don't you ask the doc" a voice said, "I'm sure she'll be able to help you".

As the word "you" faded away, one of the security men walked into the room. "I've just had a strange experience" he said. "Why. What happened?" the doctor replied. "I was standing at the end of the corridor, where I was supposed to be and I felt the air move around me, as if someone was walking past. But there wasn't anyone there. The whole thing left me feeling weird, so I wondered if you have an Aspirin, or something, that you could give me?" he asked.

While all of this was going on, Gary turned to Jack and whispered, "They're here."

After the guard had left the room, the door was closed and locked.

"Let me explain the facilities that have been arranged for this morning," Joanne said and then turning to Gary, she asked "I'm not encroaching in one of our guests' space, am I?".

Gary looked over at the 'invisibles'. He had been a little surprised when they all arrived that morning. He'd never seen the whole group together before and saw some faces that were new to him. But for now, he was able to report that everyone had arranged themselves so there wasn't any overlapping.

"That's good. Thank you Gary" Joanne said and then continued. "As you can see, this room has been re-arranged since the last time you were here and two adjacent rooms have been seconded for our use. The one that's joined to this one by the dividing door over there," she pointed to the door, "has been fitted out as a post procedure care area and the room beyond that, has been fitted out as a waiting area. A TV and a drinks machine have been installed for your use, although not for our patients, along with some comfortable seats for you all, while you wait.

"I have three nurses to assist me today and they all are affiliated to the Home Office, as I am. So they're used to working on sensitive projects. If it's alright with

Theo, I thought that you would all like to see the first procedure. Would you mind Theo?".

She turned towards Gary, waiting for an answer. "Theo is happy with that" Gary said, on his behalf.

Joanne took charge of the conversation again, saying "I feel that once Theo's procedure is over, it would be best if you all moved into the waiting area. As the same thing will be repeated each time and as the patient has to uncover their top half, it would be more modest for the female patients. I hope you can understand my reasoning on this".

"I'll take it upon myself to speak for my team," Jack said. "I think it's a reasonable request and if you were to encounter any problems, the last thing you need is an audience".

"All of your patients also agree with your suggestion," Gary said "and they thank-you for being so thoughtful".

"I'm glad that you're all so understanding," Joanne said. "After all, we're breaking new ground here this morning. Nothing like this has ever been done before, or has needed to be done before".

She stood there, looking around the room and then said,"There's no point in putting it off any longer. We might as well make a start and called one of the nurses through from the other room. There's just one more thing I've forgotten to tell you all. As this is a world's first, as far as we know, the whole thing is being recorded, if you look up you'll see the cameras up near the ceiling. With all that's going on, I completely forgot, so I hope that you'll forgive me.

Unseen by the majority of the room's occupants, Theo stripped to the waist. Emily threw her arms around his neck and in a quivering voice she said "My brave man. Be safe".

Theo looked into her eyes, watching the tears form before they started their journey down her cheeks. "Don't worry. Everything will be OK" he said "We'll both come through this without a problem, you'll see".

"I think we may have to hose those two down, Doc," Gary said, laughing. It became obvious to those in the room, that Theo had laid himself down on the gurney, as it moved slightly and indentations could be seen in its surface.

"Is every one ready?" Joanne asked "Is all the equipment switched on and waiting? Oxygen standing by? Let's make a start then. Michael, could you please give Theo the injection".

They all watched, fascinated as a syringe lifted itself up off a tray and moved over to the side of the gurney, where the patient's arm would be.

"One last time, before the injection is given. Is everyone ready?" Joanne looked around the room and then concentrated her look in Gary's direction, waiting for a response.

"Everything alright here," Gary said "Both Theo and Michael are waiting for your word to proceed".

"Let's do it then," she said. The syringe seemed to empty itself, its contents disappearing through the needle. They all stared at the apparently empty gurney. But then, slowly at first, an outline began to appear. Within thirty seconds the whole materialization had taken place, although to those watching, it had seemed much longer. Joanne, Andrew and the nurse moved in, working together like a well oiled machine. The heart monitor pads were attached, the monitor obviously displaying a flat line and the defibrillator pads were prepared. Joanne placed them on Theo's chest, called out "Clear", everyone stepped back and the defibrillator fired. The heart monitor trace shot off the screen, as the pulse hit Theo's chest and then returned to a flat line. The defibrillator's output was

increased by a hundred joules and they tried to resuscitate Theo again.

After the heart monitor's trace straightened out, it displayed a slight blip. Joanne started manual chest compressions and mouth to mouth resuscitation. Although it struggled at first, Theo's heart slowly came back to life and settled into a normal sinus rhythm. Joanne leaned back against a bench and wiped the sweat from her forehead. "Well done everyone" she said, as the nurse placed an oxygen mask on Theo's face. He slowly started to move his arms. His chest felt as if he'd been kicked by a horse. He moved his head, so he could see around the room and the success of the procedure was confirmed, when he realised that he couldn't see his friends. Theo reached up to his face, removed the oxygen mask and asked "Where's Emily?".

"Don't worry," Gary said to him, "She's right here and she says that she still loves you". A large grin appeared on Theo's face, as the gurney was wheeled into the post-procedure room. "I think we all need a hot drink after that" Joanne said, "Let's go through to the waiting area. I know it seems unfair, but as I said earlier, its best that our patients don't have anything to drink at the moment".

Gary looked at them all and a few moments later said, "They understand and thank-you for your concern." He then said they knew that before you have an operation in hospital, it's 'nil by mouth' for the patient. So they agree that it's best to be careful now.

Then it was Emily's turn, It was decided that Gary

would remain in the waiting area and be called in, if he was needed. So Emily and Michael followed Joanne and her team, back into the procedure room. It all followed the same patten as it had done with Theo, until it came to re-starting Emily's heart. It just wouldn't start beating. So Joanne took a chest needle and gave her a shot of adrenaline straight into the heart. The paddles were then applied, but apart from a couple of small contractions, her heart wouldn't respond any further.

Finally, after a couple of higher level hits from the defibrillator, mouth to mouth and chest compressions, Emily emitted a large gasp, sucking in the air, as her heart returned to it's normal rhythm. The oxygen mask was then applied, to assist her breathing.

"I'm glad we didn't have an audience for that one" Joanne said, "Can you imagine how Theo would have reacted, if he'd seen all of that going on". Andrew and the nurse both agreed with her. Joanne followed Emily into the post procedure room, to make sure she was alright and then she was able to tell Theo.

Their gurneys were placed side by side, so they could hold hands, while their bodies recovered from the trauma.

Phil was next and his procedure went as smoothly as Theo's had. Lying in the post procedure room, the three of them were trying to get used to being back to normal and were surprised at how quickly it all came back to them. But there was to be one fly in their ointment and that was Jennifer.

Try as they might, her heart would not re-start and the situation quickly deteriorated to the point that had she survived, she would have been severely brain damaged. A later autopsy would reveal that Jennifer had a congenital heart defect that she'd never been aware of, as it had never affected her everyday life. When that was combined with her advanced years, it became apparent that she was a brave woman for even considering the procedure.

Those that had already come through re-materialization, were very upset when they were told that Jennifer hadn't survived. She had meant so much to them and had always been there for them. Theo had often thought about how she coped in her early days, when she was on her own, before the rest of the group came along. It must have been a frightening time for her, not knowing what to do and not having anyone to talk to. Now all they had of her was memories, happy pleasant memories.

For Michael who was the last one to go through the procedure, found that Jennifer's death put quite a damper on things.

"The other three, who are more your age, came through with flying colours, didn't they," Frank said to Michael, "So why should you be any different?".

Michael was boosted by Frank's words and asked him, "Are you sure that you're OK about giving me the injection?".

"I've watched you very closely," Frank answered "and I'll try to make it as pain free as you did for all the others". Michael turned to Frank and grasped his hand tightly.

"This is it, old friend. If I come through this, I won't be able to do this again. So take good care of yourself and I must ask you one last time, for my own peace of mind. Are you sure about your decision?"

Frank smiled and looking him straight into his eyes, he said "Yes I'm sure, that this is what I want. Even when I was younger, long before any of this happened, I longed to live a life like this, free from the constraints of society. You could say that I'm an anti-social old sod, but that's me. Thank you for your concern and please look after yourself. Now get up on that gurney and I'll give you the injection". Michael lay there, jumping slightly as. Frank inserted the needle into his vein. He watched Frank, knowing that it would be the last time he ever saw him, until everything started to fade and then it all went black. The next thing he knew, he was conscious again and had a terrible pain in his chest. He knew that it had worked, when he felt Dr Roberts hand on his shoulder which confirmed that he was back to normal. He joined Theo, Emily and Phil in the post procedure room and they all compared notes about their experience.

Many lives changed for ever that day. Not only for the ex-invisibles but also for everyone else involved in the whole situation. Theo and his friends became celebrities for a while and were temporary fodder for the tabloid press. Although they benefited financially from the experience, to the extent that they wouldn't have to worry about money for the remainder of their lives.

Jack retired, just as he and Joyce had planned, spending his days pottering about in his garden, while he smoked his pipe. He now had more time for Joyce, his daughter's family and especially his grand children. He still kept in touch with his old force and was pleased to see the three members of his team move up through the ranks, to achieve elevated positions in the force.

Jack was also pleased to see that Dr Joanne Roberts was included in the New Years Honours list, for services to science. Of course Dave knew about it before the list was published, as in the interim period, he and Joanne had tied the knot and were enjoying their married life together.

What about Gary? He became a consultant for the Home Office, as there was still plenty of interpreting work to be done, all over the country and he built up a fine reputation. The biggest shock happened to his old friends Bill, Dave, Nigel and not forgetting Suzy. They were enjoying a drink together one evening, discussing the revelations about the invisible people.

"Do you think that's what Gary was mixed up in?" Bill asked.

"Gary?" Suzy exclaimed, "You mean our Gary? No chance".

At that moment the door opened and a well dressed and groomed man entered the bar. They didn't recognise him for a moment, until Nigel said, "Doesn't he look like Gary?". They all stared at the man. It was when he spoke to them, that the penny dropped. It was their old friend Gary, but it was a Gary they'd never seen before.

"Look at you," Suzy said, "I didn't know that you'd clean up that well" which started them all laughing and they remained together talking over old times long into the night.

Jennifer's funeral was a sad time for them all and was the first time that everyone involved had met together since the procedures. Although it became a regular meeting point for them to renew the flowers and to pay their respects. All of the invisible group, vowed to meet up there every year, on the anniversary of Jennifer's death, to remember their kindly friend.

Even though they could no longer see him, they all agreed that they felt Frank was there with them. For that period of time, once a year, every year, the invisible group was re-united once more, to talk over their lives and to remember their missing friend Jennifer,

***

EPILOGUE

Carol Brown and her daughter Jasmine, were sitting at their kitchen table, eating their tea and watching the local news on the portable TV. The door bell suddenly rang. "Who's that at this time of night?" Carol asked.

"I'll get it," Jasmine spluttered, her mouth full of food. "It'll most likely be for me". "Why couldn't they text you like they normally do?" Carol said. Jasmine bounced up out of her chair and ran into the hall. Carol heard the door being opened, heard Jasmine squeal and then silence.

"What the hell's going on?" Carol said, getting up so quickly that she knocked her chair over. Rushing out into the hallway, she half expected to see Jasmine lying there, with a knife sticking out of her. But what she saw, stopped her dead in her tracks.

Jasmine had her arms around someone. Carol couldn't make out who it was, but was able to see enough to know it was a man. She was worried for a moment that her errant husband, Art, had returned. But this person had the wrong build and any way, the hair wasn't right. As she got closer, threads of recognition began to weave themselves together and when she heard his voice, she knew.

"Theo, Theo" she called out, running down the hall to become part of the joint embrace.

"Hello mum, Hello Jazzy" the voice said, convincing them that their long lost son and brother, had returned. Theo was treated like royalty, that night. Bob, Andy and Terry were contacted and they came rushing round to see their long lost friend. Theo explained the whole experience to them and they were astounded that he had been so close to them, on a number of occasions, but they had no way of knowing. Within an hour, the phone started to ring, then the reporters arrived and were joined by TV news crews. It became so bad, that Carol unplugged the phone and drew the curtains, before it all drove them mad. That's the way things were for quite a while, with Theo, along with his family and friends becoming used to being media celebrities. For a while anyway, until some new story came along.

Similar re-unions took place all over the country, during the following months, as long lost sons, daughters, husbands, wives and friends re-joined normal life. For many of those involved, it was part of their jobs. Jack's old DCS and Dr Hedley often spoke on the phone, even though they never met, as they both tried to find out who it was they had been speaking to, when they phoned their reports in. But after the first group had been successfully returned to normality, the phone number went dead and try as they might, they always got the same answer. "There's no such number and there never has been". The cause of the invisibility was never definitively proven, although there were many different theories, which made the rounds of the scientific community.

It's possible that some of the government's more shadowy departments carried on experimenting and who knows, they may well have been successful. Although it's worth wondering how many casualties there were in the name of 'state secret', we'll never know what they achieved. But it's always possible, that someone's looking over your shoulder right now and you'd never know.

***